THE CONDUIT

Phillip Macko

To my friend

"Keep the lights
on after reading!"

The Conduit

To Dan Edelman for your incredible support, editing and storyline consulting work.

To my brother Richard for the ideas, suggestions and medical insights you provided me.

To my incredible wife and the love of my life Yixuan and her unending support - this wouldn't have been possible without you.

To the memory of dad, Papa Ted. You're forever missed.

And finally, to my dearest mom, my most valued reader.

I dedicate this book to all of you.

"In almost every act of our daily lives, whether in the sphere of politics or business, in our social conduct or our ethical thinking, we are dominated by the relatively small number of persons...who understand the mental processes and social patterns of the masses. It is they who pull the wires which control the public mind."

~ **Edward Bernays, Propaganda**

1

I've always known it was here, especially in the fleeting moments of clarity I later deny. The blackness inside me, tucked away in the place where a soul should be.

I told myself it was a tool to be wielded. A tool I could control.

I told myself a lie.

It could all be over now. It would only take a moment to snap his neck and finish this. But I won't. He's earned a slow, painful death.

He shows the first signs of coming to. A twitch, a muscle spasm. Eyelids pull apart. His mouth fights against duct tape. I rip it off as he screams, happy I've taken some of his mustache and beard with it.

A sliver of vague bluish moonlight pierces through like a sign, illuminating the clipped black and white newspaper photo of you I hold.

I'm sorry. A thousand times sorry. You were collateral damage. An innocent trapped in a narrative whose ending will be written tonight.

His beady, tombstone-grey eyes search mine for an answer through round, mist-covered wire-rim glasses. My dead-eyed glare gives him nothing. "W-what do you want?" he finally asks, in a shaky voice nearly drown out by the rush of the falls.

I suck a sharp, damp breath, and let out a slow, impatient exhale. "I think you know."

"I. I *don't*," he pleads, all color fading from the few visible patches of face not obscured by a thick, salt-and-peppered mustache and an untended beard.

I grab a fistful of his hair so he can't look away and shove the photo in his face before ripping off the porcelain mask I'm wearing and tossing to the ground.

It shatters to pieces.

Shattered pieces. Shattered like the lives I'm here to avenge.

His eyes slam shut.

"You can still let me go. I haven't seen your face."

"Oh, but you have. Open them."

Arms struggle, urgent under the rattle of chains. Hands fumble for the phone I've taken from his pocket, for the smartwatch I've removed from his wrist. His utter helplessness. Something I find myself cherishing.

"There's no way for your people to track you. Now *open* your eyes."

He fights the inevitable for a time. Then accepts it. His eyes open.

"You?"

He goes white like a ghost.

As he should.

He created me.

"Do you see this?" I ask, picking up my sword, slicing through the air before pointing it at his face. A wet circle forms on his khaki pants. The acrid sting of ammonia fills the air, insulting my eyes and nose. I make a slow semi-circle around him, tapping his head with my blade. He flinches with each strike. "Don't shut your eyes again unless it's to blink."

"¡*Ajuadame*! Help me!" He makes a wasted attempt to fight his way out of the bindings. I sit down bang opposite him, watching until he collapses in exhaustion.

"Ajuadame!" he calls out in a last, desperate plea.

"There's no one out there for you," I tell him, leaning forward and sliding my kukri across his distended belly, then sharply up his sweat covered white lab coat. Three buttons fly off and bounce on the ground, spinning like tossed coins before coming to rest on the cold stone floor near his hairy-knuckled left hand.

"You don't have to do this," he begs. The circle around his crotch grows, a puddle forms underneath him. "I can help you."

"Help me?" I spit back, the words like acid on my tongue. "Like you helped Samuel Moore's grandmother? Like you helped Paul Pellen's wife and children?" I raise up his chin with my blade. Our eyes meet. "They're *dead*, remember?"

His panicked eyes search the surroundings for the glimpse of a person, the beam from a flashlight. For someone or something to save him.

"Can I assume you've heard the stories about this hotel?" I ask.

"H- haunted," he stammers.

"No one comes here at night. I'll be long gone before staff discovers your body in the morning."

He opens chapped, spittle-lined lips. "Just tell me what you want."

I lift his chin again with my blade. "The woman in the photo. I want her life back. I want *my* life back. I'll settle for yours in exchange."

"Please," his eyes become wet again. "I don't want to die."

"Neither did your victims," I say, followed by a sharp and unrestrained slap to his face. "Take a look at the bend in your right elbow. I've already killed you."

His eyes fall, his dry lower lip begins to quiver. "You're bluffing," he says.

"Aconite, so we're clear, takes a few hours," I tell him, pointing the blade at my backpack. "The antidote is in there. If I decide to administer it in time you may just survive the night."

His shoulders fall. "Why are you doing this to me, Nathan?"

"I've already told you."

"The woman? I don't k-know her," he protests.

"But you will. For every last minute you have left, you're going to listen to me tell you her story, *my* story, on the off chance you don't know all the damage you've done. I hope it all weighs on you like an anchor for the whole of fucking eternity. Now pay attention."

NATHAN BADGER

ELEVEN MONTHS PRIOR
RAMONA, CALIFORNIA

I'm drowning. My lungs on fire with the need for oxygen. A moment of panic touches my inner core at the words, "Wake up, Nathan."

I know why they're calling me, and I don't want to go.

I push away white bed sheets, frantic, my surroundings unfamiliar, searching for my parents. My family. Someone to help me.

"It's okay, we're here," to the touch of a gentle hand.

A blurred face hovers above me, "You've had an accident." He's dressed in white, his face mostly covered by a surgical mask. "I'm here to help you regain your memories."

"Thank you, Doctor," the woman holding my hand says.

"I'm just going to place this on your head, Nathan. You don't want to be late, do you?"

"I don't want to be late," I say, fear animating my eyes.

"Don't want to be late."

"Can't be late."

"We're already late," yells the woman who pushes past me, bringing me back to the moment.

A sea of black bags winds past me to the hypnotic whir of a conveyor belt. One by one they disappear, along with the impatient passengers hurriedly lugging them.

I catch people staring at me as I rock in place, tightly gripping my phone.

They don't matter. Nothing matters. Nothing but her.

Pick up Abby. *Tell* me you're okay.

"This is Abby. You've reached my cellphone. You know what to do."

They sent me to Bogotá on the promise of her safe return. They lied.

No. She's still alive. I know she's still alive.

She *has* to be alive.

I'm spent. My body feels like I just ran a gauntlet of baseball bats. My brain's being squeezed by an invisible vise. At least the drugs have worn off. Mostly. Whatever they fed me had legs.

Three bags remain on the carousel. Now two. Now only one.

It circles again before I summon the strength to retrieve it, feather light when I packed it, now like I'd stuffed it with bricks. The rattling, wobbly wheels behind me ring in my ears like the clang of hammer on anvil. The long jog-walk through the parking lot to my car leaves me catching my breath, the drugs they administered a compressed force against my greedy lungs.

It takes me a moment to realize that the shaking finger touching the ignition button is mine. A welcome voice serenades me as the car comes to life. The Boss, my favorite song "Thunder Road" plays as my sandpapered eyes search the parking lot for an exit sign. The car flies onto the freeway.

"Like a vision she dances across the porch as the radio plays."

I find myself at the end of Scripps-Poway Parkway as "Jungleland" ends and "Thunder Road" cues up again.

I need something harsher. Something violent. Bas Rutten. The Thai boxing workout. Visualizing Abby's captors in front of me, me landing each strike in perfect cadence with Bas.

"Welcome to the Thai boxing workout..."

My hands curl into weak fists.

My throat's parched. An empty water bottle rattles around the passenger seat floor as I punch at the sky. There's a convenience store just up ahead. Can't go in. Need to get home. Need to find her. Then who took her.

I turn right and head down San Vicente.

There are four traffic signals. I catch all of the reds, impatiently pounding my fists on the dashboard through the first two. Running the last two.

I finally get down to my road, only now realizing I don't know what awaits me at home. *Who* may await me at home. But at least I've survived. So will *she*.

It's late, long past the neighborhood's self-imposed nine o'clock bedtimes. Only one house is lit, a blinking Rudolph nose. I'm reminded of the stillness of the night by the gravel crunching under my tires, by a pack of coyotes howling in the distance. Instinctively I click my

right blinker, knowing there's no one on the street behind me, especially at this time of night. I used to think
it was safe here. Not anymore.

I turn in, headlights cut through the darkness to the
top of the driveway. Tires squeal to a stop on cement.

Oh my God.

Abby sits alone, slumped like a rag doll against the
garage door. She's alive, transformed into something I
barely recognize. Scabs cover her arms. There are a few
open wounds. Her blonde hair is hacked, streaked with
blood. Patches of scalp show through.

She looks like a prisoner of war.

I bolt out of the car, desperate to go to her, instincts
and training instead forcing me to an unsteady jog until
I reach cover.

When she sees me, her bloodshot blue eyes widen
like she just got an injection of adrenaline.

I hold up a shaking finger to my lips. Be still, Abby.
I'm coming.

I click the tactical flashlight attached to my key-
chain, shooting beams through the foggy blackness
blanketing the front yard to each side of the house.
Someone may be hiding in the bushes, or farther back
where my flashlight can't reach. She may have been put
here as bait.

I'll take the chance. God helps whoever gets in my
way.

She hums an odd, familiar melody to herself for the
seconds I study the crime scene that is her before making my move.

The patches of missing hair form an imperfect circle
around the top of her head. Her bottom lip is cut, a thin

line suggesting a razor was used. Her locket is missing, there's bruising around her neck but no ligature marks. More bruising at the bend of her right elbow, roughly the size of a dime. Dead center, a small scab where a needle punctured her skin. The scab's outlined by a ring of pink.

She's sweating profusely. It's clear she's been drugged.

They drugged her. Tortured her.

They fucking *tortured* her.

It's coming. The throbbing veins in my wrist, the pounding of my temples. I know it's coming.

Recite the word, Nathan. Recite the word and stop it.

It's too late. Abby's sees. She knows.

She abruptly stops humming and stares back, eyes wide in panic. I know what she's afraid of. It's me.

"Let me help you," I plead, fighting back hard to recover. Her hands, once limp in her lap, spring to life, like those of a marionette in the hands of a novice puppeteer.

Her dilated pupils dart side to side. She stretches out her left hand. It sends a message, telling me to stop. Her head tilts, the second message comes from a blade.

She turns the knife slightly, making sure it reflects the beam coming from my headlights into my eyes before a shaking hand guides it to the side of her neck.

"Abby, no!" I yell and lunge toward her. She mumbles back at me, the near indiscernible repetition of a word as though from a long-lost dialect echoing in my head like a threat. I drop to my knees in front of her, blood dripping from my nose. A queer smile forms over her face as her blade pierces my chest.

That's all.

Then I awaken to the grisly swirl of ambulance lights.

There's blood.

So much blood.

I know this is all because of me.

This is the thought I continue rewinding while I watch paramedics tend to my wounds.

PALOMAR MEDICAL CENTER
DECEMBER 23

I struggle to open my weighted eyelids. They resist as though they're sewn shut.

I win the battle; my unprepared eyes are assaulted by fluorescent lights overhead.

I'm struck like a punch in the gut by the sight of my chest, shaved bare, and the crimson-stained bandage stretching from the tip of my collarbone to base of my ribcage.

I strain to rise, a rush of blood floods my brain. My head falls back like a dropped sandbag

And then it arrives, the brutal, breath-stealing remembrance of how I got here draws the last ounce of hope from the room.

I try fighting back, try telling myself Abby wouldn't have done this to me. But she did.

I slam down on the call button before curling my hands into frustrated fists. Turns out it's a bad idea. My right is marked with two one-inch stitch lines. I just pissed off every nerve surrounding them. My left is wrapped in pinkish-red gauze, there's a new crimson circle spreading above my palm. The dull throbbing in my chest has changed its tempo to urgent.

Guess I peeled back the morphine veil. Yeah, bad idea.

Still, I keep squeezing them tight, then releasing, only to do it again. And again.

Does the pain for a moment free me from my guilt, or do I just need to feel again? To experience the little foretaste of death that pain brings with it.

The thin plastic curtain surrounding the windows of my room finally snaps open. Here comes the team, all dressed in white. I try to read their poker faces. No tells there.

The doctor tells me it took several hours of surgery to fix me. That the knife wound in my chest would've killed me had it been two inches or so to the left. She goes on to describe my worst injuries in detail. Subclavian this, intercostal that.

"What about Abby?" I press.

"Let's keep our focus on you, Mr. Badger," the doctor responds.

"But she'll recover, right?"

No response.

"Hey," I yell back. "I need to know. I need to see her."

"The prognosis is good," I'm finally told, in a flat *end-of-conversation* tone, leaving me frustrated, without answers. Without anything.

She asks me how the morphine titration is working and if I'm ready to self-administer.

I force Abby out of my mind for the moment it takes to weigh my options.

The pain right now is brutal; the morphine helps. But I don't like the drug-dream it brings. The same one over and over. A young girl screaming for help, holding her smoldering legs. A bearded man running past me to save her. A boy in the shadows admiring the scene. It creeps me. It shouldn't. I've seen far worse in real life.

"Self-administered. When can I see her?" I ask.

"In due time," I'm told. She leaves the room after what I'm pretty sure is a lie. A single nurse remains. Once the line's fully set, I'm handed the plunger and told it's time for a dose.

I wait until she's gone before making a few futile attempts to get out of the bed and go to Abby, but my body and the tube stuck in my arm don't allow me. I fall back in my bed and tug nervously on an earlobe, as I do.

Giving in, but only for now, I press down on the plunger. The effects don't take long.

There's a monitor bracketed to the opposite wall, it's the same size as the one in the room in Bogotá I'd been kept in. It begins a slow, familiar turn, then fractures into a trio. I place a hand over one eye, unable to tell which of the three is the real one.

DREW CAVANAUGH

SHERIFF'S PRECINCT, SAN DIEGO
DECEMBER 24

Detective Drew Cavanaugh takes a reflexive draw from a mug of cold coffee she poured for herself hours earlier. Her face pinches into a grimace before spitting the bitter mud back into the cup.

"That's an attractive look," mumbles the officer at the desk nearest hers.

"Piss off," she replies.

The precinct is empty, except for her, three grumbling night shifters, and a janitor outside her cubicle who's pushing an orbital buffer and tapping his fingers to a melody only he can hear. She waits until he passes before dumping the contents of her cup in the trashcan, then grabbing a baggie filled with Peanut Butter Oreos from the bottom desk drawer. The other officer clears his gravel-filled throat. She ignores him and tosses one in her mouth.

"Mmm, hmmm, *hmmmmm!*" He rotates his chair to face her.

"Alright, already," she says, unamused, passing him a cookie. He nibbles away at the edges, glances down at his watch, then returns to the pile of papers scattered in disarray across his desk, shuffling through them until finding the one he's after, all the while mumbling to himself.

She stuffs another cookie in her mouth and opens Nathan Badger's file to a photo of Abigail Ashford taken at the scene.

The wounds tell her a story. Abigail Ashford's torture required privacy, planning. It took experience. Expertise.

If it's him, there'll be a history of violence.

She scans Nathan Badger's military record.

"What branch did you say you were in?" she asks the officer next to her.

"Semper Fi, baby," he answers, eyes never leaving the report he's completing.

She reaches out, cookie in hand. "My boy here is ex-Army. Bribe you to let me pick your brain?"

He snatches it. "Ask away."

"There's some gaps in Badger's military record," Cavanaugh pronounces in a voice hinting suspicion. "Like he just fell off the earth, at least from the Army's perspective."

"There a question in there somewhere?"

"Yeah, smart ass. There is," she says, shaking the half-empty cookie bag at him. "The question is *why*? Says here he did Basic and Advanced Military Training at Fort McClellan. Initial Counterintelligence Training at a place called USAICO. Then there's a two-year gap. He resurfaces, attends another Advanced Individual Training at Fort Huachuca. Then disappears again. Any chance he was incarcerated?"

"Not likely."

"Then what?"

The other officer holds out his hand. She shakes another cookie out and puts the bag back in her desk drawer.

"Simple. SMU."

"In English, please," she says with a sideways glance, all the while rubbing her wrist.

"Special Mission Unit. Means he probably did some off-the-books shit," the officer says, his lips invisible, buried under a thick, greying mustache.

"Off the books? Great," pain now pulsing across the scar on her forearm as it does when the job's pressures bear down.

She fires up a web browser and googles Badger's name, scanning for any entries with dates matching the ones shrouded in his military record.

Nothing.

She scrolls past his author's page, book reviews and social media profiles until a press release catches her eye. The fighter he'd sparred claimed the UFC light heavyweight belt two months later.

She studies the photo of him taken after the charity kick-boxing event. Chiseled olive-toned features, muscular build. Six-one, one-ninety or better, a boyish grin, short, scruff black hair styled into a fauxhawk, piercing chestnut-brown eyes fringed with long lashes.

You're a looker. So was Ted Bundy.

Not allowing herself to give up for the evening, she returns to the file, and the officer's notes on the Najera interrogation.

"Interesting," she says aloud, but to herself.

The officer next to her looks up, now somewhat annoyed. "What?"

"You remember the Najera case?"

"The drug dealer? Yeah, what about it?"

Cavanaugh spins her chair around so she can look him in the eyes, gauge his reaction.

"They found him bound and gagged after someone called in a tip. Found a list of other names in his shirt pocket. The enforcers, the crooked politicians, the suppliers, everyone in Najera's network. Know what else they found?"

Unfazed, the officer next to her points to the drawer with the cookies.

She reaches in, throws him the bag. "Incriminating photos. Typed directions leading the investigating officer to a stash of over thirty pounds of fentanyl and nearly one ton of heroin."

"And?" the other officer prods, digging fat fingers into the bag and pulling out a few broken pieces.

"Najera got roughed up. Half the people on that list got roughed up," she says, eyebrows raised. "Badger lived on the streets amongst the homeless at the time, smack dab in Najera's territory. He reportedly had grown close to a boy named Johnnie. Johnnie died from a hotshot of heroin believed to be Najera's product."

The other officer's face lights up. "Sounds like motive to me."

"Uh-huh." She runs the softest part of her palm over her scar again and sits up in her chair. Each described a man about Badger's height and build, but the eye and hair color didn't match. According to each, their attacker walked with a pronounced limp; they each also saw what could have been the edge of a tattoo all described as a white dragon. Badger neither walked

with a limp nor had any tattoos, but all this didn't mean
it wasn't him.

Police observed a man who could've been Badger
driving away from San Pasqual when they reviewed
the parking lot surveillance footage, but the man's face
was obscured by a hat and one of those cheap white
dust masks. Police discovered the car from the footage
near the Mexico border a few days later. It had stolen
tags, the only fingerprints found belonged to the ass-
beaten dealer.

Police brought Badger in for questioning. He admitted to living on the streets for the past several months
while researching a story in a neighborhood controlled
by Najera, but nothing else.

As for the timeline surrounding the ass beatings,
Badger promptly delivered five witnesses who all provided written statements indicating they'd been with
him the entire day of the Najera incident playing poker.
They were all former military, like him, including his
friend, Lucas Sturgeon.

No charges were brought against Badger, but the
story of the drug bust made the front pages of the *Trib-
une* when it broke, then again during the trials.

"Yeah, motive. And shows what he may be capable
of," Cavanaugh finally says. "And listen to this. Badger
went on to announce a foundation he'd created after
Najera's trial and sentencing. He donated $115,000 to
combat addiction in the young and homeless, he also
gave his time to local soup kitchens, and formed friend-
ships with the at-risk youth there. He named his foundation Johnnie's Kids. Badger is still active in the
foundation to this day."

"Tread lightly. He's a local celebrity, you know," the officer next to her warns.

"Yeah, and he's also a suspected vigilante," her reply.

It's long after eleven when Cavanaugh first thinks of Nixy, eleven-thirty when she's finally home to feed him.

The black Toyota creeps past a second time. His acne-scarred face leans out the window for a closer look. She flashes a smile, careful not to overplay it. The car slows to a stop.

"Hello, handsome," she calls out. Her heartbeat quickens.

The man slides a hand through his greased, jet-black hair. "Hello yourself. Seen you around here." The man licks his lips.

"And do you like what you see?"

"Stopped, didn't I?" He flashes a crooked-toothed smile.

"Well," she says, loud enough for the microphone hidden deep in her skirt to pick up, "how 'bout a date?"

The man reaches over, unlocks the passenger door, and flings it open.

"Challenge Me" plays over and over again on the bumpy dirt road leading to his house.

"Leroy and the Rockets, case you're wondering." He turns down the volume, reaches over and runs his fingers through her hair. She fights back an involuntary shudder.

He leans closer, pulls her face to his. "What's this I smell?" She inches a hand closer to the door handle. "I think it's pheromones."

Her stomach turns like a washing machine tumbler. The growling grows loud enough for him to notice.

"Sounds like somebody's hungry."

"Yeah, hungry." Her nerves twist like a wrung towel.

"Mebbe I'll whip up a snack for you before we, you know, get familiar. Make you a plateful of my nachos, best for miles." He cranks the radio up again, drumming a rockabilly beat on the steering wheel.

She inches toward the door. Her right hand taps the unlock button. It never reaches the door handle.

"Going somewhere?"

"Thought I heard rattling, making sure it was locked is all," she's quick to respond.

"I think it's time you come a little closer." He grabs her hair again and buries her head in his lap.

"Fifth Street," she whispers. The officers monitoring the established frequency hear only Leroy wailing out the chorus.

"Fifth Street."

"Fifth Street!"

Cavanaugh bolts up, shielding her face. Terror-filled eyes search the room. The weapon she keeps hidden under her pillow is drawn and pointed. Her free hand inches toward the lamp on her nightstand. She stares into the darkness, watching for movement as she feels for the switch.

The light comes on. She's alone.

Just like last night, and so many nights before, her trembling hand reaches into her nightstand drawer. A match gets lit. Her lungs fill with smoky solace before a Dunhill cigarette burns to its filter in the ashtray beside her as she sits, knees tugged tight to her chest, and stares at the door.

***

NATHAN BADGER

PALOMAR MEDICAL CENTER
DECEMBER 25

It's the little moments I question. Little moments I lose, drawn away like a seashell in high tide.

I'm in a crowded bar, someone waves at me, smiles. They walk over, reach out their hand. I hesitate. Their head tilts to one side, confused.

I'm in a room in my house, frozen in place, unsure of why I'm here, what I've come for.

I awaken in the living room. Abby stands over me, holding her neck.

Little moments leaving me wondering what I've done, what I've forgotten.

Little moments like this.

I had the dream again.

The bearded man. The girl holding her smoldering legs. The boy.

This is the morphine. Or my mind playing tricks. Toying with me in the way that it does since the accident.

This is not the time.

I need to get up, get out of this fucking bed. This room.

Take control. Be in control.

Start small. Test yourself, Nate.

Curl your fingers into fists. Nothing but the pinch of stitches against the tug of dry skin. Good.

Do it again.

I kick away the sandpaper sheets, freeing my feet, both swollen with a slight bluish tint. I slide my legs over the edge, they hover there for a tentative moment, then I commit. The cold floor feels good on the pads of my feet, a minor victory.

Now to these tubes. I'm gonna rip them out of my arm, change clothes and go to her as long as the coast is clear.

They've left the privacy curtains fully open, for the first time I'm able to take in the view of my surroundings through the glass wall separating my bed from the hallway. There are no guards posted in front of my door. No nurse manning the nurse's station. Good.

I give a threatening tug at the IV line and trail my eyes down the hallway, following a row of precisely hung scarlet garland until they land on a lone woman whose precise forward footfalls resemble those of a soldier. Her black suit coat and matching pants are a sharp contrast to the antiseptic, alabaster white walls and gleaming tile flooring.

She's folded the straps of a distressed-leather messenger bag neatly into her left palm, which is locked into place an inch or so from her hip by a fully extended, rigid arm. Her other swings slightly. Her fists are clenched. Every step she takes brings a slight opening of her jacket, revealing a belt with two notch marks and the discolored groove between them where her weapon should be.

She's heading straight to my nurse. She's come here for me.

My nurse leaves her in the hallway and raps lightly on the door before entering. Maibel. A black woman. Late forties, maybe just cresting fifty. Mahogany skin and big, springy hair that moves only slightly as she glides into the room with the practiced grace of a dancer. A kind face, one I'm compelled to trust.

Her eyes convey genuine concern. I need to know why.

"Merry Christmas, Mr. Nathan. You have a visitor," she says, apologetic, yet with a smile meant to reassure me. "It's a detective from the San Diego Sheriff's Department. She'd like to talk with you if you're feeling up to it."

"Did something happen to Abby?" the question sucks all the air from my lungs.

"There's no change in her condition," Maibel assures me.

I exhale the breath I'm holding, catch myself chewing a fingernail and shake my hand away.

"Merry Christmas, Maibel. It's fine." I nod my head only once. I knew someone would eventually come. A Sheriff's Detective, alone. So far, they've kept this with the locals.

Maibel lingers. A question forms on her lips but doesn't leave them. Instead, she offers me the smile I've begun to look forward to before leaving.

The door to my room re-opens. The detective's eyes lock on me. They're a brilliant emerald, no measure of empathy in them. Her aquiline, makeup-free face is framed by golden hair ending abruptly near the base of clenched jaws. Her full lips pulled tight. She stands all of five-feet-six, every inch of her seeming ready to pounce.

I know the look. She's not here to console me. Or to check on my welfare. This much is clear. The accusation she wears prominent on her face makes mine heat.

She closes the gap between us, gets close enough to speak in a whisper. Her breathe hides the hint of a cigarette behind an ineffective mint.

"Good morning, Mr. Badger. I'm Area Detective Cavanaugh with the San Diego Sheriff's Department," she says, her voice raspy, like she'd been up all night. "I'm here about what happened to Ms. Ashford. Your nurse assured me you feel well enough to talk. I'd like to hear it from you."

"Never mind that," I snap back, tugging again at the IV line. "Tell me you have a suspect."

Her face hardens further. "I *asked* you if you feel well enough to talk."

Our eyes meet, lock. I'm the first to look away.

"Yeah. I'm up to it," I say, pointing my chin toward the chairs at the end of my bed.

"I'm fine here." She drums her fingers on the bag at her side and the rapid-fire interrogation begins. My hands close again into fists.

"How long have you known Ms. Ashford?"

My fist hits the bed.

"How did you meet?"

It hits harder this time.

"How long have you lived together?"

I push myself closer to her, lean in and lock on as I answer her questions.

All the while she studies my eyes for tell-tale shifts. She's forming her baseline. Textbook.

I know what comes next. The pivot.

"Tell me about the night you found her."

Even knowing it's coming doesn't prepare me. There are things hiding inside me. Things locked away in a dark closet somewhere deep in the recesses of my mind. This is one of them.

"It's mostly a blur," I tell her, pointing at the IV still attached near the bend in my elbow. Hoping she'll just let it go. Knowing she won't.

"Do your best," she says. Her eyes bore into mine like the bit of a drill.

I open the door to that dark closet and let the memory out. The weight of recalling it slams my head into my hands with the force of a brick falling from a rooftop.

"I found her in the driveway, propped up against the garage door. She looked like she was…" I can't say it, I don't want to even think it. The door to the dark closet slams shut. "I need a minute," I finally say.

"*What* did she look like, Mr. Badger?" she presses, unmoved, not missing a beat.

I'm met with a cold stare when I lift up my head. "She looked like some ten-year-old attacked her with scissors, *that's* how she looked. She was going to kill herself. I stopped her. She turned the knife on me."

Warmth flushes my face. It's the heat of her intensity.

"I know *what* happened. I'm here today to find out *why*. We found no evidence of self-inflicted wounds. What there *is* evidence of are defensive wounds." She points two fingers at the bandage covering my chest. "*Your* defensive wounds. Given the state we found her in, I consider this pretty relevant." She folds her arms over her chest and asks, "Why did she stab you?"

I tug at the edge of the bandage with a fingernail, buying time for an answer I don't have. "Abby wouldn't have done this to me on her own."

Her arms unfold and spread wide. "Clearly she did. I'll repeat the question. Why?"

I dig my fingers into my chest and stare back blankly. "I don't know," I reply.

"Really?" she scoffs. "Your window is closing here, Mr. Badger. The team completed their SOREK testing this morning."

I held on to the ring for more than a month. It burned like an accusation in my pocket, ever hotter when those five words got stuck in my throat.

Will you marry me, Abby?

How fucking *dare* you, Cavanaugh.

"You ran a *rape* kit on Abby because you think *I* raped her?" I spit out in disgust. Without realizing I've done it, I yank the corner of the bandage away, exposing the jagged edge of the wound underneath. I welcome the pain it brings. "*You* think I *raped* Abby? She was going to be my fiancé. Of course they'll find my DNA."

A slow nod of her head, a condescending frown. "Fair enough. I'm curious though," she says, reaching for something in her bag. "How do you explain the bruises your neighbor saw on Abby's neck twelve days before the events in your driveway?"

The bruises.

Abby holding her neck.

Why is she holding her neck?

Stay calm, Nate.

Kah-thuhm.

The little moments I've grown to question.

Kah-thuhm. Kah-thuhm.

Little moments I lose, snatched away like a seashell in high tide.

She lifts her hand from the bag. "Take a good look, Mr. Badger."

Kah-thuhm. Kah-thuhm. Kah-thuhm. My pulse trips along like the foot of a coked-up drummer.

It's coming again.

"This is how we found her. *This* is what was done to her."

The machine I'm attached to sounds its alarm, Maibel rushes back into the room, with what must be a trainee in tow, and whispers words of instruction in the trainee's ear before taking her place at my side. The trainee checks my vitals before resetting the bandage.

The pain in my chest is searing now, a white-hot sword against my flesh. Cavanaugh paces the room, waiting for words that won't come. I press down on the plunger, the drug washes over me like the soft breeze of a summer day. I surrender to it.

Recite the word, Nathan.

I close my eyes, concentrate, command my mouth to move. Command words of my innocence to come.

A gallows silence blankets the air until she breaks it.

"To be continued, Mr. Badger."

2

DANIEL

Even before the electrode-lined membrane is peeled back from his scalp, Daniel Mazer knows something is wrong. He's burning up.

He scrapes the nape of his neck, unable to quell the ratcheting sting drilling into his cervical spine. Frantic hands shoot upward to his shiny head, cradling it against the pressure building inside. His eyes search the downstairs room for answers. Two bodies lying still on metal tables offer none.

Disinterested, the figure hovering over him tugs the second high boot into place, then pulls the coverall's zipper tight to his neck, tucking the mask shielding his face underneath.

The slight movement on Mazer's arm amplifies. His arms stiffen. Random ripples rise and tear their way downward, moving like a violent summer storm. The star-shaped birthmark covering the whole of his forearm burns like a brand. A vise tightens around his neck, squeezing phlegm down his throat, gagging his breaths. His trembling hand reaches out to the figure, but Mazer's fingers betray him, and lose their grip on the figure's skin-tight suit.

The figure gives thoughtful consideration to killing Mazer now. To gripping Mazer's throat in his hands until its pulse stills. To watching the last light fade in his eyes. *How nice it would be.* But this indulgence will come another day. Today his hands must stay clean. Today he must see the experiment through to its end.

Mazer's body begins to tremor. The figure's eyes darken. "Sit still." He retrieves two leather straps from the floor. One cinches Mazer's arms to his torso, the other immobilizes his legs.

Mazer's eyes plead for answers. He stares back at the shape of a man, now seeing only the aura surrounding him. His tongue, thick and purple, strikes out in dog-like pants.

The scene both amuses and displeases the figure. He steps back from Mazer, removes a spray bottle from his breast pocket, and douses Mazer's face.

Mazer chokes on the chemical sliding down his throat. When the gagging subsides, his eyes open, primitive. His pupils dilate, the last remnants of prefrontal cortical impulse control diminishing with them.

The figure watches the storm rise and recede with dispassionate curiosity. He waits until only a thousand-mile stare remains, then bends down so close to Mazer's ear that his soft breath thunders inside it.

He whispers the Gaelic word.

Athraigh.

Athraigh.

Athraigh.

Mazer fights through his stupor just enough to join in.

Athraigh.

Athraigh.

Athraigh.

The chants keep on and grow louder. Faster. More urgent.

Athraigh.

Athraigh.

Athraigh.

After the sacred thirteenth repetition, the figure falls silent, placing a finger over his lips. The empty shell that once was Mazer goes quiet too. "Here." Sliding two fingernails across Mazer's neck, he hisses, "Do it here." A throbbing vein haunts the figure's forehead like a phantom lightning bolt.

Mazer's lips part slowly. "Here." His voice absent emotion, all humanity gone.

The figure removes the two belts.

"Now go."

Ω

SARAFINA LOUNGE, DOWNTOWN SAN DIEGO
DECEMBER 26
8:36 P.M.

Victoria pauses to study her reflection, nervously twisting a thick lock of bronze hair that had fallen out of place. She's early, as is her plan. First in, and if need be, first out. If he's twenty-some-pounds heavier than the photos in his profile, like date number one, or twenty-some-years older, like date number two, she won't give James the courtesy of a hello or goodbye. She'll just leave.

She holds what feels a fool's hope tonight will be different. That maybe the third time will in fact be a charm. James' self-deprecating humor and gentlemanly manner propelled him to the top of the candidate list, a worthy accomplishment in its own right given the barrage of new suitors who message her daily. If, however, he turns out to be like the others, her night will end with Haagen-Daz and Harry Potter, alone.

The closer she comes to the club they agreed to meet at, the better Harry Potter begins to sound.

"Fuck it," Victoria spins on her heels in the direction of her car, and as it grows nearer, the resignation weighting her shoulders like a thick winter coat falls away. The little voice in her head nudges her on, assuring her she can be home in twenty minutes, cozied up in her Snuggie in twenty-five, back at Hogwart's soon after. She clutches her car keys, shaking them twice as though doing so somehow gives permanence to the deal she'd just made with herself.

The deal doesn't last long. A new inner voice protests. An argument ensues. *You have to keep trying.* She stands still as a statue, immobilized by cognitive dissonance until, without consciously directing them to do so, one hand drops the keys back into her purse, the other lets go of the door handle.

Soldier up, she tells herself as she spins around, and marches back down Market with a newfound resolve. The heels of her Jimmy Choo pumps click up to the doorman, who holds out his right palm, and steadies the beam of a penlight on her face. "ID please," he says, clearly doubting she's old enough to enter. She's grown used to it. Even her creative writing professor had joked about carding her one day before class. "Enjoy yourself," mutters the broad-shouldered Samoan with gargantuan hands, after casting several suspicious glances from her ID to her.

Victoria chooses her place at the bar strategically, a spot where she can both monitor the entrance and slip away unnoticed if the situation warrants. A glass of red from the Alsace region meets her hands not long after she sits. She places enough cash to cover it on the bar.

A rumbling knot creeps up from her stomach as the minutes tick past the agreed upon time. She drowns it in red before ordering a second. Resignation again pulls down her shoulders, she shakes her head and heaves a frustrated sigh. The argument inside picks up where it had left off, the first voice winning her over again.

She tells the bartender he can keep the change; he takes off to the other end of the bar before she's startled by a barstool thudding against the open spot she'd been holding for James. She turns toward the noise. A gasp escapes her lips before she can stop it. The dead eyes of the man next to her squeeze shut against visible pain. When they open, his pupils jump side to side. He mutters the chorus of an old children's song, which seems momentarily to calm him. His fingers trace the edges of a splotchy pink birthmark stretching from elbow to wrist. Sweat covers his arms.

"I'm sorry I'm late," comes a voice from behind her. James has arrived. It's too late to run. It's showtime.

Forgetting for a moment the odd man beside her, she sucks in a breath, and turns her head, bracing for what she expects to see. But when she sees him her full, pouty lips wet with gloss form a smile and her apple-green eyes brighten. He's handsome, far more so than his profile photos. Bonus points, he has a brilliant, beautiful smile.

He holds a bouquet of roses in a grease-stained hand. "Flat tire," he says apologetically.

"I'll grab us a table," she replies, shooing him off to the restroom to clean up. She admires him as he walks away and finds herself wondering how he feels about Haagen-Daz and Harry Potter. The idea sounds better and better as she slides into a seat at an open table.

James returns and they make small talk. She soon realizes she's happy, genuinely happy she's stayed. She's equally glad to be away from the dead-eyed man, whose foot rattles in a chaotic Morse code each time she shifts a glance at him. His presence is like a horrific accident she'd once driven by, one she couldn't stop staring at.

Should I say something?

"Hello? Earth to Victoria. Your Brazil trip?" James repeats.

"Oh, right. Sorry." She does her best to put the man out of her head as she tells her story. Nervous fingers twirl locks of hair. She feels chills when James touches her arm the first time and knows for certain the night will go well.

The waitress interrupts their moment. He orders the sea bass and a Hoegaarden. She, a strip steak, and a fresh glass of red. When the waitress peels away from the table, the man is standing directly in front of them, swaying from side to side as though to some unheard song. Victoria freezes when she sees what he's holding.

The man screams a word as he raises the knife to his throat. Before they can cover their faces, a spray of hot, arterial blood fans over them.

***

NATHAN BADGER

PALOMAR MEDICAL CENTER
DECEMBER 27

My spine tightens, my ears heat like lava rocks spewed from a volcano, a shiver strikes the arch of my back. I'm cemented in place on a ridge overlooking a campfire.

"You shouldn't have chosen me." The boy's snarled teeth bare, an eerie orange glow dances over his face.

"H-he made me!" The girl fights in vain to kick free from his grasp.

"I warned you," he says, vice-gripping both ankles and dragging her toward the flames.

Thith-thith-thith. I hear the song of skin tearing away

I will my feet to move. A scream freezes in my throat.

It's okay, the winds whisper.

My senses alert. Someone's rushing up from behind. A bearded man turns to me as he passes, holding a finger to his lips.

You're okay, the wind reassures me.

Thuzz, suzzzz, the sound of sizzling flesh. The boy's menacing eyes trail up the hillside until they meet mine as the man pulls the girl from the fire.

Look away, Nate. Look away now.

But I can't.

The scream finally comes.

Wake up, Mr. Nathan, the wind commands.

My throbbing head shoots up from my pillow. Sweat beads pop on my forehead. I slap my face; the sharp sting brings a bitter return to my current reality. I'm not on the hillside. I'm in a hospital room.

It's the little moments I've grown to question. Moments like these.

Maibel appears from the washroom door, a wet towel in her hand. "You're okay, Mr. Nathan," she assures, rubber soles squeaking across the room. She takes my head in her hand and guides it back to the pillow.

I rub the sleep from my desert-dry eyes with the back of my hand. Down half a glass of water. "Bad dream," I tell her.

"I know," she replies. She brushes matted hair from my pillow-creased face and lays a cold towel over my forehead. "Pretty bad one at that."

"It's nothing," I assure her, clearing the cobwebs from my brain.

She pulls up a chair. There's a telling frown where a smile should be.

"Detective Cavanaugh's on her way back," she tells me.

I study her face for what's hidden there, she looks away. "There's something else, isn't there?" I ask.

She places a hand atop mine. "We've been instructed to take blood and urine samples before she arrives."

Ω

It's the little things you remember, and you miss. Abby pinching my waist and wagging a finger at me as I lick Nacho Cheese Dorito residue from my fingers. Those foo-foo drinks she likes, the ones I pretended to like. The scent of perfume on her pillow lingering long after she left for her run. Me in bed, trying to plan out my day, my research, only to find myself again distracted by the smell of her perfume.

I don't know how long it's been since my eyes closed; I just know these thoughts are with me when I open them. And with them the reminder, the knowledge that the woman I love lies in a hospital bed one floor above me, and whoever took her, whoever did this to her is somewhere out there, free, living their life. I shoot up from the bed, teeth snarled.

Maibel's gone, no doubt lining up the necessary tubes, vials and needles. Writing my name on plastic bags holding test kits. I could be gone before she returns.

I don't get the chance.

The gentle rap on glass comes.

Maibel returns with her trainee in tow. I don't wait long for the poking, prodding and needle pricks to begin.

They leave once they've drawn what feels like my last ounce of blood, I fill the cup I'm supposed to fill. Whatever they fed me had legs. Guess we'll all soon find out if it also has a half-life.

I hit the call button once I finish. Maibel returns alone.

In her left hand, a clear plastic bag filled with my personal things from the night they admitted me. My keys. My cellphone. The ring.

Abby's ring.

I suck in a sharp breath at the sight of it.

She peels my clenched fingers open, places the ring in my hand, closes them around it before leaving.

The ring speaks to me. Reminds me. I have to come clean.

And I will. Now. Cavanaugh's arrived.

"Detective Cavanaugh, good morning." I slip the ring on my pinkie finger and greet her with the best semblance of a smile I can muster. It's returned by the *thup-thup-thup* of fingers on leather.

"Let's pick up where we left off," she says.

My knee jitters under the bedsheets. "I have things to tell you," I say.

She notices, sits down, straightens her pants, holds up her right index finger, slowly spinning it in the air. "I'm sure you do."

I squeeze my eyelids shut, and open the dark closet's door. "I think you need to know what went on before the night I found Abby," I say before opening them.

"Let's find out," she replies, the hint of a sarcastic smirk forms.

"Yeah, *let's*," already noting the steady pounding of the veins in my wrists. "Starting with this. My interview on *Good Morning America*."

She studies the wall behind me as she deadpans, "Caught it on YouTube. I'm curious. You're researching connections between cults and the government. You ever *belong* to a cult, Mr. Badger?"

I shoot a look. "Is there a reason you're asking?"

She smiles a knowing smile. "Just curious. We digress. The events you want to tell me about?"

My fists squeeze together until my fingers go white. This isn't easy, but all of it needs to be said. "I came home after the interview to find her locked in the bedroom. She was talking on the phone. I made out one sentence before she hung up," I say, pausing long enough for our eyes to meet. "She said, '*I couldn't stop him.*'"

"The *him* I assume is you," she blinks once, then looks away. "Stop you from what?"

I shoot up straight in the bed. "She *wasn't* talking about me."

"Then who?"

I search the ceiling for an answer. "I don't know."

"Is there some significance to this you're wanting me to pick up on?"

Fists unclench, I gently roll her ring counterclockwise on my finger. "Have you checked her phone records?" I ask.

"No reason to," she flatly responds.

"Please," I say. "Please check them. It could be important."

"Moving on," she replies." How would you describe your relationship with Abby?"

Thwack. A flash of the marks on her neck hits me. I flinch. Cavanaugh's eyes linger on me too long, her head shakes slowly, disapprovingly, before she jots something down in her notebook.

"We didn't have a perfect relationship," I finally respond.

"Yeah, that's pretty clear," she says, uncrossing her legs, only to cross them again. "Sometimes arguments take a turn. They go places we never intended them to. We say things we can't take back; we *do* things we can't take back."

She waits for her words to sink in. Waits for me to accept that she's on my side. She understands me, knows I made a mistake.

I give her nothing.

She makes a show of how she closes her notebook, then stares at the worn, dog-eared cover long enough for me to wonder when, or even *if* she'll look away from it. "You're not helping yourself here. Why don't you just tell me what *really* happened, and we can work this all out. Together."

The ring calls out to me again. Come clean, Nate. Come clean.

Alright, Detective. As you wish.

"Abby was taken," I blurt out, clearly taking her by surprise. "Sometime the day after the phone call, that's why I asked if you've checked her phone records."

"Now you've got my attention." Her face a mix of intrigue and amusement. "Do continue."

The words come together in my head, and even as they do I deny them. My lips part and I talk, detached, as though recounting the story of a character from a novel. "The morning after the GMA interview I got an email a guy named Bish claiming to have information for my book. Abby had already gone on her daily run, so I left her a note and took off for L.A. I had a meeting with my agent and a publisher in town from New York. I arranged to meet up with Bish at his hotel in La Jolla after. I told Abby all this in the note, told her we needed to talk when I got back home."

Cavanaugh's face twists up like she'd just smelled something fowl. "And we *know* how your little talk turned out," she spits out, not attempting to hide her disdain.

"Listen to me," aiming an index finger at her. "The meeting never happened. Bish never showed. I had too much to drink waiting for him at the bar, so I got a room. The La Estancia Hotel. I have receipts. I came back the next morning to an empty house. She'd left me a note of her own; she was staying with out-of-state friends. She did that sometimes."

Her eyebrows lift in amusement. "I'll play along. Did she ever call you back? Did you try to look for her? Did you call those friends?"

I place a hand over the ring, it's cold to my touch. Like Abby had become.

"I waited two days. Nothing. Day three is the first time I left the house. I needed an outlet. I went climbing. Joshua Tree. I have this three-foot gnome statue in my living room. I found it in the dining room with an envelope propped against it when I got back home. It had a note with instructions and a one-way ticket to Bogotá inside. That's when I learned she hadn't gone to stay with anyone. She'd already been taken."

"And you *didn't* call the authorities?"

"The note warned me not to. So, no. I didn't make the call."

"Duly noted," she says, unconvinced. She flips back several pages in her notebook. "I want names. Your agent, the publisher. Anyone who can verify this supposed rock-climbing trip. Let's visit something else. You have an alarm system. You're telling me someone broke into your home. Why didn't your alarm trigger?"

"They must've made her give them the code."

"Back to the contents of this mysterious envelope. Can I assume you have a note to show me?"

"I was instructed to burn it," I mumble absently into the air.

Cavanaugh spins her right index finger. "How convenient. All of it. Let's deconstruct this. You tell anyone else about the tipster guy. His name again?"

"Bish. Kenneth Bish. And no. I only told Abby."

Her pen moves quickly across paper. "There goes a part of your alibi. How about the phone call?

"No," I say, eyes falling down the bed to my feet.

"The note? The tickets? Bogotá? I'm guessing not them either. As I said, *how convenient*. We searched your house, Mr. Badger. We found no evidence of a struggle. If someone took her, and I'm not suggesting I believe this is what happened, but *if* someone took her, what I think we both know is she would've been taken by someone she knew."

Now the emerald greens are piercing through me.

"Which brings me back to you. Give me the date, time and airline you flew on for this supposed trip."

She jots down what I tell her before closing her notebook.

"I'll of course be checking this all out. The flight. La Estancia. This Bish person."

Nacho Cheese Doritos. Her pinching my waist. The smell of her perfume. It all comes rushing back again, overwhelming me for a moment Cavanaugh takes notice of.

"Look," I say, blinking my eyes to the threat of a tear, "I need you to hear me. I didn't hurt Abby. I'd never hurt Abby. I love her."

I meet her eyes again. For a moment I fool myself into thinking she's considering me in a new light.

But then everything changes. Emerald greens light on fire. She reaches into her messenger bag and takes out a tan file folder, removing a photograph as she rises up from the chair.

"I've been waiting to show you some things we found at your house," she says. "Now seems like a good time."

She pulls her eyes away from me long enough to glance again at the photo she holds as she snits the next words out. "So, you love her, huh?"

She's standing over me now, eyes locked on mine, her left hand within inches of my face. I want to look away, but I don't. My eyes blur at first, but when I refocus, I see it.

The photo is of me.

The timestamp is clear; the date is incriminating.

I'm in bed.

I'm naked.

I'm not alone.

For a brief moment an image in my mind fits the photo, as the corner piece of a jigsaw puzzle unites the abstract others once sitting alone and disconnected.

It was taken in the room I was held in. Someone staged it. Someone staged it to frame me.

I hope Cavanaugh doesn't read the recognition in my eyes.

But it seems she has.

She holds the photo there until I look away, then returns to her chair, careful to smooth her dress pants as she sits. She pulls out the file again from her briefcase, takes out a thick stack of other photos, holds them high enough for me to see.

"A young girl. Really, really young. What's a loving boyfriend like you doing in bed with her? And this one caught my attention too. The baggie on the nightstand by your bed."

"I already told you. I was *sent* to Bogotá. They held me in a room there. They drugged me." I shove my arm toward her, point a finger at the gauze taped to my arm where the needle went in. "You had drug tests run on me. You'll see I'm not lying."

She ignores me, and instead drops the hammer on the last nail in my coffin.

"You look good for this," she says, eyeing me up and down. "Maybe it's because you are."

That's it. I've heard enough. I gesture toward the door. "We're done here."

"For now," she replies on her way out.

Outside my room, she makes a call. She could place that call from anywhere, but she doesn't. Clearly, I'm meant to hear it.

"It's Cavanaugh sir. He gave me an alibi. I'll check it out."

Silence. Then a slow shake of her head.

"No, I don't think it *will*." She glares back at me as she says it. "I'm going to check on Ms. Ashford now. I'll update you after."

She's going to see Abby.

Kah-thuhm.

Abby, alone, afraid, forever damaged by what was done to her.

Kah-thuhm.

I'm a suspect.

Kah-thuhm - Kah-thuhm.

Carlos Najera vowed revenge after what I did to him. He was released earlier this month. He has connections in Colombia.

This could be him.

And I know who helped him.

Kah-thuhm - Kah-thuhm.

The woman at the bar who drugged me.

I will find her.

Open the dark closet door.

Close your eyes, Nate. Close your eyes, open the door and enter the woods.

Kah-thuhm- Kah-thuhm - Kah-thuhm.

Every vein in my body pounds, the raw skin pinched tight around my chest wound throbs in near perfect synch. It's coming again.

Kah-thuhm - Kah-thuhm - Kah-thuhm - Kah-thuhm.

Take control, Nate. Slow this down. Focus on details. Anything Cavanaugh can use to find who did this to Abby.

Anything to prove my innocence.
Focus.
Say the word.

3

You are LATE!

A thick network of vines parts before me, allowing me in, only to close again behind me. A chill wind chaps my face, whipping through the trees lining the path to the first shrine.

Thuhmm. Thuhmm.

Thin branches dance a violent dance, cutting through the night sky like swords.

Thuhmm. Thuhmm.

Just as I was taught as a child, I visualize lighting the first candle in honor of Mnemosyne and things remembered. Its flickering flame cuts against the blackness, illuminating the portrait of two children, of my first kiss with Claire, her auburn hair pulled back into pigtails. Of Claire's mother, Mrs. Lemley, presenting me a plate filled with toasted bread covered in a patchwork of dripping orange and white squares of cheese.

Of the day when my injury happened, of the neurologist. Of my foster parents telling me not all my memories will return. They tell me to cherish the ones that stay. To cherish these. Claire. The cheese sandwiches, Her pigtails. Only to cherish these. And I do.

The candle's light dies, stealing my memories away. The wind whips up in warning of an imminent storm. It whispers to me that I'm no longer safe here. I must go to where I am.

The patter of raindrops builds as I summon the view from the dining room windows of my home. I have arrived. I am safe once again.

There before the final shrine, my Buddha shrine, I light the last candle. A comforting scent of vanilla coats my nostrils as I kneel.

I focus my mind on a single word, the word I was taught. I repeat it over and over until it takes on a resonance of its own. The object I've summoned appears. Through the blue sky above me, the roar of a jet engine cuts through the crisp winter air, the place I first noticed the woman.

I will myself inside of it.

The slow-pitched roll builds into a tremor. An invisible force stirs the remaining water in my glass. Reflexes thrust my hand toward it in time to stop its fall. For a long moment, nothing, then the fury unleashes. I'm thrown violently upward, then snatched back hard by the pull of my safety belt. There is no fear, only thoughts of Abby and the promise I was made for her safe return.

I take in the others around me. Some stare forward wide-eyed, as though their heightened alert will somehow save them from the plane's seemingly imminent tumble from the sky. One head among them is lowered, it never moves, her red nails tightly grip the armrest.

It's her.

I fast forward the movie. I'm seated at the bar of a busy restaurant. It's brightly colored, eclectic, ornate. The woman touches my shoulder. She tells me her name and gestures toward a table. I notice her hands, her red nails. I take in the scent of lavender. She hands me a drink and I carelessly drink it. The world begins turning like a carnival ride.

I glide across the floor. Into a vehicle. Flashes of buildings fly by the speeding car as I fade in and out of consciousness. The car stops on a cobblestone road. Men carry me out. I'm taken to a small, dark room.

You are LATE!

There's a television monitor on the dresser across from the bed I'm strapped in. The picture's increasingly blurred, spinning. A young woman enters the room. A guard posts at the door.

LATE!

Our bodies writhe. A bearded man looks on, another takes photos. The woman rolls out of bed, I watch her leave. The bearded man stands over me, smiling a threatening smile.

He strikes me. Again. Again. My arms can't move. I can't protect myself. He looks down at me holding a syringe, demanding answers. I offer him none.

A bolt of electricity surges through me.

LATE!

I'm standing on the hillside. The bearded man runs by me on his way to the campfire. An eerie orange cast lights the boy's face as he glares up at me.

"I'm LATE!" I scream as I awaken.

Maibel's seated at my side, she holds onto my arm until I stop shaking. She takes a tissue from her purse and cleans blood from my face before saying, "I have a friend. His is a comforting voice in…in uncomfortable times. I feel like he's someone you could talk to. About whatever's going on."

I study the light coat of sweat covering my forearm. "It's the dream again. The bearded man I keep seeing."

Her heads nods knowingly, as though she expected my answer. "*Bearded* man?"

"I don't know," I say, head full, like I'm underwater holding my breath.

She shows me the card. Dr. Richard F. Eastcott. Forensic psychiatrist. "He can help you."

My Maibel. My protector. "I'll let you know. And thank you for looking out for me again. Give your husband a message for me, will you?" I ask, casting a glance at the platinum ring on her left hand. "Tell him he's a lucky man."

"I will. I talk to him every night when I pray. And I know he's somewhere listening. Better be."

"I'm sorry for your loss." I reply, overtaken in the moment by the dripping sadness thick in the air between us.

"So am I," she says, handing me a newspaper. "From yesterday. There's mention of Abby's attack in the paper. I thought you should know."

Reluctant, I stretch out my hand. This is someone else's nightmare, not mine.

She neatly creases the newspaper into thirds. As she does, I notice the front-page article covering a suicide downtown.

"Even the Lone Ranger had Tonto," she tells me. "Let me call Dr. Eastcott."

I don't stop her from going, though for some reason I find myself wanting to.

Closing my eyes, I return to the path. To my first shrine. To what lies beyond it.

The wooded path leading me to my memories isn't a place I feel safe going to. Threats scream to me in the violent winds assaulting the trees as I pass them.

They tell me to stay on the path. That I must always stay on the path.

They tell me I'm late.

But I can't listen to them.
Not anymore.

* * *

ALASTAIR KANE

NUESTRO HOGAR
SAN DIEGO, CALIFORNIA
DECEMBER 27, 8 P.M.

Dorien Wissom, ARMR founder and president, clips forward, breaking now and again into a heavy-footed jog, struggling to keep his bird legs centered underneath the sloshing mass above them in a succession of near falls. Each huffed exhale coats his glasses. Each breath he sucks back returns the smoky chocolate aftertaste of a Romeo y Julieta he'd savored on the flight over.

With the opening of offices throughout the US and Latin America, and the lucrative, multiyear contract he'd signed with Kane Industries, fortunes have changed for him, and with them have come a private jet, and new, better vices.

And now, finally, after years of study and struggle and building, of soul-searching and self-development, of walking the path, of graduating the rigors of the Discernments, after the countless SR milestones he'd achieved in his time at Paradign, his reward has come: acceptance into a coveted group of CEOs, visionaries and leaders invited to an urgent meeting at the founder of Paradign's home. But as of this moment, his reward is in jeopardy. He's late.

He shifts anxious glances through fogged glasses to the well-hidden rear entrance he'd been instructed to enter, then to his watch, as if doing so can somehow stop time, or slow its advance.

Just a few more feet, he assures himself, scanning the driveway for signs of others. He arrives nearly breathless at the vine covered entrance alone.

After wiping away the sweat weaving its way down through dense eyebrows, he gives the door an expectant yank, finding it locked. He lifts a chubby, shaking finger, presses it hard into the buzzer. Frustrated, he pulls the thick fingers of his hands together, and begins assaulting the door with hammer fists.

Ω

A security camera whirs into motion overhead. Its lens tightens in on Wissum's face.

Inside, Alastair Kane views the remote camera's feed on an HD color monitor, considering the man's situation for a long moment. His right index finger rests near the remote lock release switch.

It's nine minutes before the announcement, and six minutes past when the guests were instructed to arrive. The others long ago followed the trail of candles set out for them and found their way to the Ascension chamber, there surrounded by marble walls, there warmed by the flames dancing low around their ankles.

Kane's finger meets the cold metal toggle. He nudges the switch forward, then stops to consider.

You're late.

But I pardon you.

The locks disengage. Kane watches as Wissum wedges inside and follows the candlelit path down the hall to the room with the others.

I pardon you.

With a motion of his hand, Kane waves the thought of Wissum away, having more pressing matters on his mind: his coming performance.

The click of Berluti Scritto leather slip-ons echo off pristine Maplewood flooring down the long first floor hallway. Black Ermenegildo Zegna Trofeo trousers grip tight to his thighs, a Brunello Cucineli short-sleeve dress shirt completes the ensemble.

The mirror at the end of the hall draws him to it with the force of a riptide. He does not, cannot resist flexing like a bodybuilder and admiring his arms.

Exquisite.

He traces his finger down the softest parts of his face until it rests on the one imperfection. His one beautiful, perfect imperfection.

Exquisite.

Drawing his admiring black eyes away, he turns to his father's meditation room.

It's been nearly four months since Father sought treatment. The room betrays those many months of neglect. A sprinkling of dust coats the magenta meditation bench centered before a small shrine. On top of it, on either side of Father's gold-framed photo, dried, withered stems slump out from two blue-and-white chinoiserie vases. Brown petals coat the floor beneath. He crushes them under his heels before turning to leave. Those he's chosen await him downstairs. It's nearly time.

At the end of the hallway, he again pauses before the iron lattice-framed mirror mounted there, practicing for a final time the expression of emotion his face must later form.

He removes a keycard from his pocket and presses it against the mirror's center, counting the seconds with an impatient swing of his index finger.

Locks disengage, the mirror slides away and the now-revealed door ratchets open. A chill draft rolls over him, ticking his eyebrows, biting the tip of his nose. He steps through to the stairway after sealing the passage behind him.

Fingernails scrape along the brick wall as he descends. The hoarse melody soothes him, bringing memories of the decayed walls at Bolsiver.

An undulating yellow hue grows bright as he reaches the base of the steps, soft flames dance inside the burner lined Paradign emblem carved into the floor of the Ascension chamber where his invited have assembled. Those inside cannot see him through the frosted privacy glass window forming one-half of the room's outer-most wall. But he can see them. See right through them, right into their greedy black hearts.

Kane holds the keycard to a pad mounted near the door, a panel in the wall slides down, revealing a dial. Kane gives it a sharp clockwise twist. All eyes in the room dart to the floor as the flames shoot up, then just as quickly disappear.

Kane takes a moment to imagine himself in his audience's place; how it will feel for them to behold him.

A silence ushers over the invited as he enters, confusion moves in even measure through the room.

Thomas Anderson, CFO of Jentaine Technologies, is first to speak out. "My invitation came from Cathal. Why are *you* here?"

Kane manifests the expression of regret he practiced in the mirror upstairs. It's foreign, unwelcome. It falls away as would sand through his fingers. "Father is ill."

"Ill? And *you're* the one delivering this news? Where is Elder Dean?"

"Elder Dean is with him."

"With him *where*?" presses Anderson.

"His Ascension is near. It doesn't matter where. What matters is what I came here to tell you."

Whispers spread over the room with the force of fanned flames, a lone voice cuts through the din of the twelve.

"Through the hardship, character," the CEO of The Cohagen Group begins. Others join in. "Through the pain, clarity. Through the unplugging, awareness. Through the awareness, rebirth. Through the rebirth, deliverance."

The room quiets after. The pain of coming loss clear on the faces before him, Kane hangs his head, long enough to convince himself he's maintained the illusion that he actually cares.

"Your companies, ladies and gentlemen," he says, stepping over to the podium on his right to retrieve a remote. At the press of a button, the seventy-inch monitor mounted on the wall behind him blinks to life. A collage of corporate logos roll one after the other. Scion Bank, Epsilon Investments, The Grœbeck Fund, TetraTech, Sequence Analytics, The Cohagen Group,

Atrium Foodservice, Jentaine Technologies, Turning Leaf Media, Zephyr Metrics, Howard Regence Inc. ARMR Intel's logo appears last. "With the news of Daniel Mazer's death, each of their reputations are at risk. Paradign's legacy, too, is at risk. I'm here to offer a solution."

"Legacy?" Howard Regence says, loud enough for all to hear. "You give two shits about Paradign's legacy, or ours for that matter. I'll have no part of your fucking theatrics."

Regence heads for the door. Others follow, rising up from their chairs and collecting their things.

Kane closes his eyes to a vision. He's sealing the door behind him. Flames are dancing again at the feet of the invited. Shadows reflect off marble walls as they rise up. Shrieks of agony sing in his ears as the flames devour the invited, as they'd sung to him in his childhood at Bolsiver.

Kane opens his eyes to something he hadn't expected; Thomas Anderson blocking the door.

"Step aside, Tom," Regence demands.

"He's right," Anderson says, shaking an accusatory finger. "And you know it. Leave if you will. I for one want to hear what he has to say."

Regence raises an open palm to Anderson's face; a threat lingers in the tense air surrounding them.

To their surprise, Dorien Wissum makes his way between the two men, taking Anderson by the arm and leading him back to his seat. An angry Regence relents and eventually follows. One by one the other invited quiet and return to their seats.

Wissum exchanges a nod with Kane. "We're even," he says, before finding an empty chair in the back row.

"Say what you've come here to say," Regence says, folding his arms over his chest.

Kane does not hesitate to seize on the invitation. "Daniel's death casts yet another shadow on Paradign. The coming weeks will bring questions, investigations. Like before, our members will be subjected to all manner of scrutiny. Their families will encourage them to leave Paradign. The very basis for SR treatment will again come under public scrutiny. That is, unless we give it a bold, new face." Kane clicks the remote again. "I give you the future."

A video rolls on the television screen. A young woman wheels her chair forward across an empty gym until she reaches the camera. "I'm a person with paraplegia. After the accident I lost the use of my legs. Thanks to the Kane Industries Alpha program, I'm up for partner at my firm. And I'm growing as a person, every day." She stretches her arms to the sky as the room fills with beams of laser light shooting down from the ceiling in a pre-programmed dance. The dance ends, the beams unite together in the shape of a woman.

The hologram lowers its laser-formed hand. "What would you like to master today?" the synthesized voice asks.

"Closing arguments. I go to trial in three weeks."

"Very well. We'll be using the case of a disgruntled employee's discrimination lawsuit as our first lesson's scenario. I've identified your level of familiarity on the topic, we'll begin there."

The video fades to dark as the silhouette of the young woman rises up from her chair and thrusts her fists to the sky.

Eleven audience members sit up straight in their chairs. "She said she was a person with paraplegia. How was she standing?" Asks a voice from the middle row.

"She can stand, walk, even defend herself, all the result of recent advancements at Kane Industries. Her professional and personal development, however, this comes from Paradign."

"You're proposing what? A publicity stunt?" Howard Regence asks.

"I'm proposing Paradign takes a bold, new direction while we still can. One I will lead."

"One *you* will lead? Not without Cathal's blessing, Elder Dean is next in succession" asserts Regence. Others echo their agreement.

"Then you shall have his blessing." A coy smile washes over Kane's face. "But before we adjourn, please allow me to share the rest of my vision."

In the back of the room, Dorien Wissum listens in disbelief as he realizes what the true purpose of his contract with Kane Industries is. As Kane details his plans, Wissum, now angered, begins forming one of his own.

***

NATHAN BADGER

PALOMAR MEDICAL CENTER
DECEMBER 28

The morning sun crosses my window, the dim of late afternoon falls, then finally Cavanaugh arrives. She strides back into my room; the smug look on her face reminds me my guilt has already been decided.

Her dress pants are pressed to precision. I take note of the care she again takes to smooth them as she sits. Her fingernails are filed short, precisely short. There's a light coat of gloss, just enough to show she'd taken time to attend to them. Her hair doesn't interfere with her face or the disapproving scowl she wears prominently. No smell of cigarette today.

"You got my call. Look for the woman, I think she works for Carlos Najera, the drug dealer who accused me of beating him," I tell Cavanaugh.

She shrugs, a slight upward twist of her lips forms a vaguely amused smile. "No one named Jan Castellano was on the manifest for the flight you told me you took."

"Bullshit!" I shoot up from the bed. "Jan Castellano was *on* my flight. She drugged me. She was in Bogotá. *You* need to find her."

"I do, do I?" Cavanaugh only smirks. "We'll circle back to that in a minute. Tell me this first, the guy you were meeting. His name was Bish, right?" She flips through her notebook, shifting emerald greens for a casual glance to confirm.

"Kenneth Bish," I state emphatically. "You want to see the email he sent me?"

Emerald greens fan across the room until they meet mine. "No. I *don't*. We found no hotel reservation at La Estancia in his name."

My arms spread wide in disbelief. "I already told you, he no-showed."

"Oh, that's right," she scoffs. "He no-showed." Her eyes narrow as she tugs at a sleeve, revealing her wrist. She rubs the scar tissue rhythmically, catches me staring before I can look away. "Of course he no-showed."

Kah-thuhm.

It's coming again.

"Your sarcasm isn't lost on me Detective," I snap back, the blackness sliding up from my stomach, squeezing my ribcage, gripping my throat.

Kah-thuhm - Kah-thuhm.

The throbbing veins in my wrist, the pounding of my temples. I know it's coming.

This is bad. This is really bad. Not now. Don't do this now.

Not now. Not in front of her.

Recite the word, Nate.

"Mr. Badger—"

The room stills, darkness falls, only the red glow surrounding her remains.

"It's not too late to change your story," she says.

"I'm *fucking* innocent. And I'll prove it," I scream back, the blackness inside a ticking time bomb that's about to explode, leaving behind only pieces of her.

She sees it. Recognizes it. And it scares her. A cavernous pause lingers in the air as she rises up from her chair and backs cautiously away.

"That's what I thought," she says, fearful eyes cast from me to the door. "Once you're released, don't even think about leaving the city without my knowledge and permission. And if you see a car parked outside of your house. One that seems to follow you down the street when you pick up your groceries. Who knows, it may, or may not be one of my friends. I'll be in touch soon. Rest assured."

Il bacio della morte.

The kiss has been given.

She makes it to the threshold before her feet lock in place.

"Mr. Badger," she says without turning to look back at me, "there's no record of *you* on that flight either."

***

CATHAL KANE

"I don't care what he's asking. You can't leave here."

Weak from the war waging in his body, Cathal Kane lies in his hospital bed, clutching a hand-written note to his chest. "If you love me, you will help me."

"A fool, stu-" A torrent of tears break through the wall Elder Dean Wallace had built against them. He dabs them dry with the sleeve of his shirt; quivering lips betray the false hope he musters. "The chemotherapy's working. You just need a little longer."

Cathal offers a weak smile. "We both know that's not true."

"But it can be. You just need to stay." Dean lifts his thin runner's body out of the chair, pushing a wisp of salt-and-pepper hair from his eyes. His sixty-eight-year-old frame crackles as stiff joints straighten. Arthritic fingers clutch the cold hand of his love, placing it over his heart. "Please stay."

Cathal directs his eyes past the cobweb of tubes to a newspaper lying neatly folded in half on the nightstand beside him. "Daniel Mazer is dead. Paradign needs me. My son needs me."

"I need you too. I need you to live. To grow old with me." Dean's sienna-brown eyes plead for a reply he knows he won't hear.

"Make the arrangements." Cathal points a weak finger at the entrance to his private room at The Oasis of Hope.

Dean bends down to kiss his love. "There's still time. Finish your treatment, then go."

"No. Daniel is *dead*." Cathal presses the paper he'd held into Dean's palm. "Alastair has arranged a gathering tomorrow night. I will tell him the truth, and then I will tell the others."

Dean takes Cathal's hand and caresses it. "Then I go with you."

Cathal's face hardens in resolve. "I confront this alone." The flush of palest rose blooms in his cheek, as though life has decided to return to him just for a moment. He points a shaky finger. "But if I'm too late, if I can't convince them, you must do as I've written."

Dean unfolds the paper Cathal hands him, unable to mask his horror as he reads. Outside, the sun sets, taking all hope and warmth with it. "Your journal? You can't ask this of me. I won't be party to the destruction of your legacy."

"The story must be told." With a slow nod of his head, Cathal closes his eyes.

It is decided. Dean knows he must do as he's asked.

"As you wish, my love."

He signs the necessary papers before arranging for a car to take Cathal to the airport early the next morning.

NUESTRO HOGAR
DECEMBER 29

The San Diego morning skyline is awash in a maze of brilliant reds and oranges. A view Cathal treasures. One he will miss. His brittle thumbnail creases backward as he fights with the seatbelt; a veil of thin, watery blood forms near the tip of his finger. No pain registers. He dabs it dry with a fresh tissue from a pack in the glove compartment, then rubs the atrophied remnants of legs, and, for a moment, pretends they are still as they were.

Outside the car, Alastair Kane shields his eyes from the mid-morning rays of daylight with a crooked salute as he presses in the digits of the combination. The tumblers click into place, the weather-worn hinges cry their familiar lament of resistance.

A cancer-filled cough escapes the lips of the man he calls Father as he gets back in the vehicle. Kane eyes his father's emaciated body up and down before muttering, "Avoidable," under his breath and starting the engine.

Kane's 1965 gunmetal Aston Martin DB5 hums along the winding driveway, passing the black oak, pecan, and rosewood trees lining it. They arrive at the front entrance of the Spanish Colonial Revival-inspired mansion to the sound of Loreena McKennit's "Lullaby." Surveillance cameras pan above them, tracking their progress.

"All I'm asking for is your support," Kane's voice tinged with contempt as he climbs out of the car, his words the first to cut through the dense silence between them.

He opens the passenger door, Cathal waves him away, clutching the bag to his chest like a treasured toy in the hands of a child.

An atrophied arm lifts one atrophied leg out of the car, then the other. Kane waits by the entrance, counting the moments with an impatient swing of his finger.

"You *owe* me this," Kane demands.

Under a sheet of quiet, Cathal enters the home. Taking measured steps, his grey-veined hands pressed against the wall for support, he inches down the long hallway toward the east-facing meditation room. Kane reads the last of his texts, glancing back now and again to note the old man's progress. All will attend.

Don't deny me, old man, Kane says to himself.

Cathal pauses at the threshold to catch his breath and does his best to awaken his numb toes before setting down his bag and shedding his clothing. He stands shakily before a bowl of water to wash his feet, then dabs them dry with a gold-trimmed towel he'd taken from an antique hook near the doorway. He dons a ceremonial robe; the hood covers all but his forehead and face.

Cathal approaches the meditation room shrine, falls to his knees in prayer for Daniel. And for the strength to say the words he must to his son.

As night falls, he finds them and searches the empty house for his son before feeble legs strain up the stairs to his bedroom.

In Cathal's dream, he has all his hair. In his dream he is mighty again. In his dream he bounds up the steps to Bolsiver in time. Before fires are lit. Before ammunition is loaded. Before knives are wielded.

He's awakened by birdsong warbling in from the window. He refuses to open his eyes, to see himself once more as he is, refusing to let go of the dream's promise.

Just as every morning before, he prays for forgiveness from the others he left behind, knowing none will be given.

And prays for the souls of the two children he saved.

An unsettling flutter strikes his chest at the sound of the door opening down the hall. The click of heels down the hallway leading to his room grow louder, as does the pounding heartbeat in his eardrums.

Cathal opens his eyes to the reality of the next day of his last days, and to the man he calls son propped against his bedroom door.

"There are things you must know. Things I've come home to tell you." The effort to raise himself up from the bed leaves him catching his breath.

"The only thing I'll hear from you is your words of support."

"You know I cannot."

"Then there's nothing more to talk about."

Cathal continues to rise. "Joseph. Bols..." inter-
rupted by a torrent of coughs.

Kane steps back into the hallway and taps a command into his phone. "Some things are better left unspoken." The bedroom door closes, the lock engages,
leaving Cathal imprisoned and alone with the memories of Bolsiver, of the flames, and the young boy he'd
saved, only to lose him again.

***

4

ELDER DEAN WALLACE

NUESTRO HOGAR
DECEMBER 30

Alone, locked away in his room, Cathal's weak fingers wrap around the newspaper he'd secreted out of his messenger bag hidden under the bed. Eyes wet with regret look away from the front-page article covering the very public suicide of his friend Daniel.

All the screams cloud his head; the sizzle of flesh, the foul sulfurous wafts of smoke sting his eyes as though he's back there. Back at Bolsiver watching them die. Allowing them to die. Letting them slice their own throats just as Doyen Daniel had done.

The newspaper slips from his hand, joining with particles of dust in a downward dance to the resting place they now share, the marble floor flecked with cracks of gold.

I brought this on him.

Pushing a weak hand against the side of his knee, the stick of sunken skin and bones moves slightly out from beneath the sapphire sheets of his bed.

Shaking hands held high in the air, he calls forth the energy of the universe, directing it through the remains of his withered, skeletal shell. A foot jerks to life in response. Two stick legs quiver, they begin their fragile slide over the edge of the bed. Icy feet meet warm slippers. He rises, light-headed, weak.

Determined.

One foot, then the next, fighting forward as though through the headwind of a hurricane.

Cathal never reaches the door.

Ω

Two floors below, ignoring the din of the assembled, Elder Dean looks up at the bedroom window, hoping for a glimpse of his love, unable to shake the foreboding, questioning if he'll never see Cathal again.

Alastair Kane takes his place in front of the group, taps the microphone twice before calling them quiet. With skillfully manufactured sorrow he announces the passing of Cathal, who, according to Kane, died peacefully.

All bow heads in prayer except Dean, who collapses, heart bursting with grief as though it could shatter, sending shards and blood splatter to the ground.

Dorien Wissum guides him back to his feet. Wissum's whispered words of conspiracy, of standing up against Kane, are near lost in the air between them.

An aperture blinks closed near the edge of the yard, capturing the two of them together before Wissum peels away and the crowd dissipates, leaving Dean alone, stricken with the paralyzing realization that without his love, all is lost.

Ω

DECEMBER 31

Dean catches his reflection in glass. A lost, sunken-cheeked stranger stares back.

Three days ago there was hope. Now all hope is lost.

His grip tightens on the note in his hands, desperate to tear it into tiny pieces and toss them to the sky.

Knowing he can't. Knowing he'd made a promise.

The heavy front door of the bank pushes open. In a daze, Dean enters.

The banker takes him to a private room where he delivers a lockbox.

"Take as much time as you need," the banker tells Dean before leaving.

An hour passes. Two, before the broken man that is Dean musters the courage to rise from his chair.

Per Cathal's instructions, he places the contents of the lockbox into a large, pre-addressed and stamped flat. He mails the package containing Cathal's journal to the FBI's San Diego Field Office before returning home.

Alone inside the four grey walls of his living room, he flips through a photo album until reaching a page in the middle. On it, Cathal stands to his side, arms around him. Cathal, whose absence makes each breath difficult. Surrounding them, the men, women and boys from the shelter.

Dean runs his fingers over their faces, and considers which of them will be next, before dialing the Carlsbad, California Headquarters of ARMR.

"ARMR Enterprises. How may I direct your call?"

"Dorien Wissum, please."

"Is Mr. Wissum expecting your call?"

"Tell him it's Elder Dean."

"Hold please."

Wissum ends his meeting and clears the office once he's told who's on the line. He answers Dean's call after the last person is gone.

"I've thought about what you said last night," Dean tells Wissum. "You're right. It *should* be me."

Together they plan a meeting of the Paradign Doyens. One Alastair Kane will not be invited to.

***

Drew Cavanaugh

Goff Halfway House
North Park, San Diego
December 31

Carlos Najera ran drugs for a Colombian cartel. Until he got tuned up. Presumably by Badger. Then hauled off to prison. Early into his incarceration, Najera had not been a model prisoner, this is what made his redemption so notable. Shortly after getting stabbed in the eye by a rival gang-member, he found God and rehabilitated. Warden Wilcocks himself recommended him to be released to the Goff half-way house in North Park. The house director, Ari Simmons, helped arrange Cavanaugh's meeting with the now God-fearing ex-convict.

She arrives at the halfway house a few minutes before 8:30 p.m. The pungent ammonia-like urine smell and the stench of rotting rubbish from an over-filled dumpster permeate the cul-de-sac. In the shadows, what appears to be a drug deal comes to an abrupt end, the participants scatter when they see her.

A front stoop consisting of sun-blanched, decayed boards sits squarely in front of the door, flecked with red paint. She steps up on the porch, half expecting it to give way under her feet, and raps the antique gargoyle door knocker twice.

Inside, a small metal cover swings away from the security peephole. Soon after the door opens.

"Detective Cavanaugh, I presume?" The septuagenarian house director holds out a leathered hand, which she accepts. "Carlos is expected shortly. Please make yourself comfortable."

Cavanaugh brushes away the dust from a green velvet tub chair before lowering herself into it. She tries to ignore the stains on the rug, smoke smudges on what might've been yellow walls in a different lifetime. Everything seems halfway between broken and fixable. Much like she imagines the occupants of Goff House to be.

"Old bed and breakfast?" she calls out to Simmons.

"Seen better days, I'm afraid," he replies. "Funding's been cut again. We do the best we can with what we have."

She makes a show of checking her watch. Simmons picks up the house phone. The door swings open. Cavanaugh slides her legs out of the way to let a man and woman pass. The man, looking more sixty than the thirty-year-old he likely is, lifts up a shaky hand to her. She holds hers up in response. The woman next to him, mid-to-late twenties, every inch of her betraying the difficult life she's lived, flashes a yellow-toothed smile. A tinge of pity for the couple pulls at Cavanaugh's throat.

As the 9:00 p.m. curfew draws nearer, the door opens several more times. Once for a man with several ink-blue teardrops tattooed under his left eye. Once for a woman sorely in need of a shower.

Then for him.

Carlos Najera stands five-foot-five, every inch chiseled. His right and left arms are stained with blue ink, there are notch marks on one side where an eyebrow used to be. An eye patch covers the other eye. He glances over at Simmons, who nods his head. Najera's one good eye sizes Cavanaugh up. "Tough neighborhood, maybe you shouldn't have come alone."

"I can handle myself," she responds, her sudden defensiveness surprising her.

He gives her the once over again, it makes her feel dirty. Like she's just been violated. "I'm sure you can, *chava*."

She knows what the word means. "Thought you were a man of God now, Mr. Najera." She shoots an angry glance at Simmons.

"I still have one good eye," he says, with a flirtatious smile.

"Mr. Simmons?" Deflecting.

"You can use my office. Take as much time as you need, Detective," says Simmons, ushering them inside and closing the door behind him.

Ω

Like nearly every night before, it's long after 10 p.m. when Cavanaugh first thinks of Nixy, who greets her with a discordant, full-throated chorus of mews when her key finally hits the door.

She thuds a can of albacore into his bowl, runs a hand down his body to his tail. Nixy ignores the attention and shoves his muzzle deep into the bowl. She scribbles a few items into her notebook, appending the list from two days ago she hadn't found time to fill. A half-empty bottle of Gentleman Jack calls out to her from the counter. Instead, she grabs an orange Gatorade from the fridge and plops down on the sole piece of living room furniture not belonging to her home office, a La-Z-Boy that slightly cants to one side when the leg-rest is fully extended.

Najera was no help. No, he never saw the man who attacked him. No, he didn't know who ratted him and his crew out, and even if he did, he had no right of retribution. This he left to his Savior.

"I don't buy it," she tells Nixy.

He's hiding something.

***

NATHAN BADGER

PALOMAR MEDICAL CENTER
JANUARY 1

Tell it to yourself, Nate.

Call it out, shine a light on it.

And accept it as truth.

I *was* on that fucking plane.

I'm going home today. I'll find my proof.

But before I'm released, I *will* see Abby.

I've already changed into my jeans. Glad there were no witnesses to that fiasco. I pad toward the door, toes fat like balloons.

The trainee's there at the nurse's station. She looks up from the clipboard she's holding. "Can I help you?" An expression I can't really define appears on her face.

"I'm going to see my, um, my fiancée," I flatly assert, my voice nearly drowned out by the dinging and opening of elevator doors. Maibel's inside.

"Goin' upstairs?" she asks with a knowing nod.

"I'm *going* to see her."

"Maybe I can help you," Maibel whispers.

"I hope so."

"No guarantees, Mr. Nathan."

"I know."

The doors slide shut, sealing us inside, doubt gnaws at my stomach like a hungry termite.

Maibel lightly touches my hand when the doors open. "No guarantees."

"I know," I say to myself as a man dressed in a skin-tight designer shirt and dress pants pushes past her, bumping my shoulder on his way in.

"Excuse me," he hisses, before reaching the back of the car.

He turns back to face me. His black eyes meet mine. *Kah-thuhm.*

The man's head tilts to one side. His mouth forms a slow smile as the doors start to close.

A slow, unnerving smile.

Kah-thuhm - Kah-thuhm.

The little moments I question. Little moments I lose, drawn away like a seashell in high tide.

"Wait here," Maibel says, motioning to the nurse's station on the right and breaking the momentary spell.

She and the floor nurse exchange words. A head shakes a third and final time.

Maibel returns, her soft eyes meet mine. "I'm sorry, Mr. Nathan. Abby said no."

Kah-thuhm- Kah-thuhm - Kah-thuhm.

The words stab my chest like a knife. Like Abby's knife. "Just tell her…" I start, but the words fall back in my throat.

We ride down to my floor in silence.

"Hospital regulations say we have to bring you downstairs in a wheelchair." She scans the now empty nurse's station. "Looks like they haven't sent it up yet. Should be here in the next five or ten minutes, though. Do you have someone you can call for a ride home?"

The man in the elevator. His eyes. Those black eyes.

Little moments.

"Mr. Nathan?"

"Huh?" I stammer. "Oh. I'll Uber it."

"I'm sorry about what happened upstairs," she says with an apologetic smile before turning to the paperwork I imagine to be waiting for her at the nurse's station.

I go back to my room for the last time. That's when I find the note left on my bed.

Kah-thuhm- Kah-thuhm - Kah-thuhm.

"Who the fuck *are* you?" I yell, charging toward the door, nearly crashing into the trainee pushing a wheelchair.

"Everything okay?" Maibel calls out from across the hallway.

Kah-thuhm - Kah-thuhm
Kah-thuhm.

Little moments.

Say the word.

"It's nothing," I answer, forcing anger down my throat like a dry-swallowed pill, balling up the note and stuffing it in my pocket before settling frustrated, angry into the chair for my ride down to freedom.

Maibel goes with us. She makes small talk, an effort on her part to ease the tension creasing my face, slipping in how much she loves gladiolas, and Finnish chocolates. Fazer chocolates.

We get out of the elevator and traverse the lobby, reach the front entrance and spill out to a parking lot resembling a busy ant hill. Maibel grabs my hand and holds it a little too long and a little too firmly. The scent of her perfume lingers in the air, it's both agreeable and appropriate. "This is my friend's card. Call him." A graveness weights her words.

"Thank you for everything. I hope our paths cross again, different circumstances obviously."

"Call him," she repeats, handing me the newspaper from my room before she turns gracefully, walks away and out of my life.

I don't wait long for my driver. I toss the newspaper across to the other side of the back seat before climbing in. He confirms my address, sounding like what happens when Texas meets Bourbon Street.

He tries to make small talk, but when I look up from the folded note I've pulled out of my pocket and catch him watching me through the rear-view mirror he goes silent.

She was never yours.

That's what the note says. The note's wrong.

Cavanaugh asked about the first time we met; it was at the Starbucks in town. She sat with her back to the door, her tone, runner's body hugged tightly by a crimson turtleneck. She played with her glistening blonde waist-length hair, sometimes twirling it in her fingers, sometimes tucking it behind her ears.

All of it, every bit of it affected me in a way I still don't fully understand.

Turn. Show me your face, I thought.

Then she did, and I saw her. I stood there, foolish, embarrassed by the fleeting fantasy that for a brief moment played in my head. The spell lifted when she looked away.

I stayed a long second, watching her shop for electronics online. She didn't look back.

I ran through the day's itinerary in my head while I waited in line behind a mom and two young children as she prodded them to make up their minds. I had a phone interview in one hour and began to wonder if I'd still be here in line behind the family when it came time for the call.

Then I heard a voice from behind. Hers.

"Let me guess. A salted caramel latte." Delicate fingers appeared from over my shoulder, taking hold of it and turning me toward her. And right then I felt it again. She felt it too, I could tell. Raw, unbridled animal attraction. We could've thrown down together right there on the floor in front of the cash register. In the bathroom, in my car. Anywhere. Everywhere.

Her full, red lips parted into a knowing smile, and I knew in the moment she'd read my mind. "My name's Abby," she said, tossing her head as though she'd just stepped into a photo shoot. "And you're Nathan Badger. The author."

"You know me?"

She placed the tip of her finger on top of her button nose and wiggled it from side-to-side in a way that reminded me of a TV show I watched as a child. Her cashmere-painted fingernail captured and reflected all the lights in the room like a ballroom's mirrored chandelier.

"I do now."

"Nice to meet you, Abby," with what I remember to be a clumsy smile.

I asked her to join me once my drink order arrived, but she had to run. An appointment with her life coach. That piece of scum.

She agreed to meet me again. Same time, place, next week.

Before she left, I asked her how she knew my coffee order.

In response, perfect glossed lips pressed into my coffee cup.

"I'll never tell," her response.

This is how it began. And back then it was good.

She *was* mine. She was.

Maybe not anymore. Maybe she's his now. The black-eyed man from the elevator.

Kah-thuhm.

There's a darkness inside. A foul, faceless darkness, real as blood. Real as throbbing veins, as fingers curled tight around the handle of a blade.

Real as screams.

Recite the word, Nate.

Ramona, California

Tock.
Tock.
"Thirdy-See…"
Tock. Tock.
"Ah said, thirdy-six-eighty-eight gonna cover it."
Tock. Tock. Tock.
Huh? Where?
I awaken to the metronome click of a turn signal.
Tock, Tock, Tock.
Oh my God.

"Stop the car!" I yell, frozen in the realization he's about to pull in my driveway and see the painting in blood at the top.

"You don't need to yell," he says, reaching out to take the fifty-dollar bill I've pulled from my wallet.

"Keep the change," I tell him.

He looks back at me through the rear view, then scans the back seat. "You gonna take that paper with ya' now, aren't ya?"

Yeah. Sure.

I'm careful not to slam the door behind me.

He skids out of the driveway, hitting the cross drain in the road too fast. His car's chassis grinds against the highest edge, shooting sparks. Taillights disappear behind a bend in the road before I reach my car, which is locked. Just how I left it.

I take a deep breath and hold it, not fully ready for wait awaits me at the top of the driveway.

I've seen my share of these kind of scenes. Other people's scenes. Too many of them. We don't always choose our paths in life, sometimes they choose us.

Or do they?

My first real case, the McEverley double homicide, a contract hit staged like a burglary gone bad. I was twenty-one at the time. Then came the Roll-Away Bandits, as they were nicknamed, and the fitting end their ringleader Sargent Lee Chance met. Apparently someone didn't like the cut he took, so they beat him to death with an entrenching tool.

By my last year in the military police, I processed the Soliz Brothers' home, solved a cold case and in doing so identified the Cryptogram Killer, witnessed the aftermath of Wallace Harmon's bloody rampage, and worked dozens more cases like them.

None prepare me for seeing this crime scene of my own.

The top of the driveway looks like a wine-splotched Rorschach test. Two crude half-circles of dried blood stretch out from where I knelt.

Where I knelt before Abby. Where she stabbed me.

Where she saw the blackness coming to life inside me and she stabbed me.

Kah-thuhm.

Ω

I don't know how long I've been standing here in this new little moment.

Keep going, Nate. Harden yourself, as you do. As you always do. There was a crime. It needs to be solved. Focus on that.

First things first. Whoever took her may have my security code.

They could have come back. There's a chance they could be here waiting. I need an equalizer.

I slip into the garage and toss the newspaper into the trash before tapping the false wall twice. It opens, revealing the wall safe holding my weapons cache.

Left nine, right fifteen, left seven.

I choose the kukri, and start my sweep of the grounds, sliding through the wooden gate leading back to the patio to the right of the courtyard. The padlocks on the doors to my white-washed, walk-in tool shed are intact. No one's hiding inside. Further down, and to the right of the sidewalk is a twenty-five-foot strip of yard filled with lava rock. I grab one of the rocks, toss it over the roof of the tool shed and wait for movement. All is still.

There are four living room windows looking out over the area. The plantation shutters to all are closed, like I left them. Still, I crouch below them and quietly work my way across the patio past the sofa and the sliding glass door to the other side of the house.

Once cleared, I move back through the courtyard to the house.

The front door's unlocked. Is there someone inside waiting for me? Carlos Najera and a few of his boys perhaps, come back to get a little get-some?

Time to fucking find out.

My search ends in the master bedroom. The house is clear, but my head isn't. Abby left a glossed kiss on the bedroom patio sliding glass door. Did she do it before she was taken? Maybe a peace offering?

Stop it. No time to get all twisted up.

Focus.

Get your proof.

I head down to my office and fire up my laptop.

Now to the flight.

American Airlines website. User ID. Password.

Kah-thuhm.

I log out. Log back in. "The fuck?" I yell to no one. Pound frustrated fists into my desk and am rewarded by a resonant stinging and a new fan of blood spreading over my palm.

There's some kind of mistake. I'm on hold for less than a minute before the agent confirms there is no record of me boarding a flight.

This is bad, really bad. I *was* on that flight.

Wasn't I?

Kah-thuhm - Kah-thuhm.

Oh God. It's happening again.

No. It's not. There *was* a note. She *was* taken. I *was* on that fucking flight. I *was* sent to Bogotá.

The word isn't working. I need something else. I need a drink.

I cover the hallway at an urgent half jog, prop the kukri against the kitchen counter, plug in my phone to a charger cable and fling open the fridge. There are only two of those foofy apple cider drinks she likes and a half-empty bottle of de-fizzed Moscato.

Fine. Fuck it. I down them all, but they don't help.

Only one other thing will.

I need to stab something.

I collect up three throwing knives from the garage, and head to the back yard and my target.

G80PGTK GI Tantos. Well balanced, utilitarian.

Number one sings a beautiful song.

Thwack.

Ring three. Focus.

My hand begins to shake. I fight it steady.

Ready. Aim.

Loose.

Ring two. I'm coming back.

I slide a finger down number three's blade. It's sharp. Razor sharp. Unlike the blade used on Abby.

Kah-thuhm.

Her hair was hacked away unevenly. Either swiped at with scissors or sawed off with a barely sharpened implement.

Abby was swiped at with a blunt instrument. And I'm not there to stop it.

The third blade flies from my hand and strikes the center ring with violent force.

I pull the knives out of the three-quarter inch plywood sheet with a bullseye painted in Captain America colors.

Colors.

Kah-thuhm.

The contusions on Abby's face and under her eyes were a mix of purples and browns, meaning they were days old. She was held somewhere private. Someone had her to himself.

Kah-thuhm - Kah-thuhm.

I see a face in the target. See an arrogant, chilling smile. See his black eyes.

A terrible answer is better than having none at all. At least it's something to hold on to, gripped tight like a mallet I slam into my head again and again until it all fits.

***

KENNETH BISH

In a sealed-off panic room on the second floor, the figure touches the screen of a closed-circuit monitor on the table in front of him, his fingers finding and caressing the image of Vivian Marcus as he awaits her transformation, which grows nearer with every movement of her silver spoon to her mouth. When it slips from her fingers, and she struggles again to hold it, he table-taps fingers in anticipation of what is to come.

Seconds tick to minutes, pushing the sweeping hand of the grandfather clock on the dining room wall toward its target. When the clock chimes for the third of eight times, Kenneth Bish rises and quiets the room.

In time with the last of eight chimes, five guests in fine dining attire look up again from their soup bowls. Then the movements commence.

The figure watches as Charles Breen's face twists in pain. Watches as Breen claws at the base of his neck in jerked, awkward grabs. A red spiderweb spreads across the back of his white Oxford shirt. Manuel Ortiz points a finger at Breen and laughs.

He sees Ellen O'Bannon stare at her arm. Sees her roll up her sleeves, watching, seeming to battle the urge to recoil. A nervous laugh escapes her lips as the sensations take physical form, moving in waves down her arm like ripples across a wind-blown pond.

He watches as Edward Shea's narrow eyes dart back and forth between the room's two exits. Shea's hands press against his chest; rage builds on his weathered face; a face time has not been kind to. He forms fists. They strike the mahogany table once, then again, rattling it, sloshing the drug-laced soup remaining in his bowl across the herringbone pattern.

From a speaker mounted high on the wall comes the hiss of the figure's voice. He bares his teeth, says the word again, and watches as all eyes in the room below widen. A wry smile lifts the corners of his mouth. He repeats the word until reaching the sacred number. Then he waits.

In near synchronicity, the dinner guests tilt their heads, their eyes squeeze shut, the last of their humanity fighting against the command they've been given.

Among the many he'd auditioned, the figure had pre-selected a familiar piece for this moment. One to move them. To inspire them. A fitting aperitif for the carnage to follow. His hand reaches out, a knuckle taps the play button.

The dinner guests sit motionless for one verse of "Gnossienne No. 1." All eyes open, savage, as the second verse commences.

One by one, each reaches beneath his or her chairs, removing the blades left for them there in thick, cardboard sheaths. One by one, compulsion drives the limbic system of each to fixate on the beautiful symmetry of ninety-six equally spaced releases of the life blood, which runs through and unites us all.

One floor above them, the figure's bony fingers touch invisible keys on an invisible piano as he admires the black ballet below. Bish lands the last strike before lying down on the floor and slicing his throat left to right.

When it's over, the figure removes each of the sheaths from under the chairs, fires up the heaters he'd rigged earlier to ignite, then arranges the bodies in the manner he'd seen as a child.

* * *

MICHAEL CAVE

SORRENTO VALLEY, CALIFORNIA
JANUARY 2

Michael Cave graduated Quantico at the top of his class. He arrived for orientation at the FBI's San Diego field office full of swagger. Over the twelve soul-crushing weeks since, his swagger died eighty-four sequential deaths.

Missy stares at her husband, who's pushing peas back and forth across his plate. "You wanna talk about it?" Her tone optimistic, her expectations low.

"The usual, honey," sliding a pea up the stiffened slope of his untouched mashed potatoes.

"The guy a few cubicles down from me got his assignment today, which is good I guess."

"Put down the knife and fork and look at me." Her smoky brown doe eyes alight in a playful gleam. "Or I'll call her."

"*Don't* call her."

"You wipe that frown off your face or I'll do it," she says, wagging her index finger in warning.

The frown remains.

"Here she comes." Wiggling fingers reach toward his ribcage. "The tickle monster cometh."

If he were strapped to a chair and administered sodium pentothal, he'd go to the death before admitting how much he hates the tickle monster thing she does. But hate it he does.

"Okay, okay." A half-smile appears. "Put her away."

Missy crawls her hand back across the worn table like a long-legged spider. "She'll be waiting," she warns, bringing with it a titter.

"I don't want to live a rinse-and-repeat life," he says, his voice suddenly empty,

"Is that what you call us?" She socks him playfully on the shoulder.

"You know what I mean. Every day, the same damn thing. It's not enough for me."

She spider-walks her fingers back toward him. "I warned you."

"Babe, I'm serious. This isn't what I signed up for." He reaches out to the hand crawling towards him and stops it. "Come next Monday, I'm gonna say something."

"Michael, honey, love of my life. Say the words with me."

"I love you?" This time she thwacks him hard. "Ouch. Okay."

Eyes closed, they recite in unison together, "I am the author of me. I am the composer; I am the conductor. I am not part of your world. I am of the one I create."

"The one *you* create Michael. You're an amazing Doyen, they love you already. Time to practice what you preach." She takes his hand, guides him up from his chair and toward the staircase. He motions back at the table. "It'll be there waiting in the morning. Right now we have something more important to do." She leans in for a kiss, then denies him. "You know the way. Carry me."

Cave sweeps her up in one fluid motion. The laughter begins on the steps. He carries her into the bedroom, lifts her up high enough up to be sure she'll bounce, then drops her on the pink comforter he bought her on her last birthday. "That's payback for the tickle monster."

He slides in next to her as she fidgets with her iPhone until a song starts to play.

"Barry White?"

"*My darlin' I, I can't get enough of your love babe,*" Missy sings along in a full-throated contralto that takes him by surprise.

"I didn't know you had it in you."

She continues. "*I don't, I don't know why, I can't get enough of your love babe.*"

Cave joins in with his best, but a terrible Barry, "*Oh, some things I can't get used to, no matter how I try. Just like the more you give the more I want, and baby that's no lie.*"

Barry finishes the rest of the song alone.

Ω

A shaft of early morning light pierces through the kitchen window as Cave grabs his apple and heads to the door.

"Forget something?" Missy, dressed only in a white Dobby evening shirt she'd stolen from his side of the closet, spreads her arms wide.

"Never," he says, carelessly tossing the apple he'd been munching on over his shoulder in the direction of the couch. "How could I?"

She stays on his mind as he weaves his motorcycle in and out of the usual morning traffic, blasting NPR news, his daily morning indulgence. She walks side-by-side with him through the front doors of the FBI Field Office, past the screener, through the metal detectors, all the way to his cubicle, where an email awaits him.

Finally.

A long row of other first-years look up from their respective stacks of papers, curious, envious. As Cave whisks by them they reach hands out for high fives on his way to the staircase in the far corner of the massive room filled with cubicles.

He takes the stairs three at a time until he reaches the top floor, the seventh floor, the restricted access floor, all the while humming Barry White. This is her, she did this. He knew when he'd married her, she wouldn't just bring him good luck, she'd *be* his good luck.

Cave places his right eye over the retinal scan, it reflects back at him bright, brimming with anticipation. A green light illuminates, the locks disengage.

At the end of a long hallway lined with windowless, unmarked doors, Cave finds the room he'd been directed to, empties his pockets as instructed and places the contents, including his phone, into the metal drawer and pushes it shut. The door's lock disengages, the door opens, and he enters.

"Nice," he says, admiring the solid wood boat-shaped oak conference table with eight empty chairs.

He scans the Parma-grey walls for hidden cameras, doesn't find any. A few photos of past directors hang on the walls, freshly dusted. Just in front of the middle seat opposite the door, next to a phone with no dial pad and only one button, there's a sealed box and a hand-written note.

Welcome, Agent Cave. Please open and read.

Cave slides the note off of the table, shoves it into his pocket, opens the box and removes the copied pages of a handwritten journal from inside.

December 20, 1986 11:10 pm

I sit alone tonight before a raging fire. I should appreciate the crackling of applewood. I should savor the smoky sweetness. I should sink down in the cushions of this leather chair, surrender into it as it calls me to do. I should relax in the safety we've found, celebrate in the knowledge that we're a world away from where we were just days ago.

But I don't. I just want to know you're okay.

I heard your cries earlier and held you as you fought through a nightmare again. You struggled in my arms as you did the day we boarded the plane. Sebastian warned this would happen. He says it will take time for the visions of the flames to go away. If they ever do.

As for Amelie, maybe your sister's innocent dreams are of cornfields. She sleeps so peacefully beside you, never stirring, even when you cry out.

I checked back on you both just a moment ago; I saw your hand interlocked in hers. It brought me relief. I silently meditated at your side, envisioning the days before things spun away.

I can close my eyes now and see you searching for Amelie, see her hiding amongst the rows of corn stalks, hear her laughter as it betrays her hiding spot. I can smell the musky ground you trod through after the midsummer morning rain on the day I arrived. I can see the outfits you and your sister wore, which doll she held tight in her tiny hands.

It's all there, in the movie of my mind. Where only I can see it, where it's mine and mine alone. May I one day forget how the movie ends.

These are my first written words since Bolsiver. Reducing my thoughts to writing is not something I do easily or naturally any longer. Not since Joseph. After him, my life's aim is to be in the moment, to create new memories I can store away somewhere deep in the recess, only to one day present themselves as would unexpected but welcome guests at my door. To pry away the tendrils of the past from their hold on my future. Our future.

But too much has happened. Too many important, terrible things, things I may one day have to tell you of. So I write, and I read and remember, and I prepare for the story I may one day have to tell.

Maybe you'll understand. Maybe you'll embrace me for what I did for you, what I saved you from. What we saved you from. Because of Sebastian and I, you are safe. Because of us another took your place in the flames.

DECEMBER 21, 1986 9:15 PM

Sebastian called. I told him how I'd found you both. That you'd lined up Amelie's dolls in a row, and marched back and forth in front of them yelling out orders. I told him how your sister moved the doll's heads up and down to acknowledge your commands. When you saw me, the look on your face brought back memories that scared me.

Sebastian had other, more pressing matters on his mind. The news from Bolsiver has spread like a virus since the day the first bodies were discovered, and though we expected as much, I must confess how on edge I've become. Today while you were both with him, someone knocked on the door, sending my heart into my throat. I would be lying to myself and to you if I said I didn't eye the handgun Sebastian gave me and consider answering the door with it in hand. How foolish I would've been to do so, and how scared the poor paperboy, who only wanted to collect his money, would have been had I not resisted the impulse.

The burglar alarm company's techs arrive later today, before you both return. They'll check the sensors on each window and door and test the auto-dial before leaving. They'll place the control panel and siren next to my bed.

I'm having cameras installed in every room. A monitoring station will be set up in the safe room.

The safe room. Pray we never have to use it.

Sebastian tells me it's okay for you both to sleep together, he thinks it will help you adjust. Though I don't completely agree, I'll honor his advice. He hasn't misled us so far. He facilitated our escape, and so he is a friend to me and to us.

I watched you earlier tonight through the camera's lens as you fought the imagined enemy hiding under the covers, as you awakened and rose, as you stood over her, watching her. I know what comes for you in your sleep.

Because of this, Sebastian tells me tomorrow's treatment will be rigorous, so I've decided to prepare a special surprise for you both tomorrow night.

When I met you and your family for our first night together, we dined on rice porridge and scraps of chicken with potatoes that your mother magically transformed into a delicious stew. I barely had the strength to raise the spoon to my mouth. My hands and arms rested heavy on wood when you slipped me another piece of chocolate, your last. After dinner, she pulled the splinters from my hand from the weather-worn picnic table your father had reclaimed and repurposed into a dining table. The dirt floor beneath us, the cold night air that invaded through the cracks in the door and the windows, none of it mattered. The humble, wonderful grace of your family made up for it all. I miss that.

But tomorrow we'll experience something far different. The grand table arrives while you're gone, and though it seats twelve, we'll take our places next to one another by the back window, where we can see the pine trees shift in the wind, where we can watch the snow dance through the air as it falls. Our place settings will be of the finest herringbone china; we'll use imported stainless steel cutlery, not crude wooden bowls or wooden spoons, not our fingers. When the grandfather clock on the wall strikes six, dinner will be served. Hot cocoa and a story when it strikes eight. I wonder how it will be for you both.

Considering this gives my tired brain a rest from the thought of cameras and intruders and dreams. I think I will close my eyes.

1:17 AM

I awakened again to your screaming; this time Amelie cried out too. You'll stay in the bedroom closest to mine from now on; she'll sleep alone two doors down. I'll have a motion sensor installed in the hallway separating your rooms. It will alert the control panel next to my bed if it's disturbed. You'll not do this again to her.

Don't lose faith son. All will pass. The nightmares, the moments where all you experienced paralyzes the goodness in you, they will pass. It takes faith. And determination. You possess both.

Sebastian has a new plan. He's brought a boy with him and intends to recruit the boy's friends too.

Bolsiver. The suicide cult. Joseph LeMay. *Why am I reading this?*

Cave fingers through his French-cropped brown hair, rubs his eyes. He stands up and contorts in a massive, mid-morning stretch.

The phone rings twice before he snatches it. "May I call you Michael?"

"Yes. Who am I speaking with?"

"Soon enough. Put the phone on speaker and please have a seat, Michael."

"Show, meet road," Cave mumbles, surprised by the rumbling of nerves in his stomach.

"I'll get straight to it. What do you know about the events leading up to the Bolsiver mass suicides?"

"I know they called themselves the Celestial Temple, we touched on what happened at Quantico. I have a feeling I'm about to learn more."

"You are. A journal containing the excerpt you just read was mailed to me. I've read it cover to cover. I'd like a second set of eyes on some of the content."

"Of course. But may I ask why?"

"We'll get to that too. This room is yours now, you'll have full and private access. I'll ping you by email when you need to come."

"And what am I looking for?"

"Whoever sent this didn't provide a reason. I have some ideas. I want yours. Also, maybe you've already seen it in one form or another. Online, local news. The Wheaton dinner party massacre."

"I heard about it on NPR this morning. They found the bodies laid out in a circle, like Bolsiver. Is there's a connection?"

"The house our diary's author wrote about in the journal. It's the same house as the massacre."

"Then Kenneth Bish was the son I read about in the journal?"

"No, Michael."

"I don't understand."

"You will. Let me ask you a question. According to your personnel file, under religious beliefs, you indicated *other*, with no further details. Why is that?"

Cave, taken by surprise, fights a rising defensiveness. "I don't know. What religion are you?"

"I'm not here to challenge your beliefs, just to establish them," answers the voice.

After the accident, his family felt broken. His faith, their faith helped them piece it back together. It gave his mom a voice for her pain: it gave his dad the fortitude to be by his daughter's side through the surgeries. There were many. It returned hope to a family who could have abandoned it after the doctors broke the news to the family she'd never walk again.

His little sister, now a strong willed, accomplished person with paraplegia, graduated Harvard Law School with honors, and was recently made partner at her law firm.

"Agent Cave?"

"I'm a Paradignist. But I think you already knew."

"I understand your position there got recently elevated."

"I replaced Daniel Mazer as Doyen," Cave replies.

"After his suicide, the incident at the Sarafina Lounge."

Cave closes sad eyes. "He was my friend."

"Please take the manila envelope out of the box. Inside, you'll find his forensics report."

Cave says a prayer for his fallen friend, then opens his eyes and removes the report as instructed. He scans the page. "Why are you showing me this?" Cave asks, the report clasped tight in his hands.

"I'm sorry, Michael. This may be hard to hear. The same drugs found in your friend's system were also found in the systems of all five victims of the Wheaton massacre. And their alleged killer, Kenneth Bish."

Cave closes his eyes again, sees Daniel Mazer's smiling face. "You didn't call me here about the journal or the house, this is about Paradign."

"Let's just see where the investigation takes us. Have a nice weekend, Michael. I'll be in touch."

***

6

"Stop wasting time. Give me the antidote," the man struggles under chains to wipe a bead of sweat from falling into his eyes.

I study him, and for a moment visualize the violence I could choose to unleash. Then remind myself. A slow, painful death, that's what he deserves.

"There you go, thinking only of yourself again." I say, grabbing a syringe from my backpack and giving it a good shake on my way to the windowless ledge. Chill mist clings to my clothes in tiny silver droplets. "Maybe I should just toss this, since it's become such a distraction."

"I know you, Nathan. You wouldn't."

"Yeah. Go with that. Carlos Najera. Let's talk about him. I lived on the streets nearly six months researching my story on the homeless epidemic downtown. I learned how it works, how to survive."

"Give it to me," he says, reaching out, desperate hands shaking. A prayer forms on his lips.

"Najera had the heroin market locked, no one dared fuck with him," ignoring his plea. "But he got greedy. Started cutting with fentanyl. Killed a lot of people no one cared about. Killed someone *I* cared about."

"*Give* it to me!" he screams.

"No one can see you when you're homeless. You're a ghost, invisible. Ignored, even when you shouldn't be. Najera and his crew never saw me." I grab my kukri and place it under his chin. "*You* never saw me. Did you, Sebastian?"

He sucks a few breaths and stares wide-eyed back at me.

"It must be thirty degrees. I can see my breath. Meanwhile, you're sweating like a pig. Tick tock, Doctor."

"I'll tell you something," he stammers. "A show of good faith."

"Look at me," I say, pointing double-barreled fingers at myself. "I'm all ears."

"I work for the Defense Intelligence Agency. My work is sanctioned. Everything I've done has been in the country's best interest. You can't punish me for what I did in the service of my country."

The back of my hand meets his sweat-covered face. I wipe it off on my pant leg in disgust.

"Stop me if you know this one, Doc. Samuel Moore comes home from his job at an auto repair shop. He takes a shower, cooks dinner for his grandmother, who he's lived with since childhood. They watch *Jeopardy!* then *Family Feud* together before he helps her upstairs and tucks her in. Early the next morning, Moore sharpens a machete, marches back upstairs, and strikes her seventeen times before he severs her head, which he drains of blood before placing it in a burlap sack and heading off to Begley Hall, where he sits on the steps, grandma's head next to him, and waits for the police. He was one of yours, so tell me. What part of this story best captures you acting in the country's best interest?"

His face hardens. I've struck a nerve. "Great break-throughs require anomalies. For his one story, there are tens, maybe hundreds you'll never hear about. Foreign officials compromised in order to advance our agenda overseas. Attacks averted on our sacred soil. You should be thanking me."

"Should I? How about this one. Paul James Pellen begins hearing voices after he joins Paradign. Just so happens their SR process brokers in rewriting memories, as *you* well know. They uncover something he's not supposed to remember. More specifically, they trigger the failsafe you or your team planted to make *sure* he doesn't remember. Pellen loses his job, becomes increasingly despondent until one day he snaps. A hostage negotiator gets him on the phone. Can't talk him down though. The tactical team busts down the door, but they're not in time to stop him. He points his shotgun. He takes out his wife and two children before he does himself. But hey, greater good, right?" I say, now pacing the room.

He stares back, defiant. "You beat Carlos Najera within inches of his life, Nathan. What right have you to judge *me*?"

I turn on a dime and pounce on top of him, raising a fist. "My point exactly. I'm one of yours too."

Fear animates his eyes. "I have n-nothing more to say."

I grab a fistful of beard hair and stare down at my hands, considering just what they're capable of.

"No?" I yell back. "Well, I do."

Nathan Badger

Ten Months Prior
Badger Home
Ramona, California
January 2
11:20 a.m.

Kah-thuhm. Kah-thuhm.'

I need to know if I'm right.

"Palomar Hospital, how may I direct your call?"

The words trap in my throat, I fight to release them. "Abbigail Ashford's room."

"Hold, please."

My fingers beat an impatient rhythm through two cycles of a familiar Celtic melody.

"Nurse's station, may I help you?" a hurried but pleasant voice says.

"Abigail Ashford's room."

A long pause followed by the shuffling of papers. Then a sigh. "I'm sorry, sir. We've been instructed not to put any calls through to Ms. Ashford."

"Instructed? By whom?" I demand.

"The Detective on her case," the detached response.

"*What* are your visiting hours," I press, charging off to the bedroom closet for a change of clothes.

"Are you immediate family?" the pleasantness gone in her voice.

"Immediate family?" I spit back, caught by surprise. "Is this a new rule or something? She had a visitor yesterday," I say, ripping shirts from their hangars.

She doesn't answer my question, only replies with frustrating, call-ending pleasantries.

"Wait," thinking fast, "there's a nurse named Maibel. I was her patient until yesterday. Could you please call down to the third floor and see if she's on duty?"

A pregnant pause. "Hold, please."

The same Celtic melody. Enya, maybe.

"Personnel office. I understand you're calling regarding a staff member."

"A nurse named Maibel," feeling the slightest hint of hope. "I was her patient. I need to speak with her," I say.

"I'm sorry, sir. She's no longer with us."

"Check again," I demand. " I just saw her yesterday."

"I'm sorry. I can't help you." And with that, a dial tone.

I grab the last remaining clean shirt from the closet. Abby's favorite shirt. My head throbs, I try avoiding my reflection in the mirror but can't. Key gripped tight in my hand like a prize, I march down the long, window-lined hallway. That's when I see her.

Cavanaugh's come alone. At least I know I'm not getting arrested today.

"Detective, please come in." I point toward one of two pneumatic stools at the kitchen counter, both out-of-place modern black pleather pieces in the room they share with a beechwood table and matching china cabinet. Instead, she walks past me to the shrine at the back of the dining room.

My shrine. My Buddha shrine. The home to my memories.

"Nice touch, Mr. Badger. Are you Buddhist?" she says, reaching out to the statue in the center.

"Don't touch it," I warn her, hands pressed on my hips. "I called the hospital. Why are you restricting her calls?"

Cavanaugh glances back, dismissive. "You should know the answer, given your background. She's started talking," she says, matter-of-factly, "I need to hear what she has to say, without any outside interference or influence."

"That's bullshit. You know it." I point an accusing finger and watch her hand slide toward the weapon holstered at her side. "There's nothing I would say or do to stop her from talking. I *need* her to start talking. And *you* to find out who *really* did this to her."

Cavanaugh's hand relaxes at her side. "She *has* started talking. In fact, she told me a few very interesting things." Cavanaugh looks me up and down with something far stronger than mere disapproval. "You two liked it rough, is that right?"

A flash of my hands on her neck.

Kah-thuhm.

"We're back to that, are we? Let me be clear about something for the record. *She* liked it rough."

"Really?" Cavanaugh asks, sarcastic, looking slightly amused. "I don't have to remind you, but I will. *She's* the one still in the hospital now." We lock eyes, anger fires in mine, accusation in hers. "Does the word *Althraigh* mean anything to you?"

Kah-thuhm - Kah-thuhm.

"What did you-"

"Althraigh, Mr. Badger."

The word Abby repeated as she raised the knife to her neck. As I kneeled down in front of her, praying her to stop. As the blade pierced my chest.

I've remembered.

Althraigh.

There's a darkness I've come to embrace.

Althraigh.

ALTHRIGHT!

"Hey, hey. Sit down."

The bearded man. The room I was held in. Abby. The knife.

The knife.

Abby.

Little moments.

My vacant body is guided to a stool.

Little moments I lose, drawn away like a seashell in high tide.

Little moments like these.

Cavanaugh eyes me suspiciously.

"Nosebleeds," I tell her, suddenly defensive, looking away. "I get nosebleeds." I yank a couple of tissues from the box on the counter, pinch my nose with them.

"Abby told me this word. I looked it up, it's Irish. Means to change, to alter. Strange safe word you guys had, but hey, consenting adults and all."

"We've been through this. We didn't *have* safe words. We didn't *need* safe words."

Cavanaugh taps the counter to get my attention. "You sure about that?"

I look up, purse my lips in resolve. "Enough, Detective. She had a visitor yesterday. Who?"

"That's not your concern," her response. "What *should* be is the results of the test we ran. What should be your concern is what Ms. Ashford will be telling me next. You still have a chance to get in front of this." She points two fingers at my chest. "Be a man. Tell me what you *did*."

There's a darkness inside me. It's coming again.

"I told you," bolting to my feet. "I didn't hurt Abby."

She takes a step back, hand on her weapon again.

"Why are you here?" I demand, sitting down to diffuse the situation.

She takes her hand off the weapon and stares in the direction of an air vent. "I came for a tour. Show me around."

She starts off toward the master bedroom. I bolt in front of her, blocking her way.

"You and your team already searched the house. There's nothing more you need to see."

"So it's *no*, then?"

"It's no."

"Fine, guess I'll have to come back with a warrant."

"Guess you will."

Her eyes scan the wall a final time before she turns to leave. "One more thing. The man you were meeting. The supposed tipster, Bish. He's dead. Murder, suicide. Rest up, Mr. Badger. Tomorrow could be a big day for you."

Ω

I watch her leave before scrambling to my office and firing up my computer to confirm it.

Kenneth Bish is dead, along with his five dinner guests. It was a massacre. Ninety-six stab wounds found on the bodies. The only one without defensive wounds was Bish, the man they've pinned the murders on. The man who claimed to have information for my new book.

I don't understand. This makes no fucking sense. I vetted him both professionally and personally before agreeing to the meeting. I found nothing in his background to indicate he'd be capable of something like this.

With murderers there are markers. This I know.

Wallace Harmon's mother told me after his arrest that he wet the bed until the age of seven. Marker. He was socially backwards and regularly bullied at school. Another marker. When the family cat went missing, Harmon placed water and food on the back porch every night, but in her gut she knew it would not be returning home. A neighbor down the street found the cat's skeleton stuffed in their mailbox two days later. Animal cruelty. Another marker.

Harmon began weekly sessions with a local psychiatrist at age nine. He was prescribed Risperdal, an anti-psychotic. One night, after a bloody brawl with his younger brother, he waited until the boy fell asleep before hammering a one-inch nail into his brother's back.

He was discharged from the Army for excessive drinking during his first year of duty at Fort McClellan. This was the tipping point.

Harmon made his platoon sergeant watch as he executed every member of the family before murdering him. I was the one who laid down the evidence tags at the scene.

There are markers. Kenneth Bish had none.

Bish and his alleged victims grew up in the Theosophical Society, like me. As a practicing Theosophist, like my foster parents, he embraced all religions. Like them he believed in reincarnation, astral travel, woodland creatures. Unlike our family, he and his alleged victims stayed active. Him, right up to his death.

He was an accountant for a real estate holding company. Roncate. He was a family man, married with a young daughter. The photos visible on his Facebook page showed them camping in Yosemite, on a gondola in Venice, having a snowball fight in Alaska. Hosting backyard cookouts. Playing Scrabble together. Solving word puzzles together.

Not the profile of a murderer, but he's been labeled one during the press conference I'm watching on YouTube.

"Ladies and gentlemen." The police chief is young, maybe early forties. Deep black bags line the sockets of his sunken eyes. A stiff breeze hits his hair, cut in a crew. He wears an expressionless face; his uniform is pressed to precision. The Mayor by his side. "As you all know, the discovery of six bodies has gripped our city in fear. Luckily for us, officers arrived before a fire in the dining room of the home could compromise all of the evidence."

There's a rumbling of comments from the press corp. He raises his hands above his head until it stops, then continues. "These murders were savage in nature. People feared for their safety, believing a killer could be on the loose. I'm here tonight to assure all of *you*, and the good people of Wheaton, we now know conclusively, one of the bodies found in the dining room is the man responsible for these brutal acts."

He goes on to describe the scene. It's eerily similar to the one I researched for the book. Bolsiver. The Celestial Temple. Joseph LeMay.

The five bodies of his victims were laid out in a circle. Bish lay next to them, forming what police described as a *macabre number ten*. His throat had been slashed; the wound believed to be by his own hand.

"We now suspect Mr. Bish laced the wine he served his guests with a drug called scopolamine. We're informed this drug lowers inhibitions. With a strong enough dose it makes those it's administered to susceptible to suggestion. Simply put, they lose their will to resist. Once this drug took effect, we believe a second drug was introduced to them in their soup."

This drug the police do not name.

My fingers fly over the keyboard. Google spits out results. The drug is odorless, tasteless. The victims had no way to know they'd been poisoned.

Scopolamine. Burandanga. Devil's Breath. Whatever you call it, its effects are similar to the date rape drug Rohypnol. Confusion, increased body temperatures. susceptibility to suggestion, amnesia. In Colombia, there are stories of tourists having it blown in their faces and waking up to find they've been raped, their organs stolen, their bank accounts emptied. And they never remember.

In its raw form, scopolamine is a white powder, resembling cocaine.

Kah-thuhm.

The photo Cavanaugh showed me at the hospital.

Colombia.

Whatever they fed me had legs.

Kah-thuhm. Kah-thuhm.

The realization smacks me like a two-by-four.

I've read about someone showing these symptoms.

The newspaper article. The downtown suicide.

I've lost count of how many times I've re-read the witnesses accounts of the incident involving Daniel Mazer. Seven. Maybe ten. I don't know.

The turntable spins, the needle hits vinyl. The song begins. I dance the intricate dance of denial until the music stops.

It's one thing to suspect, to fight back the gnawing feeling climbing up from my gut like a rat, clawing, digging, tearing at every hope I hold on to that I'm wrong.

It's something very different to hold the confirmation in my hands.

Daniel Mazer walked into the crowded club, dazed, confused, sweating profusely, and cut his own throat.

Less than a week after Mazer's death, Kenneth Bish allegedly uses the same drug on his victims, administering it before he butchers five people, then turns the knife on himself. He too cuts his own throat.

I stopped Abby from doing the same.

The little moments I question, snatched away like pebbles in high tide.

Abby.

The driveway.

Drip.

Althraigh.

Drip.

ALTHRIAGH!

A pool of fresh blood covers the worn wooden edge of my desk nearest the keyboard. I drag a tissue through the seeping red mess until it's sopping wet, at once confirming and denying the realities.

Less than three percent of all suicide attempts, successful or not, involve someone taking a knife to their own throat. There's a fifty-two percent mortality rate. Slicing your own throat is number two on the *most painful ways to die* list. It comes right behind setting yourself on fire.

You want to take your own life, you get a gun. You hang yourself. You don't choose this way.

But two people did. And Abby tried.

I push back from the desk as though doing so somehow changes things. But it doesn't. I'm slapped by the cold-water-in-the-face realization again and again, until I accept it.

These cases are connected. Period.

Jesus. I need help. I need resources.

Luke and I haven't spoken since I left the life.

While I was a part of it, he and I went places I don't talk about. Did things *we* don't talk about. Luke has *connections* he never talks about.

He will now.

"Luke here."

"I need your help. Abby was kidnapped. I'm the prime suspect."

"All this time." I listen to him take a deep breath. "You just walk away. Not even a phone call, not until you're in trouble." He huffs a long exhale. "What do you want?"

"I'm going to be served with a search warrant any time now. I need to tie some things together first. The murders in Wheaton, you know about them?"

"It's been all over the news," his curt response. "What about them?"

"The guy who did it. Bish. I was supposed to meet him the night Abby was taken. He had information for the new book. He's the reason why I wasn't home," pointing an accusing finger at my computer monitor.

Dead silence thickens like fog between us, the *thuush* of a match head igniting is his only reply.

"They found Devil's Breath in all the victim's blood in Wheaton," I say, my words slicing through the awkward air. "Abby was drugged too. I suspect a guy named Daniel Mazer was as well."

I picture the cloud of smoke as he exhales. "Mazer. The downtown suicide."

I tap the screen of my phone to unlock it, tap the speaker icon and search through my contacts. "You still have your connections on the SDPD?"

"Last time I checked," his wooden reply.

"I need to see Mazer's toxicology report. They ran tests on Abby and me at the hospital. I need those too."

"There's no fucking way my guy can pull records from an active case without someone noticing."

"Then get Mazer's," I demand.

"I'll see what I can do," he mumbles, half-hearted.

"Listen to me," I say, shooting up straight in my chair. "You owe me. You fucking *owe* me."

A few more heavy exhales. "Fair enough," he says. "Anything else?"

"Yeah, there is. I need to talk to the witnesses who saw Mazer kill himself. I'll text you their names. Have your guy run them, I need their addresses and phone numbers."

"We're square after this. Hear me?"

"Yeah, we're square, The last thing. The kidnappers flew me to Bogotá after they took her. There's no record of me taking that flight. Who has the power to wipe flight records?"

A pregnant pause as Lucas Sturgeon taps out a text, then, "I think you already know."

Thack-thack-thack.

"Nathan, honey. Open the door."

"I don't *want* to go."

"You don't *want* to be late."

"I won't go. I hate him."

"Nathan, honey. The Doctor is waiting."

"I won't go back there!"

Thack-thack-thack.

Thack-thack-thack.

Thack-thack-thack.

Huh? I jump out from my office chair.

Shaking the memory loose from my brain I see shadows cast through the front door.

It's Cavanaugh and two uniformed officers. One is rapping his giant meat-hook-sized hands into my front door. The other has a German Shepherd in tow.

I stumble to the front door and open it.

"Good morning, Mr. Badger. This is Officer Parks and Officer Smith." They nod in unison. "We have a warrant to search the premises."

"I'm sure you do," I tell her. "I want to see it."

She holds up a metal clipboard. "As you wish."

I grab it, shake it at her. "You already searched once. What's this really about?"

She points to the table. "We got a warrant for the tests they ran on you and Abby at the hospital. The results came back positive. Why don't you save us all some time and tell me where you're stashing the drugs you used on her?"

"There's nothing here," I snap back.

"We'll see, won't we? Any questions before we get started?"

I sit down. She sits next to me, watching me as I skim through the warrant. Studying my face. My body.

"Do what you came here to do," I say, slamming the clipboard down on the table with a loud metallic thud.

She gets up from her chair, rolls up one sleeve, revealing the devastation beneath it.

She catches me staring. Again. "I need you out of the house. Take a walk, go for a drive, don't go far. I have your cell number. I'll text you when we're done."

I reach the courtyard before she gives the signal, watching with a mix of anger and disbelief through the windows as a German Shepherd heads straight for the hallway leading to the bedrooms.

I take a drive to the neighborhood store and buy something strong.

Ω

I arrive home just in time to see Officer Meat Hooks loading a full box of electronics into his squad car's trunk.

Cavanaugh greets me in the driveway with Abby's locket sealed in an evidence bag. She waves it in front of my face. "Tell me about this," she demands.

"It's Abby's."

"Yeah, no shit. I'm only going to ask you this once. Where are you keeping the rest of the drugs, Mr. Badger?"

She holds the bag to my face again, I shove it away. "Why don't you ask Abby the same question?"

"Trust me, I will," she tells me as the officers climb into their cars, and she into hers.

I watch them pull away

Things are moving quickly. I don't have much time.

Luke hasn't called back yet. I have another idea.

I scramble for my phone and call Bonny Bish, Kenneth's widow, hoping for something, anything to latch on to.

She tells me three things. She's selling the house and moving in seven days. She has no idea why her husband contacted me. Third and final thing: don't ever call her again.

Ω

Bahhhhring.
Bahhhhring.
Bahhhhring

Back at the precinct, the desk-phone in Commander William Ward's office bleats out a tenth time before he reaches it. "Ward here."

G2X Deputy Grey Gullen doesn't mince words. "I understand you let your detective execute a search warrant and that you're planning an arrest. I believe I made myself crystal fucking clear, how did you let this thing escalate?"

Ward nervously fumbles with the phone cord. "He's a DNA match. The blood tests run at the hospital showed he and Ms. Ashford had traces of the same drug in their systems. The hospital already notified the DEA. If I had shut down the arrest, how do you think it would've looked?"

Gullen lets out a sarcastic laugh. "Listen to me. I'm sending a specialist. See to it he gets cleared at the hospital to see Ms. Ashford. Alone. Am I understood?"

Puzzled, Ward's stares in disbelief at the phone. "What about the DEA?"

"Let me deal with them," Gullen says before clearing the phlegm from his throat. "One more thing. You're going to reassign the detective on the Badger case. She'll liase on a case downtown."

Ward's back arches. "That's not our jurisdiction."

"I've already made the handshake."

"What's the nature of the case?" Ward asks, still puzzled.

"The homeless disappearances."

"May I ask, why her?"

"No. You may not."

Gullen's next call is to Kane Industries.

***

7

"I said, open the door *now* young man!"

My eight-year-old self huddles hidden away in the closet.

"Knock it down," from outside my room.

"Leave me alone. I don't want the memories anymore."

Thack.

I squeeze my hands against my ears, unable to drown out the crack, crack, crack of splintering wood.

"Clear."

No. Please no. I don't want to go back.

Kah-thuhm.

Kah-thuhm - Kah-thuhm.

"Nathaniel Badger. This is the San Diego Sheriff's Department. Answer us if you're in here. You have five seconds to respond."

I back up slowly toward my closet.

Bodies rush forward down the hall and through the open bedroom door. I'm shoved down. A knee goes heavy into my back. My face meets the once-white carpet of my bedroom floor.

She waves her handcuffs in my face, just like Abby liked to do. But I never let Abby use them. I won't have a say this time.

"Listen up. You have the right to remain silent. Anything you say can and will be used against you in a court of law."

She reads me the rest of my rights. I'm stood up on my feet. There's a taser gun pointed at my ribcage. "No sudden movements," I'm told by the officer holding it.

"Do you understand each of these rights I've explained to you? Having these rights in mind, do you wish to talk to us now?" Cavanaugh asks.

Where are you darkness? Where are you now when I need you?

A simple twist of my hips would move the taser offline long enough to kick it from his hands. That leaves the other two, who are both armed.

I calculate the odds in my head and arrive too close to zero.

"Let's just go get this done," I reply.

SHERIFF'S PRECINCT, SAN DIEGO
7:17 A.M.

We turn into the precinct through a near-empty parking lot, save two parked squad cars and one uniformed officer out for a smoke, and down the ramp as the black metal gate completes its ascent. A flashing light inside casts an undulating crimson hue over the uniformed policeman pointing a tactical shotgun tracking our progress as we pass, his stern, chiseled face a silent, unnecessary warning. The door's alarm bleats until metal meets concrete and I'm sealed inside. The last breath of freedom escapes from my lips as the car slows to a stop. The shotgun's pointed at the me as the inner door to the jail opens. Out of the door walks the officer with meat hooks for hands. Parks.

"Let's go," he commands, leaning my head down so it doesn't strike the top of the car as I exit.

Even now I deny what clearly is happening. I've been arrested. I'll be charged. An innocent man will take a fall. "Shouldn't you be looking for the person who actually did this?" I ask flatly, a question met with a fist in the small of my back.

Parks takes his place behind me once I'm clear. One hand firmly grasping my arm, the other, I imagine, on his weapon.

A buzzer screeches as we pass through the open door, I stumble forward, dazed, unable to deny anymore. In the eyes of the law I'm guilty. I did this.

The lock snaps tight and I'm led down an egg-shell white hallway lined with doors trimmed in blue, flecks of paint peeling back against age and neglect. We reach the third door. Parks guides my face into the wall, the giant fist of his other hand digs again into the small of my back.

I hear the rattle of a doorknob and the squeal of hinges before being led into a small room with a heavy metal table and heavy air. Two chairs are opposite the one I'm placed in. Parks locks me into a hefty retention chain and takes the seat diagonal to me, a comfortable leather backed secretary's chair like mine. The two-way mirror to my right separates us from the adjacent observation room. The wall to my left holds just one wall hanging, a Norman Rockwell reprint, the one with the cop and the kid sitting next to each other at an ice cream shop.

As for me, I'm Algernon. In my cage and observed. By the camera in the observation room, by whoever's in there with it, but not by the man seated in front of me, who's busy flipping through my case file.

We sit in silence as the clock on the wall ticks away time. At minute twelve I strain against the chain securing my handcuffs, but I'm unable to reach the irritating itch gnawing at the small of my back.

The clock reaches forty minutes before a twist of the door handle brings him to his feet.

"Give us the room, please."

"Detective." Parks nods and gets out of his chair. Cavanaugh takes the seat across from me, stares me down until Parks is gone.

"Abby had a lot more to say. Thought you'd like to know."

"You can't hold me here without a warrant," I snap back, defiant.

"You sure about that?" She runs a finger down the checklist clipped to a metal clipboard, flips pages in her beat-up notebook until she's cross-referenced every line from her list. "Cause I'm *not*."

"Pretty sure I want my phone call," I tell her.

She leans back in her chair and raps on the door. Parks peaks his head in. "Mr. Badger would like his phone call," she says. Parks barely nods and leaves.

He returns, running the cord from the wall to the table, and placing the phone within reach.

"Anything else, Detective?" Cavanaugh motions him to come closer. She whispers new instructions. He leaves after.

"Turns out," she says, "the woman in Bogotá you told me about at the hospital, Jan Castellanos, is DEA."

"DEA?" I grab the phone and start dialing Ash. I know who can wipe flight records. Agencies. Three letter agencies. The *fucking* DEA.

Cavanaugh clears her throat to be sure she gets my attention. "I caught you staring at my wrists a few times now. It's time I tell you a story," she says as she slowly rolls up her sleeves, and for an uncomfortable moment I study the aftermath I've caught glimpses of. The scar tissue travels in a pattern of mangled knots up her arms. "Not my first time, Mr. Badger. Not by a long shot."

I want to look away, but I can't. I hear Ash's greeting as the phone falls from my hand.

Thuuukkk. Cavanaugh smacks the table, lifts up her reddened palm to show me. She leans back in her chair, proceeds to crack each knuckle one at a time before speaking again. "I know all about men like you. Let me tell you how I got these."

I have an idea what could do such damage. The scar tissue begins below her wrists, a molten tracery in dull red and blues climbing her arms like a topographic map of some remote alpine region. And like a map, that angry flesh leads me to some truths about Cavanaugh.

"The others didn't see it at first, but I knew. I *fucking* knew." She chucks those three words out of her mouth with a shrug so full of anger she momentarily forgets herself. She recovers. "He had a genuine appetite for it. Men like him. Like you. You just get hungrier and hungrier, don't you?"

She blinks down hard once, then again, grinding her teeth, tightening her lips. I sit staring now at the phone, at my lifeline. But I'm frozen, unable to move.

"A cigarette burn. That's how we think he got started. The victim filed a complaint. We took him in. I watched the interview from the observation room. The officer conducting it sat him down, same way you got sat down. But who's gonna believe a prostitute's word? I mean, she's a drug addict, she sells her body. Who's gonna believe her over a county employee of twenty years, right? But I could tell. I knew."

She's chosen to tell me her story. I want to know why.

"No charges were filed. Everyone went back to their lives. Her name was Beth. Beth went back to the streets. His name was Curtis Havens. Havens went back to the school district he worked at. And me, I waited for the next shoe to drop. It took over a year before girls started disappearing. Beth was the second. When we found the bodies, Beth's included, they were all left with a distinct signature." She holds up her wrists, the ruined flesh colored like a summer sunset promising a storm. "We got our first real break from a survivor. I held her, literally held her for the first twenty-or-so minutes before she talked. She gave us the house. We put it under surveillance and stationed a plainclothes at the school." She's bursts out of her chair as if to some unheard fire drill, turns her back to me, and paces the room. "I was bait. Every night."

I feel the heat of her intensity as I did at the hospital. Her fists clench and unclench.

"It took six nights. Six *long* fucking nights. Finally, he stops. He asks me for a date. I say yes."

I watch tears beginning to form in her eyes.

"He just kept on talking, laying on compliments. Playing this song, the same song, over and over. 'Challenge Me.' I didn't know for sure he'd made me until it was too late. All I remember is the sound of a camera lens zooming in. I knew then he'd been filming me. That he'd filmed others. Then it just happened. I shielded my face with a plate before he threw the acid at me. I was screaming the duress code long after they found me."

And there it is. Her story. Horrible what the darkness can do to a person. I know.

"I'm sorry for what happened to you, I am. But why are you telling me this?"

"Because you're just like Havens. Which means there'll be more. More like Abby."

Kah-thuhm.

I choke back a frustrated scream.

"Nothing to say? That speaks volumes." Cavanaugh snaps her fingers. "Oh, and about the search yesterday. The cameras were right where Abby told me they'd be. We imaged your computer; we'll see what you recorded. Unless you'd like to tell me."

Kah-thuhm - Kah-thuhm.

"Cameras?" I jerk back reflexively, metal bands bite into my wrists. "Recorded? What are you talking about? My security cameras?"

"Maybe your weakest lie yet. The cameras in the air conditioning vents. Abby told us you liked filming her. I don't need to remind you. Those IP cameras all have addresses."

Kah-thuhm - Kah-thuhm - Kah-thuhm.

I grab the phone.

"Yeah, call your attorney," Cavanaugh snipes, then as almost an afterthought, "What's his name?"

I look down and away. "Ash. Ash Davis," I tell her. "And he's good," looking down at the chains.

"I'll let the front desk know to expect a Mr. Ash Davis. And hey, be sure to ask him about *County of Riverside v. McLaughlin.*"

I give her a blank stare.

"Go ahead. He'll tell you. We have plenty of time together." She glances at her watch. "Forty-six hours or so before we have to formally charge you or let you go. That should give us and the DEA more than enough time. I'll let you know what we find once we watch your videos. But I suppose you already know what's there." She grants me a condescending smirk. "Can we get you a water, or maybe some coffee while you wait?"

How can there be videos on my computer?

Unless.

The bruising around Abby's neck. Me coming to in the bean bag, not remembering.

Little moments.

"Nothing," I tell her.

She hesitates at the door and turns back to stare me down. "Save us some time, Badger. Just start talking."

Little moments I lose.

"I have nothing more to say."

***

NEAR THE GASLAMP QUARTER
DOWNTOWN SAN DIEGO
11:55 AM, JANUARY 3

Lucas Sturgeon pushes his sandy-blond hair under a filthy, dark hood and lays an equally filthy sleeping bag on the cold cement sidewalk. On the landing above and to the right of him, a gaunt man in his fifties missing several front teeth doles out Styrofoam plates and utensils. The grateful hands of addicts, alcoholics and unfortunates accept them on their way to a much-appreciated warm meal.

Sturgeon begins speaking earnestly to an invisible companion. His hands make animated gestures to no one. Meanwhile, he hones in on the conversations from the serpentine line moving past him toward the steps of the shelter. There's no talk at all of the disappearances.

Sturgeon recognizes the man known as Elder Dean when he emerges from the entrance. Many in line pat his shoulder and thank him as he passes. Sturgeon discreetly clicks a remote tucked under the sleeve of his hoodie and snaps a few photos of the elderly man.

As Dean nears him, the telltale tingling begins. He jams a tremoring hand into his pocket and digs out two pills. He downs them with a huge gulp from the first of three cold quarts of Miller as the noon sun approaches. His hands soon still. The seizure is averted.

He settles in for the long day and night ahead.

Ω

"There's no fucking way this is right," Cavanaugh hisses at Ward, snagging his arm as she chases him up the stairwell.

"Get your hand off me." Ward's eyes burn red. "And don't challenge me. It's done." With a violent snap he shakes his arm free from her hold, turns, and continues the brisk, angry march up the stairs.

She catches him at the top of the staircase and spins him around. "Number one, you know about Havens, the song he played. Poor choice of words. Beneath even you. And number two, I had her talking to me. You didn't need to send someone else in. So why *did* you?"

Ward points an accusing finger. She lets go. He storms past Lana, his secretary, and yanks his office door open. Cavanaugh flies in behind him.

"Sir, the briefing." Lana calls out, her voice squeaky and loud, like she's yelling for her girlfriend across a crowded techno club.

When the argument inside Ward's office spills out the crack in the door, and the sound of her yelling threatens to reach the conference room, Lana tiptoes over to the conference room and closes the door.

Inside the office, Cavanaugh reaches her breaking point. "This is my case. *My* case. She gave him up on the cameras. We've got his computer. We *got* his fucking DNA."

Ward picks up the framed photo on his desk.

"This expert you brought in," Cavanaugh says, annoyed that Ward seems so fascinated with the photo that's has been on his desk for years. "Where'd you find him? He's not one of ours."

Ward sets down the photo, but his eyes don't leave it. "Ms. Ashford has recanted her story. It's over. Now listen. There've been some homeless who've gone missing downtown. Five so far. Two of them from near the shelter above the post office. You're authorized, on the department's behalf, to liaise and assist with the investigation."

"But that's not our jurisdiction," Cavanaugh protests.

"The handshake has been made."

"So that's it? I'm being reassigned?"

"That's it, Detective."

"Answer my *question*, why did you send someone else?"

His head shoots up, cocks, his eyes widen in warning. "I said, that's it." He points at the door.

She bites down on her bottom lip. An angry tear threatens. Her middle finger begins to extend, but she stops it.

This is bullshit. I know it. He knows it.

Cavanaugh leans down and places her palms on Ward's desk. "Yes, sir. Thank you for the *opportunity*, sir." The last word escapes her mouth like the threatening hiss of a snake.

She yanks open the door; Lana spins her chair around. Cavanaugh flashes warning eyes at her. Lana ducks her head behind her computer. Cavanaugh stands holding the doorknob until she counts to five, and the need to slam it shut with all of her might fades.

Ward waits until he sees her return to her desk before picking up the receiver and padding in the number he'd been instructed to call.

"He's being released from our custody." A long pause follows. Ward cradles the phone under his chin, picks up the framed photo on his desk again.

"And the detective on the case?" Gullen demands.

"Reassigned. Like you requested."

"Let's get clear on something. I *don't* make requests. Next time, if there is one, you will do exactly and only what I say from word one. Is there anything unclear about what I just said?"

"N-n-no, sir."

"Take good care of that lovely daughter of yours." Then a dial tone.

"All for you, little one," he whispers, setting down the photo of his twelve-year-old daughter on his way out the door to the meeting he's now fifteen minutes late for.

***

8

NATHAN BADGER

SHERIFF'S PRECINCT, SAN DIEGO
JANUARY 3, 3:00 P.M.

The door to the holding room finally opens. Judging by the vast shadow cast across the floor, it's Officer Meat Hooks.

"You're being released," he says, tugging at the keyring attached to his belt.

Words I deserve to be hearing. Words I don't fully believe.

"There have been some developments." He unlocks me, takes a step back and half-turns with the precision of a West Point cadet. He motions to the open door and the freedom awaiting me through it.

I lock in place. "Tell me you found whoever did this to Abby." I press, nervously chewing a thumbnail.

A slow shake of his oversized head, a giant finger again points at the door. "You are to notify the department before making any out-of-town trips." A dead-eyed warning from a dead-eyed giant.

There it is. I'm not cleared of this yet.

We go wordlessly down the hall, him thudding size twelve-or-so boots authoritatively down the hall, me spinning scenarios in my head like a roulette wheel.

We make it through a few secure doors and into the lobby. I'm free. For now.

"We're gathering the evidence we secured from your home," Meat Hooks tells me, nodding his head at the Evidence Room sign hung above a doorway on the opposite side of the lobby. "You're welcome to wait here, or you're free to go and come back for it tomorrow."

"I'll wait." I reply.

Nineteen minutes later, Ash's six-foot-six frame fills the front entrance of the precinct. He's dressed for battle in a Gainsborough-grey, notch-lapeled suit showing no sign of ever being worn before today. His sandy-blond hair is cut smartly, held in place by a what I imagine having been a palmful of gel. He doesn't know it yet, but there will be no battle fought today.

He heads straight to the front desk; it takes a real effort and a lot of throat clearing to get his attention.

I motion him over. He lowers himself onto the bench seat to my right, looking like an adult crammed into a child's chair at a pre-school. "Didn't expect to find you *here*," he says. "What's going on?"

"I don't know," I tell him, honestly. "Waiting for the stuff they took as evidence."

"You can fill me in on what you *do* know on the way to your house," he replies, pointing his chin at the security camera opposite him.

"There's nothing to tell," I say, catching my first whiff of antiseptic cleaner mixed with the welcome fresh air of freedom from the now open lobby door, where a fit, middle-aged officer in a blood-stained uniform leads a stumbling, handcuffed drunk inside. "One minute they're breaking into my computer and I'm in chains. The next minute I'm free." I make the gesture I saw Cavanaugh make, the one that reminded me of a magic show I once saw.

He fidgets with his tie. "So you're officially cleared?"

The door leading to my freedom closes, and with it, a reminder. "They told me not to leave town."

Ash wags a finger in warning. "Then you're still a suspect. Don't forget it."

From down the hall I hear the rattling wheels of a metal pushcart. A beer-bellied officer wearing Coke-bottle glasses pushes the noisy cart to a stop inches from my feet.

"Please verify that the items listed in the paperwork are all here." His breath smells like tuna.

My computer. Five cameras. A stack of photo-graphs. Abby's locket. Evidence once meant to be used against me.

Now, maybe, finally, it's my chance to turn the ta-bles.

I formulate my plan as Ash studies my face. Digital analysis of the photographs may provide me with a lo-cation for where I was held in Bogotá. Reflections in the mirror in one of the photographs may provide me a face Luke can run recognition software on. Her locket, and the cameras found hidden in the air vents at home...

Wait a minute.

Cameras Abby told Cavanaugh about.

A nagging thought burrows through my brain like a malevolent worm. Abby shopped for electronics the day I met her at Starbucks.

Officer Coke-Bottles repeatedly taps the metal cart handle with a cheap, plastic pen. Eventually I take the hint.

"All here," I reply before absently signing the form.

We're out the door in less than a minute. Ash grabbed a money spot next to the entrance. Coke-Bottles guides the cart behind us, every now and again pushing up the glasses sliding down his nose as he struggles to keep up.

He arrives, huffing, at the now open trunk of Ash's car. A bead of fresh sweat forms on his forehead.

I grab the photo Cavanaugh showed me at the hospital and Abby's locket. I put the rest in the trunk before Ash's pearl white E350 roars to life, pronouncing itself above the afternoon din like the roar of a hungry lion declaring its presence to its prey. Ash clicks into reverse while eyeing the rearview camera, then punches it into drive, spinning a tire mark into the pavement with a *phooosh*.

He takes a sharp right turn out of the driveway and spills out onto the street. We're a mile or so from the freeway before I've told him everything.

Almost everything.

"This, Ash," I say, shoving the locket in front of his face. "They served me with a search warrant yesterday. Brought drug-sniffing dogs. They found this."

He takes his eyes off the road to snap a quick glance. "Damn sure ain't yours," he says, turning back just in time to narrowly avoid running over a squirrel with an apparent death wish. "Abby did drugs?"

The inside of the locket has been thoroughly cleaned. No surprises there. "This is a long shot, but I'm gonna ask you anyway. They did drug tests on me and on Abby at the hospital. I know a guy who knows a guy inside the force, but there's no way he's getting his hands on the tox report."

"You want the ones from the hospital," he glances over, offers a disapproving shake of his head.

"Can you *do* it?"

Both palms slap the steering wheel. "This conversation never happened," his emphatic answer. "You got that?"

I offer a noncommittal nod of my head and just stare out the window.

Many mile markers and exit signs pass. "They also found this," I finally say, showing him the photo, breaking the tense veil of silence between us.

He glances over, then back at the road. "Cocaine?"

"Scopolamine. I think it's what she had in her locket."

"Nathan, I've known you a long time. Shoot straight with me." His eyebrows crease with concern. "What the hell have you gotten yourself into?"

"Nothing. I mean, I don't know," for the moment I push my eyes closed I see her standing over me holding her neck. "The drug causes blackouts. I've *had* blackouts," jabbing at my chest with an open fist. "I *need* to see the toxicology reports from the hospital. If it shows what I think it will, that's proof. That's my verification. The photo, Abby's locket." I stop myself before telling him about Bish, Mazer. The flight being erased. Ash is a rational man. All I have right now are hunches and conspiracy theories. Neither works with a guy like him.

He pushes a hand through his hair, taps his forehead a few times with a knuckle. "I see it like this," he says. "You go see your doctor. You tell him about these blackouts. Tell him you don't know why they're happening. He'll run all the tests. If what you say's true about Abby, they'll all come back negative. Bam," he smacks the steering wheel again. "there's your confirmation."

I stare out the window at passing cars. "I don't think I have that kinda time."

"Find a way to *make* the time," he commands. "You go see the doctor, Nate. You start fucking around with hospital records, you're gonna get yourself back in handcuffs."

"I need to know," I tell him, waiting for the blowback.

He heaves a heavy sigh, stares out at the road. "One last time I'll pretend I didn't hear you."

In time with his words, my phone comes to life in my pocket.

Two text messages. Both from Luke.

One containing the phone numbers of the couple who witnessed Daniel Mazer's suicide.

The other contains his toxicology report.

Kah-thuhm.

"Nathan?"

They found scopolamine in Mazer's system.

He's dead.

Kah-thuhm - Kah-thuhm.

They found it in Kenneth Bish's blood. And in the blood of his victims.

All of them dead.

"Hey, Nathan."

Abby took a knife to her throat. Like them.

I wasn't meant to find her in the driveway.

She's meant to be dead. Like the others.

Bah- BAHHHH.

BAHHHH.

Ash thuds the steering wheel again, this time the horn blares long. "You look like you seen a ghost. Why?"

"Wha?" My pulse pounds in my wrist, my hands shake, my head a giant balloon, stretched to its limits and ready to burst. "Nothing. Just worried about Abby," I lie.

"Bullshit," Ash says, shaking an angry fist in the air as he rounds a bend in the road and my house comes into view. "You hear me? Bullshit. I been in enough courtrooms, seen enough defendants on the stand to know when I'm being lied to. I'm your lawyer, for fuck's sake."

"Just Abby," I reassure him. I make him stop on the road in front of my house. Slam the door behind me and yell through the now open window. "I'll be in touch."

It takes everything within me to wait until he's gone.

It takes everything I have to sacrifice these precious seconds with Abby at risk before placing the call, only to get their automated message.

"You have reached the San Diego County Sheriff's Department. If this is an emergency, please hang up-"

"Operator," I scream into the phone as I reach my front door. A shaking hand enters the wrong access code. Twice. "*Operator!*"

"Please choose from the following menu."

Fucking *fuck*.

Maybe it's a man dressed in a blue lab coat, thick black glasses and a name tag he stole or had made. Maybe a nurse, dressed in white, gloves up to the wrist, syringe filled with poison hidden away in a pocket.

I know it. I see it. Someone's coming for Abby.

"Operator!" I scream, thudding my finger repeatedly on the number zero.

A nonchalant, matronly voice finally responds.

"Welcome to the San Diego Sheriff's Department, how may I-"

"Detective Cavanaugh. It's urgent," I say.

"What is the nature your call?" I'm asked.

"Put me through," I demand. "I think someone's in danger."

"I'm connecting you to our 911 opera-"

"Cavanaugh!" I demand.

"Hold, please," I'm told before my ears are assaulted by their tacky on-hold music.

Pacing the floor, I run through it all in my head. Hoping I'm wrong. Praying I'm wrong.

Every instinct tells me someone will come.

And finish the job.

"This is Detective Drew Cavanaugh. Please leave your name, phone number and a description of the nature of your call after the tone."

Even as the words leave my lips, I'm out the door, in my car on the way to the hospital.

"This is Nathan Badger. I think Abby may still be in danger."

I'm halfway down the 78, a two-lane, serpentine stretch of switchbacks, when Cavanaugh calls.

"I can't get through to her room," I yell, flying past a long string of cars and back into my lane to a chorus of horns and a few extended middle fingers. "*Tell* me you've already checked on her."

"Where are you right now, Mr. Badger?"

The film of sweat coating my hand makes the steering wheel slip through my fingers. I overcorrect, skidding toward an on-coming car I barely miss sideswiping. "On my way to the hospital."

"I'll save you the trip," she states flatly. "She's been released."

I smack the steering wheel hard, shooting pain through my palm like a bee sting. "*Released*?" I yell back, angrily yanking the car to the side of the road in a cloud of brown dust, spitting gravel and dirt at a passing car.

I snatch the phone from the passenger seat and text Abby. *Are you okay?* The vein in my wrist drumbeats, threatening to explode.

"Listen to me," Cavanaugh says, sounding like a principal scolding a ten-year-old. "I take calls like yours very seriously. *How* is it you think she's in danger?"

"Do you believe in coincidence?"

Her answer drips with impatience. "What's your point?"

"The *drug* is my point," I snap back. "You found traces of scopolamine in the blood tests you ordered on Abby and me. You found traces of it in her locket."

No response.

"*Didn't* you?" I demand.

There's a rustling of papers in the background.

Still no response.

"Call the Wheaton police," I demand. "They found scopolamine in Kenneth Bish's blood too, and in the blood of his alleged victims."

"Bish? The tipster?" More rustling of paper.

"He's the reason I wasn't home the night Abby was taken. And he has the same drug in his system. Coincidence? I think not."

"I researched it," she tells me. "It's a commonly prescribed drug. Used to treat nausea and motion sickness. You claim to have taken a trip. Bish allegedly planned a trip to see you for this supposed tip. Trips. Motion sickness. This would appear to explain it."

"Did you not *hear* me?" I yell. "Every *single* victim in Wheaton had it in their system. Five *dead* people and Bish had it in their system. Then there's Daniel Mazer."

It takes her a moment. "The downtown suicide. The Paradignist. What about him?"

"I have a screenshot of his toxicology report. They found scopolamine in his bloodstream too."

"How exactly did you get a copy of the toxicology report, Mr. Badger?"

"Doesn't matter. Point is I did," I tell her.

"Text it to me," she snaps back. I fire it off, drum my fingers on the dashboard and wait.

"What am I looking for?" her half-hearted reply.

"Scopolamine. You see? And oh, by the way, Mazer's estimated body temperature at the time of his death was between 103.6 and 104.1. They ran a P80 panel. That's how they found a second drug. Alpha-PVP. Flakka. Made a guy in Florida who took it chew off someone's face." I wait a beat to let it sink in. "Do me a favor. Flip open your notebook to where I described how Abby looked in the driveway."

More rustling of papers.

"I'm there," Cavanaugh answers.

"Here's the symptoms of Flakka. Uncontrolled eye movements. Increased body temperatures. Anxiety. Paranoia. Psychosis. Look familiar?"

No response.

"These cases are connected. Bish and Mazer are dead by their own hands. Abby tried to kill herself. What if she wasn't *meant* to be stopped?"

I don't wait long for her answer. "This is all circumstantial at best."

"You really want to be the one responsible for taking that chance?" Frustrated, I fling the note pad at the window. It smashes, then falls to the floor next to an empty water bottle. "You know better. *Do* something," I demand.

"I'm off the case," she says. "All I can do is report what you've told me to my commanding officer. It's up to him what he does with it. Unless there's an imminent, verifiable threat. That's all I can do."

"No, it's not. You can *help* me," I scream, pointing an accusatory finger at the windshield.

"Maybe you didn't hear me," she yells back. "I *can't* help you. But I *suggest* you help yourself. You're not yet cleared as a suspect."

"I bring you proof," I finally say, with a frustrated shake of my head. "I show you these cases are connected; will you help me then?"

"No promises. Good luck, Mr. Badger."

The calls ends there.

Fine.

Excellent.

Understood.

My next call, Victoria. The witness.

It takes a shit-ton of convincing, but she agrees to meet me.

The movie of the night in the driveway, of Abby, of the haunting melody she sang to herself, the word she said. It plays on an unstoppable loop in my head the whole way to the bar.

Ω

EAST VILLAGE TAVERN
7:30 PM

Ooonce. Ooonce. Ooonce. Ew-Ew- Ooonce. Ooonce. Ooonce.

Every bass beat rattles my inner ear, makes the hair on my head move, pounding in the reminder I need to act fast. Abby may be at risk.

A sheepish DJ flies out of the restroom door to my right and bolts on stage, spinning the volume dial somewhere below the 85 decibels it seemed to be set at.

"My bad, everyone," he holds up an apologetic hand. The microphone shrieks out deafening feedback.

The EDM bass-beat momentarily stops, the whole place quiets just enough for me to hear the crashing of pins from the adjacent, five-lane bowling alley. East Village Tavern. A place I'd once taken Abby. The place Victoria chose for us to meet.

I fling my backpack over one shoulder and hold my phone over my head so everyone can see it and scan the bar. I spot the only woman seated alone and charge toward her. Before I get there a bearded guy wearing a Harley Davidson t-shirt and leather vest with thighs for arms wraps his arms around her from behind.

"Daddy! Thought you weren't coming," the young girl with a freckle-filled face turns and says before being swept up in a bear hug.

I text Victoria again with a *Can't find you*, check the bar a final time, then head back to the entrance, checking my phone for a response from Abby a few times on the way.

Outside on Market Street, sirens wail, bells ring a third time at Bootlegger down the street. At the entrance here, the barrel-chested doorman wearing a ragged pair of jeans and an *I'm a Belieber* concert shirt mumbles, "ID," to an attractive girl with bronze hair who appears way too young to be legal.

Finally. Maybe.

She digs through her purse for her wallet. He rattles a too-many-Monster-drinks tempo with his foot while eyeing her. All of her. Some parts of her longer than others. She eventually finds her wallet and busts him, before handing over her ID. He looks over his shoulder at the line of ten or so people behind her, then inspects her ID for a long minute, turning it at different angles, flipping it over and reading the back.

"Hey, I come here all the time you know," the young woman says as she takes out her cell phone. She reads what I assume to be the message I sent her. I step over to where she's waiting. The doorman lets her in.

"Victoria?"

She wears the outfit of a runway model. Black pumps. Silk nylons, black as well. Her blouse is a brilliant vermillion. The pashmina covering her shoulders and neck is multicolored. Quality. Expensive. She stares back through sparkling, apple-green eyes. There's a slight turn to her nose, her one slight imperfection.

We make eye contact. I manufacture a pained smile. She doesn't smile back.

I extend a hand, she takes it limply in hers, all the while scanning the bar.

"James couldn't make it tonight," I tell her, answering her question.

"Figured as much." The rose-red disappointment coloring her cheeks transforms to bright embers of anger, then to ashen acceptance. "Asshole," she mutters to herself.

We find the second to last open booth.

"We've got a few minutes before my date's supposed to meet me," she tells me, after an unnecessary glance at her watch. "You said this was urgent."

"It is." I check my phone again, still nothing from Abby.

A waitress bolts by. Victoria clears her throat loudly. The waitress stops, frazzled, hair disheveled, name badge proclaiming *My Name Is Angie* loosely pinned to a baseball jersey, hanging by a few threads and cockeyed.

"Vodka tonic," she says, trailing her eyes over the crowded bar as though James may now magically appear.

"Didn't see you there, honey," the waitress replies in a heavy smoker's rasp. "Hanger 1?"

"Nothin' else but," Victoria replies, giving up on her search.

The waitress points her chin at me.

"Oban. The fourteen. Neat. Make it a double, please." The waitress peels away, the DJ finishes his set and heads to the bar. We're left only to face what we've come here for.

"It hardens you, you know," Victoria says, flicking a finger toward the waitress' back. "One minute we're ordering dinner. Next minute, shit goes sideways. You can't unsee it. Believe me I've tried."

Be gentle, Nate. She's in pain.

"Why don't we wait until the she brings our drinks?" I say, fully aware of what I've asked her to re-live.

"I want to get it over with," she answers, eyes hardening on mine.

Brave girl. Thank you, Victoria.

Mazer's blood alcohol level indicated he had only one drink that night. Where he had it matters because I suspect it was laced with a drug.

First line of questioning, establish where the drug was administered. Then go find the source. Like I did with Carlos.

"Do you remember him ordering a drink at the bar?" I ask.

Her eyebrows furrow, her eyes close for a moment long enough to recreate the memory. "No. He looked drunk or high when he got there."

"You're *sure*?" I press.

"Yeah," she replies, head cocked, curious. "Why?"

"He had a blood alcohol level of oh-one-eight. That's one drink for a guy his size. A drink he had before you saw him apparently."

Her lips tighten. "Why's it matter where he had the drink? Point is he was wasted."

It matters. He didn't self-administer. Of this I'm reasonably sure now. I grab pen and paper from my backpack and sketch out a rough map of the area. Scopolamine's effects are near immediate. Mazer encountered the drug somewhere nearby. Paradign's Causa is walking distance. Fucking *everything* downtown is walking distance.

Item one, where? Need to narrow this down.

Item two, Flakka. Start with a symptom.

Increased body temperature.

"Did he bump into you or touch you? Did you notice him sweating?"

"He was a sweaty mess," she says, looking away in disgust.

Eliminate variables, Nate.

"Was it hot inside Sarafina that night?"

"Chilly," she says, "it was chilly."

Kah-thuhm.

Chilly, like the night in my driveway. The night I found Abby.

The night everything stilled, and I studied the crime scene that was her as she hummed an odd, familiar melody to herself.

Kah-thuhm - Kah-thuhm.

The melody. That fucking melody.

How she hummed it, how her dilated pupils darted side to side as she hummed it.

"Ah-hmm," Victoria says, tapping her watch. "Urgent, remember?"

"Sorry," I say, recovering. "Uncontrolled eye movements."

"What?" she replies, confused.

"A symptom. Anything strange you remember about the way he looked at you, about his eyes?"

I see the facade begin to fade; the corners of her mouth fall slightly. She looks away a few times before answering. "They reminded me of my cousin's, when she got off on of those shitty spinning rides at a carnival we went to."

Just like Abby's.

"He had stimulants in his system," I tell her, and for the first time I touch her arm.

She glances up and away to the left, then again scans over the crowded bar. "James ghosted me right after. Didn't take him a week."

"That's just shitty," I assure her.

"Yeah, it is."

The waitress whisks by with our drinks. I hand her my credit card, then check the time on my phone. Gotta hurry. "Did he say anything to you at the bar?"

"No." She grabs her glass and downs a healthy slug. I do the same. "Humming," she says, scrunching her cheeks. "He was humming."

Abby. The driveway. The odd, familiar melody has a name.

Kah-thuhm.

Kah-thuhm - Kah-thuhm.

Kah-thuhm- Kah-thuhm - Kah-thuhm.

"Ahem. Mr. Badger? My date, remember?"

The scene plays in my head like a horrible movie I can't look away from. "It was Ring around the Rosie, wasn't it?" I finally say.

"That's one hell of a lucky guess."

"I wish it was."

Her eyes fall away. Her lower lip starts to quiver. "He, um..." She blinks her eyes shut. "He was fighting it. I think he tried to fight it."

A flash again of Abby in the driveway. How she tried to resist. How her hands moved as though powered by some unseen force. "What do you mean, fight it?" I ask, leaning in.

"Rubbed his birthmark. A lot. He just stood there rubbing the birthmark on his arm. And humming." She grabs her drink. Takes a hit. Sets it down. Picks it back up and does it again. "I'm sorry. Look, I don't know how this helps you, but my date will be here any second now."

"Please," holding up the palms of my hands to plead. "I have just one more question. In your interview you said he yelled a word at your table, just before he did what he did. Do you remember the word?"

"I'll never forget. He yelled the word *schema*."

Wait a minute. I know this from my research.

Schema. SR. Paradign's signature, controversial practice of re-writing past memories.

Paul James Pellen murdered his family, then himself. Claimed it was because of the SR treatments he'd undergone.

Schema.

Paradign.

She checks her watch a final time before shaking her head. "Hope you got what you're after. I'm gonna go freshen my face. Shove all this outta my head for as long as I can, and then I'm gonna sit at the bar and wait for my date. You got the tab?"

I nod, give her a smile tinged with gratitude and concern. "Already done."

I watch Victoria walk away, a near-broken girl fights to regain her composure. She offers unconvincing smiles to the people who recognize her on the way to the restroom to freshen up and go on with her life.

And I go on with mine and carry the tension gnawing at my gut like a parasite all the way to my car. Then my phone bursts to life.

"The answer to your question is *no*," Cavanaugh tells me, to the mewing of a cat in the background. "I *don't* believe in coincidence."

"Thank you. I'm glad you called." I tell her everything I just learned about Mazer.

"Owwww, *Nixon!*" she yells, a gentle thud of claws meeting floor in the background. "I made a call. What you told me checked out about Bish and his victims," she tells me. "But that's as far as I can take it in any official capacity."

"What about unofficially," I ask.

"You already know my answer," her reply.

"You can inform your superiors I'll be making an out of state trip," I tell Cavanaugh, the darkness hardened like cured glue. "And make sure Abby's okay."

I hang up and drive off, ride most of the way home in silence. The occasional street light illuminating my face. And then my phone screen lights up. A text message alert.

From Abby.

I'm fine. Don't text me again.

There's a darkness inside me. I've always known it was here. Crack my skull open like a walnut and pull back the bone. Look inside. It is there.

A darkness that hardens me like a soldier advancing in battle.

It's time I embrace it. I need it now. And it needs me.

Ω

Near the Gaslamp Quarter
Downtown San Diego
12:55 am, January 4

The bottom half of Sturgeon's body is on pins and needles. He's hungry. There's no more beef jerky left. He's thirsty, but the last quart of Miller is hot and tastes like piss. All things considered; this assignment's a cake walk compared to others in recent memory.

Just like last night, and the many before, Sturgeon watches the streets fill with short black dresses, hears the click of spiked heels and the padding of the legions of guys chasing after those dresses. Later on, and just like last night and the many before, he sits through the chorus of vomiting twenty-somethings, watches the parade of bleary-eyed dudes in their bedazzled Ed Hardy shirts and True Religion jeans on the way back to their cars.

The call comes in just after 2:00 a.m. The subject has left his property. Three tagalongs took turns following, then peeled off the object vehicle. At 2:17 it's confirmed the object vehicle's taken the last offramp of the 163 heading downtown.

Sturgeon's team covers a six-block radius, Sturgeon himself waits at ground zero.

No more homeless are getting taken tonight. Not on his watch.

***

9

MICHAEL CAVE

FBI FIELD OPERATION OFFICE, SAN DIEGO
JANUARY 4

The slow drip of diary pages over the past several mornings has left Cave with more questions than answers. This morning, unlike the mornings before, he doesn't bound up the steps, he takes each drudgingly one at a time on his way to the seventh floor, taking notice of the reflection of a bloodshot eye in the retinal scanner.

After placing the contents of his pockets into the drawer, the door snaps open and he enters the room, notebook and pen in hand. Again. Unlike the past few mornings, there's a steaming cup of tea and an iPad on the table.

His feet jackhammer the floor. He chews a knuckle, takes a sip of tea, fights the urge to stand up and leave without explanation. Missy would still be asleep. If he hurries, he can join her in bed.

"Good morning, Michael." Cave's legs still. "You no doubt have questions."

Cave glances down at his notebook. "No doubt," he says, skipping over the first question he'd written, deciding to save it for last. "The children, do we know their full names? And what does it mean *others took their places*."

"The journal's author went to great lengths to mask the identities of the children he took from Bolsiver," the voice tells him. "The reasons, his reasons, have no bearing on your work here."

"Ohh-kay." He scratches a line through question two. "Did Joseph abuse these children?"

"We don't know for sure. We have little to go on except for this journal. But we suspect."

Cave thuds his notebook down on the table. "*Where* were the local authorities then?"

"You don't investigate what you have no cause to suspect," replies the voice.

Cave scratches his head. Stands up, begins pacing. "There weren't any signs?"

"You should know this from Quantico. The children of Bolsiver were schooled there. It met all the province's requirements."

His arms spread wide in frustration. "You're telling me one from the outside ever saw the children?"

"We assume not."

"But you *can* request the records." Cave says. The one question that matters most to him remains unspoken.

"Assume we can't. Michael, there's reference in the last journal entry I left you regarding a treatment the boy underwent. I'm interested in your thoughts on that."

Cava again takes a seat, scratches two lines under question one on his list. "They deprived him of sleep. It breaks down cognition." Textbook.

"More to the point, it breaks down resistance. They kept the boy awake for the better part of three days on a steady diet of ginseng tea, if we're to believe the journal. Do *you* believe the journal?"

He looks up, surprised. "I have no reason not to."

"I see. Please power up the iPad on the table, enter MCave as the password. Capital M, capital C, the rest lower case. Then tap the video labeled with your name and put the phone on speaker."

Cave doesn't need to watch the entire thing. He knows exactly what's on it. And when it was recorded.

"Paradign doesn't allow recordings of any kind during the Discernments. You had a warrant? I hope you had a warrant." His chair slams into the wall as he bolts to his feet.

"Sit down, Michael."

"Who? Who'd you plant?" Cave runs the roster of new names and faces from the Causa in his head.

"What *are* the Discernments, Michael?"

"Answer my question."

"No. You answer mine," the voice claps back.

Cave turns toward the door; he tries it and finds it locked.

"How about I tell you," the voice says. "Serenity One - Belongingness. Paradign initiates have the deepest, darkest secrets they shared during SR sessions exposed to a panel of members who sit in judgment of them. They are ridiculed, hazed. Made to justify themselves, their lives. Not all advance from Serenity One, only those who show true repentance. Am I correct?"

"*Tell* me who you planted," Cave demands.

"Serenity Two - Acceptance of Love. Initiates are accused of being unworthy of the love of those they most care about. Family, friends, everyone who matters. Serenity Three - Rejection of the Old. Initiatives must renounce their former lives and commit to life anew as a reborn Paradign Member. Four - Disinhibition. Initiates must recruit twenty new potential members, at least five of which must attend at least one SR session. Five, this is where it gets interesting. Tell me, Michael, what possible reason could Paradign have for depriving a member of food and allowing only six hours of total sleep across an entire seventy-two period, all while enforcing strict silence?"

Anger bubbles inside until it reaches its boiling point. "You *saw* the video. I went through it all, right there with them. What *exactly* are you accusing me of here?"

"And you led the confessions afterward."

Cave turns toward the phone, anger transforms. "Schema Realignment is *not* a confession."

"Then what exactly *is* SR, if not that, Michael?"

The final straw. He's heard enough. "Leave Paradign and me alone. I want no part of this," lining up on the door and readying a front push kick.

"Before you do that, I'd like to talk about Paul James Pellen."

Cave stares forward in disbelief, a fist reflexively clenches. "Really? That's where this is going? Not everyone can be saved from themselves."

"But isn't that exactly the promise of Paradign?" Asks the voice.

"Open the fucking door," he says, threatening to let loose the kick.

"You need to read the diary passage from October 1985, it's the other file on the iPad. Once you've done so I'll release the locks on the door. If you still want out afterward, so be it."

OCTOBER 21, 1986

My time of Ponderance is complete.

I endured the isolation. The darkness.

The daily buckets of warm water and stale slices of bread sustained me.

And in these three days, I have learned. I have need of so little.

And have been given so much.

Through the eyes of today, Bolsiver is more beautiful than any church I've visited, any pictures of palace grounds I've ever seen.

Bolsiver, my Camelot, stands majestic against the horizon.

Bolsiver, with its view from the edges of the smoke-filled chimneys and the tiny, ant-like bustle of the unenlightened below.

It is sacred. As am I.

I am Celestial Temple.

Tonight, after the gathering, I will be given my name.

Tomorrow I will celebrate, and I will ask Aodhan to dance.

10:35 PM

Joseph honored me with the retelling of a story, and of his vision.

During his wanderings through Ireland, he'd first been told of the Morrigan myth. The Phantom Queen foretold death and victory. She appeared in the form of a crow, encouraging warriors to bravery, striking fear in the her enemies.

Such a bird had appeared to the man telling him the story. On January 12, 1980, an IRA unit's ambush claimed the man's life.

"I too have been visited," Joseph said.

Then he told me of his vision.

In it, a great raven circled above him, its shadow covered Joseph in darkness. A voice called to him from the void. It shook the very ground where Joseph stood.

"I am Morrigan," it said, as shadows dissolved, and the warrior appeared. "Such are the times that lie ahead. Prepare for this battle. Honor me and prepare, and I will bring you abundance."

The warrior waved her battle-clad arm. Great fields filled with soldiers felled by fire shone before her.

"Such will be the destruction. Such will be their Ascension. Honor me and they return. Honor me and they are yours."

The warrior loosed a word that moved across the field like a violent storm. Where once were flames and destruction now rose the ravaged bodies. Now appeared the land healed.

"Althraigh," Joseph said. "We will be purified by the Ascension. You will help lead us. You battled back from cancer. I must ask you to do battle again. From today, you are my great warrior. From today you will be known as Cathal."

Ω

The sound of an iPad skidding across the table is followed by glass cracking as it hits the floor.

"Please pick it up," comes the voice from the phone.

"Open the door."

"Pick it up," the voice demands.

Cave, in defiance, lost in thought, doesn't move.

"Destroying an iPad doesn't change what you just read."

Anger builds to a boil.

Cathal. The heart and soul of Paradign. It's reclusive founder. The man few ever met. Cave feels the weight of it all, the responsibility for it all. And is prepared to defend it, regardless of the cost to his career. "Paradign saved my family. You have no right to attack it. Now open the *door*."

Locks disengage.

"It's not me who is or will be attacking Paradign should this information get out. By the way, the other man you've read of, his name is Sebastian Allende."

Cave keeps walking.

"Allende is DIA. After China Lake, he got defunded and needed a new place to carry on his work." A pause. "You know about China Lake, don't you Michael?"

"The DIA doesn't operate domestically," Cave replies.

"Exactly. They *don't* operate domestically *unless* they're under the umbrella of the FBI, which they were. Which *he* was."

"The agency sanctioned China Lake? Bullshit!"

"After China Lake was defunded, the DIA began covert programs, targeting cults and other fringe groups. Access to children and adults done under the cover of the cult's activities. I've known it and sat here powerless for years, never sure who in the agency to trust. Now, with this diary, I might just have the proof I've needed to blow it wide open."

"This is why *me*? You're targeting Paradign."

"Paradign's founder was a member of the Celestial Temple. With the help of Allende, he and two children escaped the Morrigan Night. They escaped while knives were taken to throats. While Bolsiver laid down in circles to burn. You're damn right I want to take a closer look at Paradign."

The notebook falls from Cave's hands as he turns to leave.

"There's a reason Cathal sent me his journal. Why he's drawn this connection. Don't you want to be there to help find out why?"

For the first time since his assignment there, Cave tells his supervisor he's urgently needed at home. He is.

He torques the throttle of the BMW Motorrad K1300 he gifted himself after graduation, manifesting the pressure welling up inside.

The red lights favor him all the way home, where he slams to a stop, leaves the engine running, unlocks the front door, runs inside, pulls Missy to him. He whispers a plan in her ear, to which she responds *duh*, and scurries off after kissing his cheek.

She throws a change of clothes and some toiletries into a bag. He packs less. They lock the door behind them, and drive to Julian, where they rent a cabin for the night, one they rarely leave.

Ω

The next day, Cave drops Missy home at 6:15. He recites the Discernments. He showers, enjoys a cup of tea. Packs a banana. Hops on his motorcycle at 6:40. Arrives at his desk by 6:55. At 7, a new stack of papers arrives. From 7:01 to 11:55, he checks for typos, he verifies procedural integrity, he flags issues with sticky notes. At noon, he puts on a weighted vest, exits the building, starts the timer, and runs mile two of five miles before stopping to scream at the top of his lungs.

* * *

10

NATHAN BADGER

The morning sky is an ominous swirl of reds and oranges, gusts of wind shove my tiny Ford Focus rental across the empty road. Its tires crackle and crunch over the hardened snow blanketing the street lined by little matching boxes, all in a row, reminding me that within them are ordinary people living ordinary lives. Something I've never experienced. Maybe never even wanted.

A few overly bundled neighbors push snowblowers up and down their driveways in an unwinnable battle against winter. One by one they turn as I drive by them, pink-faced, smoke-breathing. Some wave, none smile.

"In five hundred feet you will have reached your destination," Siri tells me.

The Bish residence is a modest, one-story postwar bungalow. Shingle roof, attached one car garage. I guess it to be all of twelve-hundred square feet, maybe fourteen at best. The hunter green eaves are lined with icicles of varying sizes. What remains of an inflatable snowman lies in tatters in the yard. The only distinguishing feature on this street full of Monopoly homes is the sign mounted in a concrete-filled bucket at the edge of the driveway proudly proclaiming that another home has been sold, courtesy of Roncate Realty, Bish's former employer.

An unexpected rush of adrenaline jams my foot to the brake pedal. I slide to a stop in front of the sign and take one last look at the house before getting out.

A young girl pokes her head through the living room curtains and watches my feet sink in exhaust-grey snow as I make my way to the front door.

I count four vaporized breaths as I hear the muffled voice of the girl calling out to her mother. When the door finally opens, my eyes drop to the tiny figure before me, she's all of five or six. "Mother'th on her way," she says. The S escapes through a gap in her teeth.

"What's your name?" I ask her, bending down until I reach her at eye level.

From inside, "Bethany, *what* did I tell you about talking to strangers." Then Bonny Bish sees me. I watch momentary confusion transform into recognition, then rage.

Her eyes flash a warning at me. "Downstairs, little one," she orders Bethany, not ever looking away.

"Yeth, Mommy."

Bonny Bish is all of one-hundred-ten pounds, a feather in the wind. Chestnut-brown hair pulled into a messy bun and held in place by a single chopstick. A monotonous brown dress swallowing the tiny frame underneath it. Yet it's clear she's a formidable force, even through all she's endured. Bonny Bish's angry blue eyes are sunken, lined in pink, she's been crying. She points a shaking finger at me. "I know who you are, and I told you to leave me alone."

"I need your help."

Tears build in the corners of her eyes. She wipes her face dry with a wrinkled brown apron hung from her shoulders.

"How dare you?" She says quietly. "Do you have *any* idea the nightmare we're living? I had to take Bethany out of school. Reporters show up here all hours of the day and night. I can't even go to the grocery store. And you want *my* help? Leave. Now."

There is only mission and outcome. Right now, *she* is my mission.

"There's something I need to show you." I say, opening Mazer's toxicology report on my phone. "What if your husband wasn't the one truly responsible for those deaths?" Her eyes register a mix of anger mixed with something. Maybe hope.

Maybe not.

"My *husband*," she says, as though the words are foul, unworthy of speaking. "My husband killed five people and took his own life. Get out."

I hold up the phone and pinch the screen to zoom in. "This is from a suicide in downtown San Diego. Same drugs as they found in your husband and the other victims."

"Which proves nothing," she says, pulling her own phone from a pocket, and holding it up as a threat. "I'm calling the police."

"Wait. Wait!" I yell back. "Your husband sang a nursery rhyme, didn't he?"

"Just get--what did you just say?" The phone falls from her hands, hands now closed into fists. "What did you?" Fists slam into my chest.

Despair, its own kind of gravity, pulls her to the ground next to her phone.

I kneel down beside her. Our eyes meet.

"He sang 'Ring Around the Rosie,' didn't he?"

Through grief's thousand-mile stare I get my answer. "Yes."

"So did this man," I say, holding up Mazer's toxicology report again. "So did others. I need your help, Mrs. Bish… Bonnie. And I think you need mine."

She rises up, unsteady, opens the door wide and gestures me in. "This is for Bethany."

* * *

Michael Cave

FBI Field Operation Office, San Diego
January 5

Cave returns from his run, awaiting the 1:30 stack. In its place, a sealed envelope arrives, one he's made to sign for. Inside, clear instruction on how and when he's to return it.

He glares at his nosy cubicle neighbors until they look away before taking the copied journal pages from inside.

Ω

December 6, 1986

Yesterday came and went as all other days have. Twenty-six of our women, all dressed in matching beige overalls, were marched out to the fields. The rest came with me and a handful of the men and together we slathered mortar on brick to rebuild the crumbling walls of the castle.

There were comings and goings after quiet hours last night. In the moonlight I saw the silhouettes of many men carrying long boxes. All except the large one with the beard. He carried nothing. He walked alone.

Joseph returned this morning, and soon after chose twelve, the strongest men in the ranks of Bolsiver. They were given automatic rifles. A group of three now guard Joseph at all times. Nine others take positions around Bolsiver's perimeter. For the first time since my arrival, Bolsiver is weaponized. And we are imprisoned.

There is a tension in the air today. Tonight is another white night. Again, we will practice the ritual.

I never mustered the courage to ask my Aodhan to dance. Now, there will be no more dances, no more music. Only white nights. Only the ritual.

Day and night Joseph reads from his handwritten pages. All to the melancholy soundtrack of a solo piano piece, repeated over, and over. And over.

It's been impossible to sleep since the rituals began. And when daytime once again comes, I'm greeted by the sunken, black-circled eyes of the others on their way to work assignments and under guard.

Still, I have thoughts of him to cling to.

I have Aodhan.

He is the highlight of each day, the single thing I look forward to most. How can I tell him what I cannot say, what I'm not allowed to feel?

When he laid hands on me yesterday and said the prayer, I wanted to burst. I wanted to wrap him up in my arms and tell him. Instead I stayed silent. As we all now must.

There are trade-offs in life. I've accepted this. And mine is that I must hold onto the love that's grown inside of me for him, the first I've ever felt in my life. I must never speak it aloud, for it is forbidden.

I risk all even writing of it. If any were to find this my fate would be the same as the others. I'd be taken away.

Today, just like yesterday and the day before, Joseph's voice thundered through Bolsiver, and Aodhan hung on his words.

Tonight, just like every night, the men came again, carrying more boxes through the cornfields edging Bolsiver.

DECEMBER 10, 1986

Joseph is changing. Right before my eyes, before all of our eyes. He no longer reads. Instead, he gives rambling lectures dripping with fear, contempt, conspiracy. All to his chosen soundtrack. I've grown weary of its foreboding melody.

More armed members surrounded our work party. I counted seventeen today. Joseph is building an army.

Aodhan was taken to the castle just after lunch three days ago. He returned after sunset today, in time for the nightly gathering. Bolsiver's re-education, it seems, has now claimed the nearest and dearest to me.

I sat in the back row of benches at tonight's mandatory gathering, so far behind Aodhan I knew I'd not be able to see him. Still I thought only of him.

A woman sat next to me. I caught myself staring at the port-wine birthmark stretching from her left eye to her ear. I looked away only when Joseph began speaking.

He told us the men I'd seen in the cornfields had warned of an imminent attack. They were friends of Bolsiver. They'd brought him the guns. And medications. They'd trained the men patrolling the grounds, and those supervising the work parties.

Bolsiver will stay vigilant. Bolsiver will defend itself.

To the death if need be.

The woman next to me raised her hand, interrupting him.

"We deserve the truth, Joseph," she'd said. Two more stood up in support of her demand. "Tell us all why you're taking our people."

Joseph did not take kindly to being questioned in this way.

DECEMBER 11, 1986

My hand shakes as I write this. This is wrong. All of it. I know it is. I must go. I must take Aodhan and go.

Last night the ritual changed. We did not stand together in circles around the fires. We were made to lie on our backs and wait, until one by one the blindfolds were removed from our eyes. I know this. They removed mine first. I alone saw what the others couldn't. The woman with the port wine-stained birthmark and the two others who stood with her being led away at gunpoint.

After the white night drill finished, we were sent to our huts.

Gunshots rang out when the moon grew to its fullest. I laid still on the floor as instructed. Sirens wailed, Bolsiver lit up bright as the sun.

It had come under attack.

We were brought at gunpoint to the grotto, where a bloodied Joseph awaited us.

"Ready yourselves for The Morrigan's coming," his only words, words that chill me to the bone even now.

I am not a warrior. I am a captive. We all are captives.

DECEMBER 12, 1986

I saw the bearded man again. He stared at me through the moonlight tonight, waving a hand meant to gain my attention. He motioned to me. I understood.

Be patient. Wait.

Can I trust him? How can I know?

If they are all friends to Bolsiver, as Joseph said, then how can he be trusted?

DECEMBER 13, 1986

His name is Sebastian. He knows something's wrong. He sent word to the people helping him back in the States after the Ascensions began. He'll tell me when preparations are complete. And then he will take only me and two children away. It's okay. Aodhan is already lost to me now.

I shredded the note he gave me before leaving my hut and joining the circles. I laid down, feet nearly touching the flames, and awaited the moment when my blindfold would be removed, or when I would be led away at gunpoint. When they removed the blindfold, I saw Yves holding a gun.

DECEMBER 14, 1986

Tomorrow night The Morrigan comes.

* * *

NATHAN BADGER

THE BISH HOME
WHEATON, ILLINOIS

"I'll put on a movie for her downstairs, then you're going to tell me everything else you know," Bonny Bish says, her patience pulled taught as a bow string. She points past stacks of boxes labelled by room in black marker. "Bathroom's down that hall." She's on her way downstairs before I can thank her.

At the end of the small hallway there's a room sprinkled sparsely with the occasional toy. The single bed is covered in Barbie sheets and a blanket. Next to it, on a nightstand holding a collection of three well-worn dolls, a framed crayon drawing of a family of two.

The damage done. A daughter without a father. A wife without a husband. A family torn irreparably and permanently apart.

Kah-thuhm.

I owe them answers. I owe them what I came here for.

I stare down at my wrists, foreign, beating an out-of-control drumbeat.

Kah-thuhm - Kah-thuhm.

Clues, Nate. Look for clues.

Look here.

Bish's spartan office is across the hall from the bathroom, a converted guest room, maybe one-hundred square feet in size. His glass-top desk is empty, there's a clean rectangle surrounded by dust where his laptop computer once was, no doubt now in some locked away evidence cage gathering dust.

Opposite the door is a three-shelf bookcase. A Zen garden protected by a row of nine candles on top. The first shelf is filled with albums. Sonny Boy Williamson. Robert Johnson. John Mayall. An impressive collection of blues records, sixty or so. One outlier. *Goodbye Yellow Brick Road*, Elton John.

The next shelf is empty. The bottom holds a book.

Mine.

My feet draw me closer. My hand reaches out.

Kah-thuhm.

Yellow slips of paper mark two pages; yellow high-lights mark two passages.

Only two passages.

The first, from the opening chapter.

A single drop of blood falls on the floor of the office.

A new little moment.

What's the significance?

The first sentence propels me though time. I'm back there, in the hot sweat of summer and death.

There are nearly 10,000 miles of railroad tracks stretching across the state of Illinois. In the heart of Chicago, at the 75th Street Corridor, is the chokepoint, where the first bodies were found.

A passing conductor alerted the nearest station that he'd seen a blackish liquid seeping out from out from a TFI liner headed northeast to Canada. It turned out to be thick, black blood.

Three mutilated corpses were discovered inside.

The investigation began with the maintenance crew at 75th Street, who were interviewed, and cleared. From these shabby, unheated maintenance shacks, the investigation moved quickly to the highest levels of TFI. Carl Matheus Tryggstad, owner of the privately held Tryggstad Freight Incorporated, pledged his full cooperation and that of his staff. Beginning with his second in command, Carl Matheus Tryggstad II, down through every TFI employee, each were interviewed. Some interrogated.

All were cleared within days of the discovery of the next bodies, which were found discarded in the woods near a set of train tracks 6.2 miles from the 57th Street junction. Each of the women, prostitutes or runaways, had several distinguishing marks. Their left breasts were removed, their arms were marked with needle scars. All were reported missing from the city of Evanston.

In the following months, three more mutilated bodies were discovered across Cook County, Illinois. Two floated to the surface of Lake Michigan and were found by a fisherman taking his family out for a day on the water. The other woman's dismembered body was found in a wooded section near the shoreline, her arms and legs were lined up in a row.

To this day, Tryggstad Jr. and his accomplice claim to have no memory of the horrors they inflicted.

This is their story.

The words *have no memory* are underlined. Why?

The second highlighted passage is the story of Nadean Cool.

As they dug through the memories, using hypnosis, conducting Amytal interviews, and employing recovered memory therapy techniques, Ms. Cool became convinced she'd been part of a satanic cult. And worse. By the end of it all she believed she'd been raped, believed she'd had sex with numerous animals, believed she had eaten children. She believed multiple personalities inhabited her body. One-hundred-twenty of them.

But none of what she remembered was true. The courts agreed she'd been the victim of therapy gone terribly wrong and awarded her damages.

I began asking myself, what is the memory mechanism? And how is it so easily fooled?

The last sentence is also underlined twice.

And in blue ink, written next to it in what I assume to be Bish's handwriting, one word.

Brazil.

Brazil. My last excursion with Luke. What made me walk away.

"Bring me a chocklie milk too, Mommy," a voice calls up from the basement, followed by thudding footfalls up the stairway.

I dart out of the office, still lost in my head somewhere between the freight yards of Chicago and Rio de Janeiro, and slide into the bathroom before Bonny Bish reaches the hallway.

"Mr. Badger?" she calls.

What did Bish know about Brazil? What do *I* know about Brazil?

There's a small tub full of toys, brown-tinted linoleum flooring, an off-white tiled vanity, a mirror covered with toothpaste stains, and just to its right a framed embroidery of a nonsensical word. *Wyhabyt.* Stitched below it, *sleep tight little one.*

"Mr. Badger?"

"In here," I finally respond.

Through the toothpaste-streaked mirror, an angry face stares back at me. It warns me the Doctor is coming. It warns me I'm late.

I wash my hands, then grab a fistful of toilet paper and rub the mirror clean as though doing so somehow erases the raging reflection I cast.

Wait.

Toothpaste. Hands. *Wyhabyt.* Wash your hands and brush your teeth. A reminder for the girl.

Bish used mnemonics. Duly noted.

Still haunted by the passages Bish highlighted, and the memories that dance in my brain like a flickering candlelight, I make it back through the maze of boxes and take a seat on the couch before Bonny finishes delivering the milk to her daughter and returns. She wags a finger at me in warning. "If she comes upstairs, you're leaving."

"Of course," I reply.

Across from the couch on an otherwise bare accent table is a photo of her husband in a frame you buy at Walmart for one dollar or less. Her eyes fix on it. "How did you know about the nursery rhyme?"

"I told you. There were others." I say, handing her the newspaper article from my backpack. She holds it in a trembling hand. "Daniel Mazer took his own life in the same manner as your husband. I met with a witness. She told me she heard Mazer singing the same nursery rhyme. She thought it comforted him."

Her eyes shift to me. In this moment I see the glimmer of hope she holds on to.

I go on.

"I saw the press conference online. The dinner guests with your husband were slipped a drug in their wine. People exposed to the drug are highly susceptible to suggestion. They do things they don't remember doing. Sometimes they do very bad things."

"My husband killed five people," anger, betrayal coloring her words a deep red.

"Listen to me," I tell her, conviction weighting mine. "I'm working on a book connecting cults with government agencies. Your husband contacted me, claiming to have information. I think it got him killed."

The newspaper slips from her hands. She turns back toward her husband's photo. "You can't know that."

"I can. Because on the day he'd arranged for us to meet, the very day you reported him missing, my girlfriend was taken."

"Which means exactly *what* to me?" she demands, anger replaced by suspicion.

"Abby was badly beaten. She had the same drug in her system. She hummed the same nursery rhyme. It's not a coincidence. I need to prove it. And when I do, maybe it will bring you and your daughter some closure. Will you help me?"

"I have nothing to offer," she says, sunk deep in her resignation.

"Yes, you do. I know this may be hard, but please think back to the days before your husband went missing. Did he act differently? Did he tell you anything unusual? Talk about *anyone* unusual?"

I pick the newspaper up off the floor, she stares across the room, absent, numb in her pain. "He said he was meeting someone. He never told me who."

Meeting someone. Noted.

"This meeting, was it on the day he went missing." She nods. "What was he like before he left for this meeting? Nervous, scared?"

Her head sinks. "You don't understand. My husband was…" she fights back tears. Her face hardens. "He was good at many things. Working with his hands was not one of them."

"I don't understand."

"H-he was making something," she tells me. "Before he left. Before the last time…"

"Making what?" I press.

"Making something out there," she says, pointing to the kitchen where a door leads to the attached garage.

"Show me," I tell her, pressing up from the couch.

***

PRESENT DAY
HOTEL DEL SALTO
TEQUENDAMA FALLS, COLOMBIA

The first hints of daylight break above the thundering crush of the falls.

I let out a few vaporized breaths and turn to my captive.

"Eventually the person you're hunting makes a mistake. But I don't need to tell *you*, I mean here you are."

He's ignoring me, preoccupied with checking his pulse.

I need his full attention.

"Hello in there," I say, sliding my blade down the side of his arm until I reach the thumb he's pressed into a vein. "Every fucking detail, remember? Shit you take with you to eternity."

"I don't care." He pins his chin to his chest, tombstone-grey eyes glare up at me through mist-covered, wire rim glasses. "You hear me? I don't fucking care anymore."

I raise the blade over his head, threatening to split him in two. "You're *going* to listen. And you *will* answer my questions. Ticktock, Doctor. Antidote's right over there."

"I'm sick of your cat and mouse games, Nathan. Just let me d-die," he says, squeezing his eyes shut as though bracing for the impact of my blade.

"Games, huh?" I say, incredulous. "You think this is a game? Cool. Here's a new one. Let's make this interesting. You play my game and pass my test; you get a reward."

He opens his eyes, lets go of his wrist and studies my face. "What reward?"

I tap the backpack with my sword. "Listen up. I went out to the garage, found a wood-boring drill bit in Bish's toolbox. It had a thin coating of wax on it. Based on what I've already told you, what makes the drill bit significant?"

"I don't know," he replies, thumbing anxiously at his beard, shifting glances at my backpack, then me.

"Oh, Doc. You disappoint. That's just lazy. Now *think*!" I grab his fat hairy face, then push it away in disgust. "*What* makes it significant?"

He lifts shaky hands and swings them through the air like a drunken conductor. His symphony, the rattle of chains. "I said I don't know."

"Let me help you get your logic-train rolling. Pay attention to this helpful vignette about a cold case I solved. Happened in 1966. Two girls lived on base in Fort McClellan with their families. They're best friends."

He looks away and out the crumbling window at the falls. As his reward, a stiff backhand that lights his cheek red.

"As I was saying, they're best friends. Both brunettes with waist-length hair parted in the middle. They graduate high school together. They go to a park nearby the school to hang out with their classmates after the graduation ceremony. One by one the other classmates leave. The girls stay. It's the last time they're seen. The first envelope gets mailed to a Fort McClellan military police sergeant. Inside, a word puzzle. *You must stop me* is written in red crayon at the top of the page. Thirteen weeks later, another girl goes missing. What color hair does she have?"

"Brunette," he says, holding his face. "Long."

I circle around him, every now and again smacking the top of his head when he looks away. "Second envelope goes to the same sergeant, a new word puzzle inside, same writing on top of the page. A full year goes by before the next envelope arrives; you know the rest. The count jumps to five missing girls. Now here's what's important. Each of the word-puzzles in the letters consisted of seven columns, each row contained exactly forty letters." I grab his fat face again. "*Why's* this important?"

His eyes widen. "There's a pattern. It's the same killer," he says, anticipation lights up his face. He points eagerly at my backpack, "Reward."

"Not yet," I reply, his fat face falls, his eyes meet the floor. "The very last letter arrives exactly seven months to the day later. One final girl disappears. One last puzzle. But this one has eight columns, not seven. The letter count changes too. Thirty-eight this time."

"There's something significant about the column and letter count," he says, beginning to pant.

"Exactly. Remember when I told you he'd written *you must stop me*. He wanted to be caught, so he gave clues. The word puzzles revealed he'd buried the bodies in an old abandoned Monsanto chemical factory in Anniston, Alabama, which was a short thirteen-minute drive from the base. I solved that part using a substitution code cipher. The row and column numbers gave clues too. He revealed his MOS in the first two letters he sent, and the new unit he transferred to in the last. The 838th MP unit, where he served for five years before dying of liver cancer caused by PCB poisoning from the Monsanto dumpsite in Anniston. Fitting end, you ask me. You get the point now? The answers sometimes are hidden in plain sight, and no one sees them. Final guess, *what* made the drill bit significant?"

He searches the air for an answer. "You said there were candles on the bookcase," through a new fit of coughs.

"And albums below them. Sixty-four to be exact. Among them one lone Elton John record. A great one, mind you. You wouldn't happen to remember a song on the *Goodbye Yellow Brick Road* album that might play into our little test?"

Hope returns. "Candle in the Wind?'"

"Did he want me to find it? Yeah, I think he did. You see, Bish liked his mnemonics. He used the album as his. He used a wood bit to bore a hole into the only candle on his bookcase big enough to fit a prescription pill bottle inside, careful to ensure he made the lid flush to the base of the candle. Then he just put back the round paper label overtop to cover it. *Et voila.* I found a thumb drive in the prescription bottle hidden inside the candle."

He points at my backpack. "My reward." His coughs now rapid-firing like bullets from a machine gun.

I toss him a water bottle from the backpack. "Here. Have a sip of this first."

He sucks it down greedily before his eyes widen and he spits half a mouthful on the ground. "What *is* this?"

"You don't want to waste any more of it, trust me," I grab the bottle from his hand.

Understanding washes over him. "What do you-- the antidote?"

"I used the syringe as a prop. And yeah, *this* is the real antidote."

"More!"

I tease him with the bottle, keeping it just out of his reach. "Can you guess what I found on Bish's thumb drive?"

"I-I don't know anything about Bish."

"Lean your head back," I tell him. He does, and I let a few splashes fall into his mouth. "That's for being honest. I know you don't know anything about Bish. But you certainly know the people who died at the dinner party Kenneth Bish hosted. And why the bodies were found lying in a circle. And here's another thing you know. You know about a girl and a campfire. She would've been young when you pulled her out of the flames. Say around eight."

"I have no idea what you're talking about."

"You sure about that. I told you how this works." I shake the bottle up over his head. "In your mouth or on the ground. Your call."

"All right. Okay. Her name was Miriam."

"*Is*." I hand him the bottle; he downs all of it. "Her name *is* Miriam, and I know what you did to her."

NATHAN BADGER

WHEATON, ILLINOIS
TEN MONTHS PRIOR
JANUARY 5, 8:00 P.M.

"Mommy? Mommy the movie ith over."

I'm drowning. My lungs on fire with the need for oxygen. A moment of panic touches my inner core at the words, "Wake up, Nathan."

I know why they're calling me and I don't want to go.

I push away white bed sheets, frantic, my surroundings unfamiliar, searching for my parents. My family. Someone to help me.

"It's okay, we're here," to the touch of a gentle hand.

A blurred face hovers above me, "Nathan, you've had an accident." He's dressed in white, his hairy face mostly covered by a surgical mask. "I'm here to help you regain your memories."

"Thank you, Doctor," the woman holding my hand says.

"I'm just going to place this on your head, Nathan. It won't hurt."

"I don't want to. Don't let him," I plead.

The doctor yanks my arm.

Yanks it harder.

"Mr. Badger."

Harder still.

Mr. Badger, it's time for you to go…Mr. Badger?"

Wait. Where am I?

I'm in the Bish house. In his office holding a pill bottle containing a flash drive.

Focus, Nate.

"Mr. Badger!"

"I'm sorry. I was. I, um."

"Leave now."

The flash drive.

My hands sweat; knots in my stomach turn like gears on the way to the car. Bish knew things he wasn't supposed to know. Wasn't supposed to tell. Things that got him killed. Secrets I know with every ounce of my being the flash drive holds.

A flash drive *I* now hold.

Anticipation worms its way through my intestines, climbs its way up my arms to my fingers as I fire up the engine and pull the car into drive.

In no time I'm in Carol Stream and at my hotel, a Hampton Inn. I stomp through a few puddles of slush unintentionally before reaching the doors and the heated lobby inside where I'm greeted.

"My name is Chad, and I'll be helping you tonight with your reservation. Whom do I have the pleasure of assisting this evening?"

My teeth are chattering. "Badger. Nathan Badger," casting an unnecessary glance over my shoulder.

"Right. Mr. Badger. I have you for two nights. King bed. Nonsmoking."

"Room service?" I ask.

"I'm sorry. No."

"Any recommendations then?" handing him my ID and a credit card.

"Madden's for sure," he says, eyes never leaving the computer screen. "I recommend the Madden Monster. Classic Chicago thick crust, every kinda meat you can imagine. Three different cheeses. Worth every calorie."

"I'll keep it in mind," grabbing the keycard he's set down on the counter.

I make my way across the wooden lobby floor, past the bar, leaving a small trail of puddles behind me. Take the elevator up to the third floor. My room is at the end of the hall. My hands are shaking, a combination of nervous energy and the cold. It takes three tries to open my door.

The uniformity of the room is reassuring. Light blue walls, off white carpet, white comforter perfectly made up on an unassuming bed. Order. I need it. There's a fifty-two-inch TV that I'll distract myself with later. Maybe.

The security lock on the door is reassuring as well.

I toss my backpack on the beige couch, fire up my laptop, rattling a drumbeat of impatience on a nearby pillow.

The Apple logo appears. The drumbeats get faster.

I enter my password, fire up the hotspot on my phone and plug in the drive.

Showtime.

Only two things on it. A password-protected folder labelled FV April 2, 04, and an application. Second Life Viewer.

Bish was a Second Lifer. The online world you escape to when your reality sucks. I know a thing or two about it from my counterintelligence days. I used it to drop information.

I know a thing about password breaking too. Let's see about these.

One in three people use their birthdays, their children's names. The name of their spouse. But not Bish, that I'm sure of. Bish liked his mnemonics.

The folder name. FV April 2, 04. Family vacation. Did they go somewhere on April 2, 2004? Maybe it's a clue referring to an actual event. I go through every visible page in his social media profiles. Instagram. Facebook. LinkedIn. Nothing.

Think, Nate.

I fire up the Second Life application and get to the sign-on screen. Only his screen name. No password.

As expected.

My options. Dictionary. Brute force. Syllable. Rule-based. Hybrid. Rainbow.

Any one of these password attack methods could work, but my gut tells me I know this guy. The way he thinks. My gut tells me I can crack these myself.

He used an acronym to remind his daughter to wash her hands and brush her teeth.

He'll use an acronym here too.
Run the clues. Process the scene.

The bookcase. The candle. The lone Elton John record in a collection of blues albums.

The candle on Bish's bookcase.

The Elton John album.

"Candle In The Wind."

FV.

***

11

MICHAEL CAVE

ANLON HALL, DOWNTOWN SAN DIEGO
PARADIGN'S SAN DIEGO CAUSA
JANUARY 5, 9:00 P.M.

Night One of the Serenity lectures has never been Michael Cave's favorite. He added some new material for tonight's talk; it fell flat. He stammered through parts of it, his mind not on the material, or the audience, but on sizing up each of the members, wondering which of them had secretly filmed him.

Wrestling with the truth he'd just learned.

Cathal belonged to a suicide cult.

With everyone gone, he sits lost in thought, dangling his long legs over the edge of the stage.

The front door of the Causa door partially opens. A man's clean-shaven face peeks inside.

He had forgotten to lock the front entrance.

"Michael Cave?" the man calls out.

"I'm sorry," Cave checks his watch. "You missed tonight's gathering by twenty minutes. Please help yourself to one of our calendars."

The man steps into the great hall where the lectures are held, moving past rows of chairs, quickly closing the gap between them. Cave jumps to his feet, sizing the man up. Black suit coat, matching pants. Dress black shoes, shined to a gleam. Earpiece. Microphone clipped to his shirtsleeve.

One of ours?

The man steps well into Cave's personal space. Cave cocks a fist.

"Come with me, Agent," the man says.

"I don't think so," Cave tells him, heartbeat quickening.

The man reaches into his jacket. Cave rushes forward, catching the man's wrist and pinning it against his chest. "Slowly," Cave demands, a warning finger pointed at the man's face.

"Just getting my identification. Secure it yourself," the man says, sliding his arm out of Cave's now loosened grip and slowly raising both hands in the air.

Cave readies his right hand for a palm strike, moves his left against the man's chest, noting the slow, relaxed beating of his heart.

Cave inches his fingers toward the pocket the man had earlier reached for. No weapon, a thick wallet. He removes it with two fingers, right palm strike still at the ready, and flips it open.

Defense Intelligence Agency.

"We both know your agency doesn't operate domestically."

"I have my orders. Follow me," the DIA agent says.

Cave tosses the wallet back at him.

They leave the building together and take a short walk to a black sedan. The DIA agent stays outside of the vehicle guarding the door. Cave steps inside.

"Name's Lucas Sturgeon," the man inside the vehicle says, handing Cave a thick red folder. "How's the new assignment going?"

"What do you want?" replies Cave, flipping through the mass of papers he'd been handed to the black and white photo in the back. "And who's Dorien Wissum?"

"The answer to a problem, that's who."

"Who said I had a problem?" Cave spits back.

"Not *your* problem, son. Paradign's."

He goes on to tell Cave exactly what he will do with the file.

Ω

Minutes later, a stunned Cave steps out into the night air.

As the car pulls forward, the rear window slides down. "The common good, Cave. Everyone wins," Sturgeon says before the car pulls away.

*** *** ***

Nathan Badger

FV.

The first verse of "Candle in the Wind."

"Goodbye Norma Jean, though I never knew you at all."

Ten letters. Three in caps.

It's not too late. CrackStation. Brutus. John the Ripper. Medusa. I've used each.

Fuck that. I got this.

GNJtinkyaa gets the first warning. Nine more attempts before the drive self-erases.

Stay with your instincts, Nate.

The first verse followed by the date, spelled out just like it is in the file name. Warning number two.

Date in numerals. *GNJtinkyaa04022004*. Warning number three.

GNJtinkyaa4204. Warning number four.

Six attempts left.

Kah-thuhm.

April 2, 2004.

First verse.

"Candle in the Wind."

Goodbye Norma Jean...

Sixty-four albums.

Sixty-four.

GNJtinkyaa64.

Five attempts left.

Kah-thuhm.

Kah-thuhm. Kah-thuhm.

Fuck. It's coming again.

I slam shut the laptop and pace the room. Frustration drives my fist into the nearest wall. It's met with three knocks from the adjoining room.

Kah-thuhm. Kah-thuhm. Kah-thuhm.

I need an outlet. Fast. Before I lose myself.

Punches. Kicks.

Bas Rutten. I cue up it up on my phone.

"Welcome to the Thai Boxing Workout," Bas announces. "This tape has three-minute rounds, with one-minute rest. So you better get ready."

I drop into stance, jaws clenched tighter than my fists.

Kah-thuhm. Kah-thuhm. Kah-thuhm.

He yells out combinations. I move. "One-four; left jab, right upper cut. One-two; left jab, right cross. Ten right knees."

Kah-thuhm. Kah-thuhm.

"One and a three. Six left knees…"

The first round is over.

Kah-thuhm.

"You have one-minute rest, then you better be ready for Round Number 2."

Round Number Two.

Two.

That's when it hits me.

Two. Fucking two. Not the file. The missing Second Life password.

GNJtinkyaa64.

Paydirt. Fucking paydirt. I'm in.

The only place Bish visited was his Second Life home. That makes this easy.

Every room is empty except the living room. In it, there's a matching couch and love seat facing a grand river rock fireplace. A few books line the mantle above it. The titles are blurred. Normal shit I'd expect to see.

What is not normal is the statue of Julius Caesar that's pointing to a painting of a grandfather clock. The time reads 6:07. What's not normal are the three other wall hangings.

The first, a cryptogram. Ten rows, eight characters in each row, each row made up of numbers and letters.

The next, a photo of the Bish family. Each flashes a peace sign.

The last, a photo of the Hindenburg.

Every ounce of my being tells me Bish wasn't decorating his living room with these. No. These are clues. This is his password mnemonic. I'd bet my life on it. I'll bet my last five attempts on it.

"We start again in five, four, three," Bas warns. "Two. One. Round Number Two. Left uppercut, three left knees."

These are clues. Clues to the file's passwords.

"Four and a two. Six right knees."

The Caesar statue.

"One. One and a three. Two. Give me ten left knees. Two. Two and a four."

Caesar employed a code in communications with his generals, it was one of the first substitution codes in recorded history. The Caesar Cypher, one I learned in my first year of Counterintelligence training. Bish could have known this had he done his research.

But how many shifts did he use?

The time on the clock reads 6:07. Six. Six shifts. The letter F.

6:07. If six is the key code, then seven may refer to the row number.

Row seven; Dn91W1w7. Decoded, Ise6T6tc.

Warning number six. Another countdown from Bas.

"We start in three, two, one."

"Two. Two and a four. Four. Four."

Wait. Wait.

Rewind.

"Two. Two and a four. Four. Four."

Four.

Four wall hangings.

Rewind.

"Two and a three. One and a two. Two. Two and a four. Four. Four. Two, three and a four. Gimme six right elbow strikes."

There's something I'm missing. Something right in front of me. There has to be something.

Rewind.

"Two and a three. One and a two. Two. Two and a four. Four."

Trust your gut. Trust your instincts. Remember your training.

Rewind.

"Two and a three. One and a two. Two. Two and a four. Four. Four. Two, three and a four. Gimme six right elbow strikes. Two and a four. Gimme four right knee strikes."

Two and a four.

Wait a minute.

The name of the folder. April 2, 2004. 4-2-2004. Twos and fours.

It's not just the folder's name.

April 2, 2004. 4-2-2004. Four wall hangings. The first painting decoded the second, the third painting must decode the fourth. Cypher key two. The letter B.

Four. Two. Two. Four.

Hindenburg. Cryptogram. Cryptogram. Hindenburg.

Ghmcdmatqf Ise6T6tc Ise6T6tc Ghmcdmatqf

Ω

I don't remember how long ago it was when I typed in the sequence. I don't know how long I paced the floor. I don't know how many times my finger hovered over the *enter* key without pressing it.

I don't know how long ago I ordered the Madden's Monster. I don't know when I shoveled down the next to last piece.

This I do know. If I'm wrong, I'll have three remaining attempts. And exactly zero remaining ideas.

Courage, Integrity, Perseverance. The counterintelligence motto.

Courage. Perseverance.

It's time I called on both right now.

Enter.

Fucking *bingo*.

The folder contains years of ledgers, a scanned article on the Bolsiver colony, and another on Paul James Pellen.

No coincidences.

The last file in the last subfolder is a photo. A woman in a wheelchair dressed all in white. The world surrounding her appears lost in her sunken, dark-circled eyes. Kenneth Bish is pushing her outside, the plaque hanging from a post in front of the building is distant but readable.

Jade Clinic.

The file is named Miriam Hill.

The photo is date stamped. The day Bish contacted me.

Time for that last piece of pizza.

Time to investigate everything else on this flash drive.

And maybe, if I'm able, I'll get a few hours of sleep.

One thing is for certain.

Miriam Hill will have a visitor tomorrow morning.

JADE CLINIC
WHEATON, ILLINOIS
JANUARY 6, 8:47 A.M.

I slog out of bed with the mental acuity of a prize fighter stumbling to his feet after the referee's ten-count. Slap on shaving cream and peel it back with a cheap disposable razor. Wait until the coffee machine heaves its last groan, drop Visine into bloodshot eyes before facing the cold whip of morning winter wind.

My Ford Focus sputters to a start, blasts of chilly defroster air crystalize on the inside of the windshield. I rub them clear with the back of my gloved hand before shifting out of park. Siri says Jade Clinic is close.

The car finds its own way, I clutch a thin plastic cup and chug cheek-burning mouthfuls until I reach the last, which is bitter and filled with dry creamer sludge. I'm able to corral a cat-herd of random thoughts into some semblance of coherent structure only after the last drop leaves the cup.

Cavanaugh needs to hear what I've just learned.

I dial her number, pound through the frustrating directory of options and am rewarded with the same Enya-like on-hold song.

I rehearse the message I'll leave one final time as the call finally connects.

"Detective Cavanaugh here," she answers, her words sounding like they're formed out of gravel.

"You're at it early."

"Cases don't punch a time clock," she responds, to the thud of a coffee cup meeting a desk. "How can I help you, Mr. Badger?"

"I found his flash drive. You need to know what's on it," I tell her, as an elderly man wearing a red driving cap with mad scientist eyebrows and a paper-thin mustache fishtails out of the entrance to the Jade Clinic, nearly clipping my car. The blanketed road lights up like tiny embers as he jams on the brakes of his candy-apple red circa-1990 Cadillac and slides into the curb. He shakes an angry fist in the air when I pull up behind him, then speeds away before I can offer my help.

Cavanaugh clears her throat a few times. "By *him*, I assume you mean Kenneth Bish. *Why* am I interested?"

"I found the connection. I know why Bish contacted me," I say, jamming the rental into reverse, looking over my shoulder and backing up past the entrance to the expansive grounds of the clinic, which is sur-rounded on three sides by deep woods. I wind down the tree-lined driveway until I reach the snow-covered parking lot and slip into an open spot. I leave the car running.

"I have a departmental briefing to prepare," she says quietly, as though she doesn't want to be over-heard. "I suggest you get to the point."

Here we go.

"He had files on the cult at Bolsiver. On his em-ployer. On an institutionalized woman and payoffs to Bish's alleged victims. And on Paradign. No coinci-dences, remember?" I say, leaning over to fire up my laptop and open the file, fogging the window with huffed breaths filled with minty toothpaste, watered down coffee and the lingering hint of garlic from last night's pizza.

"Do tell," her reply tinged with the slightest of intrigue.

"Roncate Realty, Bish's employer, acquired the home where the massacres occurred thirty years ago, nearly to the day of the murders last December. In the same year, they paid off the mortgages of five families. The O'Bannon, Breen, Ortiz, Marcus, and Shea families. Bish's alleged victims. Tell me you have a hunch why."

She lets it linger, then says, "I don't traffic in hunches."

"Well, I do," jabbing an accusatory finger in the air. "They were covering something up. Bish figured it out, contacted me, someone killed him and the others for it. Someone with the unique set of skills to pull something like this off." And as almost an afterthought, but an appropriate one given what I suspect, I add, "Maybe someone with enough juice to erase my flight record."

She lets out a long exhale. "That's a tall order, Mr. Badger. What's your proof?"

"Miriam Hill, for starters."

"Elaborate."

"There was a photograph of Bish and Miriam Hill on the day he first contacted me. I found it on the flash drive, along with financial ledgers. Miriam Hill was admitted to the Jade Clinic on December 15, 1987, right before the Wheaton home was purchased and the victim's families were paid off. Roncate Realty has been footing the bill for her treatment."

She clears her throat, smacks her coffee cup down again. "All very interesting. Call the Wheaton Police.

I'm sure if they don't already know, someone there will appreciate the info."

"I'm not finished," I yell back. "I also found a scanned article on the Bolsiver suicides in Bish's drive. Are you in front of a computer, Detective?" I ask.

"I'll play along. What am I looking for?"

"Google Bolsiver, tell me what you find," I say, stepping briskly toward the entrance of Jade Clinic, where I pace a figure eight in the snow.

"Suicide circles. Like Wheaton," she finally says.

"Suicide circles. The file was added the same day he went to see Miriam Hill. The same day he called me." I let it rest a moment. "I don't need to remind you, Bish is the reason I wasn't there the night Abby was taken."

"No coincidences," she says, nearly sounding convinced.

"And then there's Paradign. The last file I found was on Paul James Pellen. Do you know the name?"

"Should I?" she asks.

"Pellen was a former Paradignist. Killed his entire family, then himself."

There's a long pause, 1 start to question whether she's still on the line.

"Paradignist," her eventual reply. "Like Mazer. So, assuming you're right, what was Bish on to?"

"I don't know. Yet," I assert. "But I do know this. Bodies are piling up, Detective. And Bish is central to them. You see it now, don't you?"

The figure eight grows wider, muddy footprints stack over other muddy footprints.

"Maybe." The line goes quiet long enough for my lungs to burn in protest against the sharp, biting Illinois winter air. Then this. "Report back what you learn. In the meantime, I'm taking a closer look at Mazer. And at Paradign."

"You might get to solve your old case after all, Detective Cavanaugh," I say. "And take care of that cat of yours. Nixon, right?

"Yeah, Nixon," she says, before hanging up.

Ω

"Welcome to Jade Clinic. My name is Stephanie. Please sign in." The woman, mid-forties, matching red nails and lipstick, chestnut hair cut in a bob, steps down from the platform her workstation sits atop and hands me a clipboard. I scratch out my printed name and scribble a signature. "Welcome Mr. Badger. How may I help you?"

"I'm here about a patient. Miriam Hill," I answer, anticipation knotting my stomach.

Her face becomes several shades closer to the color of her lipstick. "What *about* Ms. Hill?"

"I'm here to see her."

She backpedals onto the platform and taps out an email. "Dr. Katt will be with you shortly. Our waiting area is over there," she says, pointing across the hall. The corners of her red painted lips are wrinkled, the welcoming smile is fully gone.

"Is there some sort of problem?" I ask, her face fading from bright red to pale.

"Please," her answer, gesturing again to the waiting area.

I take a seat in one of two empty pastel-blue fanback chairs and exchange nods with the others seated there.

I'm not there long before Katt rounds the corner toward me, moving at a brisk clip despite the slight hunch and limp he walks with.

I recognize the haircut. Once a marine, always a marine.

"Come with me," Katt says, insisting, not asking, his expressionless face hardened, as though chiseled from stone. He motions me toward a locked door, presses a keycard to the wall. "This way."

I have so many questions, so few answers, and a gnawing in the pit of my stomach. What did Bish know? Why did he contact me on the day he visited Miriam Hill?

"I guess you'll be accompanying me when I see her?" I ask.

"We'll discuss your request to see her in my office," he calls out over his shoulder, never breaking stride.

To the left a small rock garden, a fountain and an empty bench seat, all covered in snow. The right window separates the hallway from an enclosed indoor common area filled with residents, each passing the time in the way they likely did yesterday, and the many yesterdays before.

We reach his office at the end of a second walled hallway lined with taupe-colored doors. He motions me in and offers me a chair near his couch.

"I've asked to be personally notified when Ms. Hill receives a visitor," he looks me up and down, suspicious. "Who *are* you to her, Mr. Badger?"

"The answer to your question is what I'm here to find out."

Katt rises up from his chair. I lift a hand up in protest.

"I've come a long way. Hear me out, please. I put out a call on national television regarding a book on connections between the government and cults I'm in the research phase of. I got contacted by a man claiming to have information. He requested we meet," I lock eyes with Katt. "He's now dead. Kenneth Bish."

Katt's face screws up. "What about Mr. Bish?"

"I found a flash drive I believe he intended to give me when we met. In it was a photo. He was with Ms. Hill. It was taken here on the grounds and dated the day he contacted me."

Katt's head moves side to side, the slow shake of denial. "Miriam hasn't spoken to anyone since Mr. Bish last visited her. I'm afraid her seeing you is not in her best interest. I'll walk you back to the lobby."

"Didn't you hear me?" I protest.

"Yes, Mr. Badger. I *did* hear you. Let's go."

And with that it's decided.

We reach the hallway lined with windows in silence before an orderly stops Katt with a question. Out of curiosity, I take a step toward the window and look around the common area. A woman near my age stares wide-eyed back at me through the window.

I recognize her face from Bish's photo.

"It's her, isn't it?" I ask, once the orderly leaves.

"Yes, that's our Miriam. Now come."

"Wait, can she see us?" Miriam Hill places a book she'd been holding in her lap and raises a shaking hand, making motions at us. "She *can* see us. What's she doing?"

"My staff will see to her needs. I'm sorry for being so abrupt, but I have patients to attend to."

I turn to go but keep eyes on her. Hers sharpen. *Thwack.* She's thrown her book at the window. Katt spins toward the noise. Outside, she points directly at me.

"You *do* see this, don't you?"

Miriam Hill slowly rises from her seat and eerily stumbles toward us. An orderly stands at the ready to catch her if she stumbles.

"You should go now. I trust you can find your way from here," Katt says, surprised eyes fixed on the woman.

"Before I go, I have a question. She was a little girl, maybe eight or nine when it happened, when she got burned in a fire. Wasn't she?"

"I believe you said you didn't know her," Katt's stunned answer.

Kah-thuhm.

Kah-thuhm. Kah-thuhm.

Little moments.

"I've had dreams."

Katt steadies me when I lose my footing and guides me back to his office.

* * *

MICHAEL CAVE

FBI FIELD OPERATION OFFICE, SAN DIEGO
JANUARY 6

Cave had asked for this meeting, citing new evidence. He convinced himself there was no other option. The operative knew where he lived. He showed Cave the surveillance photos. Missy on her morning run. Missy in the kitchen. The two of them snuggling on the couch. Her at the drugstore. Cave on his run when he stopped to scream. His sister.

The threat didn't need to be made aloud.

Sweat chills his palms, he wipes them on his pants.

This time it's not a phone call. This time the senior agent joins him.

"I have new information," he says, recognizing her as the instructor for a class he once took.

"I'm sure you do. But first I have something for you. A story."

"This is important," Cave says, thumbing through a folder filled with the evidence he was given.

"*So* is *this*," the senior agent says emphatically, while fishing a photo out of her purse and setting it on the table. It's the handsome, chiseled face of a black man in his late thirties. It's taken through the thick plexiglass windows of a prison visiting room. "Tell me what you heard of my Suspect Zero Theory at Quantico."

"They talked about it in one of the classes. You advanced a theory that a string of unrelated acts of violence and sexual attacks occurring in multiple cities around the country were all related."

The senior agent gently caresses the photo. "My husband Carl was a good man," she begins. "He'd been a drinker before we met, but he chose me over the bottle. Went to AA meetings three times a week, became a vegan before being vegan was even a thing."

Cave thinks of Missy. Of last night, when the test strip turned blue. Miles Cave if a boy, Cora Cave if a girl. Then thinks of the photos Sturgeon showed him. "He must've loved you very much," not sure what else can be said.

"I was abused by an uncle growing up. And the scars he left weren't just emotional. The China Lake case was re-opened just after I joined the Violent Crimes Against Children here. I became obsessed with it. I'd narrowed in on what I believed to be a common thread, the doctor. I tracked down Allende's last known whereabouts to the Theosophical Society headquarters. I went there. This is when I first met your Cathal, who told me Allende had already gone. I had a late afternoon flight back. Carl usually took care of the dinners if I wasn't home by six. I arrived home at eight-thirty, not even a note. They kept him two days before they contacted me."

Cave chokes back his surprise. "Someone kidnapped him?"

"Carl kept an old Chevy out in the back garage, his latest restoration project. I never went out there, I let him have his space. But I did that night. They made me."

Fearing the worst, he asks the question anyway. "What did you find?"

"The entire front grill covered in blood. There'd been a hit-and-run the night Carl went missing. Same make and model. Same color as Carl's car. They told me he'd be charged with felony hit and run unless I agreed to work with them."

"*Work* with them?" asks Cave, believing he already knows the answer.

"They made me drop my Suspect Zero investigation. In exchange for Carl."

"What happened to him?" he asks, not sure if it's out of concern for her husband or for his and Missy's safety.

"They found the driver eventually. But those days after Carl was released from jail and before they found that driver ate Carl up. He picked up a bottle, and he didn't stop. Carl died of liver failure. And you know what, on his death bed, you know what he told me? He told me I shouldn't have stopped pursuing my case. I shouldn't have tried to protect him. He made me promise I'd never stop. Never again."

Cave leans back in his chair, head reeling.

"Thanks for listening," the senior agent tells him. "Now let's hear what you have."

She suspects, he thinks to himself.

"Michael?"

Too late. I'm trapped. He does his best to recover, but inside feels the creeping tendrils of doubt rising up from his stomach.

"Dorien Wissum. A long-time, deep-in-the-system Paradignist, who, around December of last year, re-nounced all affiliation. Some sort of falling out just after Father Cathal passed. Here are some of his more inter-esting flight records," Cave says, sliding the flight log across the table.

The senior agent skims through, checking the dates. "He's there in Wheaton on the 15th. He's in San Diego when Abigail Ashford is taken. He's even there during the time Mazer killed himself. Interesting. The dates and times line up."

Cave feels the tendrils falling away.

"I just have a question. How'd you come across all this evidence?"

Cave searches for an answer that doesn't come.

"Remember the story I told you about Carl," she says, a warning flashes in her eyes.

***

NATHAN BADGER

"Lean your head back."

My brain's throbbing. I wince, he notices. "Don't need to," I tell him.

"Of course you don't," he says, unconvinced. "Scale of one to ten, how bad is the pain?"

Every nerve is ignited, raw pulsations pound in my head. I hold up four fingers. A lie.

"I see," he says. "Because I could get you something for the pain, if it were worse."

The words bang my skull like a clapper smacking the sides of a bell. Four additional fingers go up, raising the count to eight. "Sure."

Katt makes the call. An orderly arrives within the minute and hands me three Advil and a small paper cup filled halfway with water.

"Close your eyes," Katt says, turning off all but the accent lights in a cabinet holding a collection of artifacts. "When the pain allows, I'd like to know more about this dream."

"Now," I tell him, the word cuts through my skull like a drill bit.

He studies my face. "As you wish. What do you remember of it?"

"A ridge, a campfire. There's a young boy, a girl. Miriam I think. Her legs are smoldering. A bearded man pulls her out of the fire."

Through squinted eyes I see Katt is taken aback. "A *bearded* man you say. You're sure?"

"Always," I respond, hands pressed against my temples. "Always him."

"Give me a moment," he says, grabbing his desk phone.

I close my eyes, lean my head back, and tune out, repeating the word I'd been taught as a child. I open them to an orderly leaving the room.

"Mr. Badger, nearly an entire wall of Miriam's room is filled with drawings like this one."

He holds it up high. It's a crayon drawing of a round-faced man with a wild, scraggly beard.

"Does this look like the man in your dream?"

Little moments like this.

"Yeah. It's him."

"Mr. Bish said she would try to talk to him about her drawings on their walks. He said it upset her. He said he sang her a song to calm her down. That's all we know about the man in her drawings."

"He would sing to her?" I ask, jumping up from the chair, head pounding in protest.

"He would. A lullaby."

Oh my God. The lullaby.

I tell Katt the lullaby's name.

"How could you possibly know this?" he demands.

"This is the question I think both of us need answered," I say, then tell him what I'd learned about Bish, the Wheaton victims, even Daniel Mazer.

Katt sets down the drawing, picks up the receiver again and summons an orderly.

He locks eyes with me before looking away. "Please bring Miriam Hill to her room for a visitor."

Ω

We travel down the hallway together, up the stairs, and down the corridor lined with locked patient rooms, all painted a drab grey.

I do my best to keep up.

"Are you certain you're up to this?" Katt's blurry face presses near mine.

I feel my head nod, the voice grows louder. My head falls, eyes close. I lean into the wall as the voice returns.

Nathan honey, sit down here.

Yes, Mommy.

"When you speak to her, do so slowly and calmly. And Mr. Badger, no sudden moves. She can excite easily."

Nathan, honey, Dr. Brown says you've suffered a severe concussion.

"Did you hear what I said?"

Your brain was hurt honey.

"Mr. Badger, maybe now's not the best time for you to visit her."

This is why you can't remember things.

"Okay, I'm calling this off," Katt says.

His words snap me back.

"I'm fine. Let's go."

He studies my face as though I'm his patient.

"I said I'm fine."

"Needed to be sure," he says, opening the door to her room.

She sits facing us as we enter, orderlies on each side. Her black hair is streaked with ashen white shocks. Her vacant eyes stare down at a paper held in tremoring hands. A white gown drapes down the flesh-covered skeleton that is her; thick, cream-colored stockings cover her legs.

Katt's words flow like melted chocolate, silky and sweet, comforting, sedate. "Miriam, we have a visitor today. Would you like to say hi?"

She does not look up.

"These are very good drawings," I tell her.

Her right hand slowly raises up from her lap.

"Who are all these drawings of?" I ask.

Her right index finger extends.

"Can you look at me, Miriam?"

"Him," she answers, with a weak, raspy voice.

"Who *is* he, Miriam?" I ask again.

"Him," she repeats. She raises her head. Our eyes meet. "*You* could've stopped him."

Kah-thuhm.

"Stopped *who*?" Katt asks.

Kah-thuhm. Kah-thuhm.

"Doctor *Brown*!" she screams back.

I watch what comes next in slow motion. Her lunging forward at me. Orderlies surprised, frozen in place. Katt grabbing my shoulders, pulling me back toward the door.

Spell broken, the orderlies move toward her.

I spin out of Katt's grasp, hand signal the orderlies to stop.

Her lips quiver. begin to move. Words, at first too quiet to hear grow louder.

"We all. We," she struggles to say.

"We all *what*, Miriam?" I ask, holding my head to cradle it against the mounting pain.

She smiles a sickening smile. "We all fall down."

Ω

12

GREY GULLEN

KANE INDUSTRIES
TORREYANA ROAD, LA JOLLA, CA
JANUARY 7

Jeffrey Delacruz completed the firing range tests with exemplary results. He showed his skills in unarmed combat, sporting a black eye for weeks from one of the very few punches that found their way through in the five consecutive bare-knuckle matches he'd fought.

He passed strenuous written and verbal tests, extensive background checks. They found his ex-girlfriend from college and probed her for details about their brief, tumultuous relationship. To his surprise, she'd been kind in the telling. Neighbors, schoolteachers. Buddies from Basic Training. Everyone. They spoke to everyone.

And it all lead to this; his second day on the job, a VIP visitor expected any moment, and him standing guard at the most coveted post on the day's in-house detail. The entrance to CEO Alastair Kane's office.

Delacruz looks across the hallway, again measuring his stance against the more senior man, Sergeant Wilfredo, standing opposite him.

They explained in orientation that the stance he now mimicked, the *Savate*, named after the French combat sport, had been developed by Kane himself, who claimed it provided a millisecond advantage when timed in two factors against others: blocking and baton strikes.

From what Delacruz knew, there'd never been an attack on Kane Industries, any Kane executive, or Kane himself. In fact, no one had been so much as detained by the security team there. Still, based on the size of Kane Industry's most recent graduating class, the company isn't just adding new guards, it's building a small army. One Delacruz has every intention of leading one day.

He moves his right hand off the baton to check the safety on his weapon. Across the hall from him, Wilfredo clears his throat and points. Delacruz holds a hand up in apology, returns to stance. Wilfredo steps over to Delacruz, grabbing his right hand and twisting it until the new guard's palm shows. "What's *this*?"

"Paint. I'll keep my fist clenched. No one will see it." Delacruz saw active combat, three tours in Afghanistan. He's no stranger to pressure. Still his stomach tightens. "I worked on my Camaro with my son David last night. Tried thinner, gasoline. Couldn't get it all off."

Wilfredo's shakes his head and unclips the radio from his black, patent leather utility belt. "Main. Main. This is Final, over."

"Go ahead, Final. Over," the voice crackles in response.

"ETA on the Object. Over."

"Stand by." A few seconds pass, then the answer. "ETA in two mikes, over."

"Roger that. Final out." Wilfredo's tightly trimmed eyebrows furrow, his eyes narrow, a threatening finger points at Delacruz. "No time to swap you out, so here's what's gonna happen. Keep your right hand closed in a fist when Mr. Kane and his guest pass. Once they're inside, you'll be relieved. You're to make one more attempt to clean off the residue here on premise. If you're unsuccessful, you'll vacate the premises immediately. Understood?"

"But I can return tomorrow?"

Wilfredo does not respond.

Ω

A light sprinkling of rain coats the windshield of a bulletproof, chauffeured sedan. G2X Deputy Grey Gullen watches from behind the privacy shield separating him from his driver as they turn onto Torreyana Road and into the gated driveway. Beyond it lies the stand-alone, five-story Kane Industries building. The driver thuds in the key code, which is changed daily. The gate swings open when the last digit is entered.

Gullen takes the last satisfying bite of a cruller he made the driver buy for him downtown. "Second best," he mumbles to himself, thinking, as he usually does every morning, of the shop around the corner from his office in Fairfax.

He chipmunks the last remnants into the pocket of his right cheek and presses the intercom button.

"Sir?" the driver replies as he navigates a sharp left and pulls into the VIP visitor's space in the lower-level parking garage.

"Twenty minutes. Thirty max. Pick me up lunch for the ride back."

Gullen clips the weapon from his briefcase onto his belt before twisting his lineman's frame out of the back seat. He moves forward with precision, purpose, resembling a bully going after his victim, only to find, to his surprise, new additions to Kane Industries' security system.

He whips out his phone.

"Luke here."

"Kane's beefed up his security. Find flaws. Or make some."

"Aye, Sir."

Gullen presses the red intercom button and awaits a response. His right foot rattles a steady tempo of impatience. The video feed blinks to life, and the face of a clean-shaven security guard greets him as Gullen's driver backs out of his space on his way to the nearest Rubio's.

"Afternoon Sir. We've been expecting you."

"New monitoring system I see. Tell Mr. Kane I'm here and buzz me back to his elevator."

"Mr. Kane's elevator is under maintenance."

"You're mistaken, son. If it *was* under maintenance, I'd already know. Which I don't. So buzz me through."

A moment goes by before the now visibly flustered guard appears again on the screen. "My apologies for the delay, Sir."

Gullen glances right and left looking for onlookers, witnesses. His face pulls tight, eyebrows crease, arms fold tight across his chest, anger building just below the boiling point at this unacceptable, unnecessary exposure. "How about we do this *now*, son?"

In response, a loud buzz emits from a stainless-steel security door as it opens, revealing the common elevator inside. "Fifth floor, Sir," says the guard stepping out of the elevator in a firm, yet respectful tone.

"*Kane's* elevator," Gullen's demands.

The guard stands stoic, blocking all but one possible path. "Mr. Kane's elevator is under maintenance."

Gullen tastes acid climbing up his throat. He notes the guard's name before loading his bulky frame into the common elevator and pressing the appropriate button. The bile rises in time with the ascent of the elevator car. He reaches for a Prilosec from the pack in his breast pocket. When the doors open again, a second clean-shaven guard blocks his passage.

"Out of my way."

"Stand still. Arms up please." A few heads raise up from their workstations.

"*Who* told you to search me?"

"New protocol, Sir."

"Doesn't apply to me. Step away, son," says Gullen, acid coating the back of his tongue.

"Please raise your arms."

Gullen makes no attempt to soften his glare. His temples throb like some alien form is trying to burst out from inside them.

The metal detector wand begins its exploration, moving from Gullen's broad shoulders down toward his torso.

Gullen grabs it in his hand. "I'll save you the effort. There's a Glock on my right hip."

The guard takes two urgent steps back, draws his pistol from its holster and points it at Gullen. "Place your hands in the air."

"That will not be necessary. Our guest may proceed." The soft, countertenor command hisses out like a secret.

At the sound of Kane's voice, the guard lowers his weapon to its holster.

Gullen studies Kane, something's changed. Short sleeve shirt, accenting Kane's biceps as usual. Skintight silken black dress pants, designer label, the outline of Kane's thighs and calves faintly visible. Also usual. Then he sees Kane's hands.

Gullen drafts a half-smile. "Hello, Alastair," he leans in and whispers. "What the fuck are you doing parading me past your staff?"

"The guard didn't tell you?" Kane says coyly, in his nasally tone. "Come." He places a hand on Gullen's shoulder.

Gullen casts a glance at the hand, then at Kane. "You mind?" Kane lets go.

The two men move down the long hallway leading to his office. When they reach the end of the hall, Kane stops in front of one of the two guards stationed at the entrance to his office.

"You are new here, are you not?" Kane asks, staring down at the man's hand.

"I am, Sir." Delacruz focuses his eyes on Kane's shoulders, sure to avoid making eye contact, as is protocol.

Kane takes a moment to admire the stance. It's perfect. Nearly. Save one minor detail. "Your right hand," is all he says, in a voice almost too soft to hear. Delacruz stretches out his fingers, revealing the imperfection.

"You have something there. A stain perhaps? Say yes."

"My son and I were painting a car together last night."

"How nice. Your first name?" He asks after reading the man's name tag.

"Jeffrey."

"Carry on, Jeffrey," he says, before motioning to Gullen. "Shall we?"

The next set of doors open automatically. The men move through and pass the frosted-glass privacy windows. They pass the 24,000-gallon reef tank housing Kane's prized collection of puffer and trigger fish and the sole blue-ringed octopus on their way to the great circular table in the center of Kane's atrium office.

"Don't expose me like you did again. Ever."

"Apologies." Kane motions his guest to a chair at the top of the circle and then finds his place at the one farthest away. As he lowers himself down to his seat, the command chair, he speaks an alert word into the voice-command intercom next to his laptop and waits for it to buzz to life.

"Yes, Sir?"

Kane reaches into his pocket, removes a small vial of liquid marked antibacterial, sprays and wipes the intercom carefully, thoughtfully, before his manicured nails trace the outer edges of its speaker, once, then again.

"The new guard, Jeffrey Delacruz. I'd like to see his personnel file."

"Right away, Sir."

Within a few seconds an email alert dings. Kane opens the attachment, glances it over. Once he's seen what he needs to he closes the file, and next opens the security system app on his phone, tapping the camera observing Father's room, then *hers*. Kane strokes the screen as he watches.

An impatient Gullen clears his throat. Loudly. "Can I have your full attention now?"

Kane deflects. "You're late, by the way. You made a stop downtown, yet you come here empty-handed?"

Gullen ignores him. "What's with the nails?"

"They disturb you?"

"Yeah, they fucking do."

"She likes it when I scrape her."

"I'm *sure* she does, Gullen's disgusted reply, certain he knows who *she* is. "Now listen to me. Carefully. Put a stop to your night trips downtown."

"Why, Grey," quips Kane. "Whatever do you mean?"

"Don't play coy with me, son. You need additional subjects, you come to me. No more homeless."

"It sounds remotely like you're questioning my methods."

"Not questioning them, ending them. We're handling the cleanup. You'll fucking stop. Now, why I really came. Any guesses?"

"The Conduit," Kane answers.

"We're talking national security here."

"I'm aware."

Gullen slams his fist down on the table. "Are you? What do you think happens when we can't deprogram a Conduit? When one starts remembering?"

"Badger *wasn't* one of mine," Kane snaps back.

"Need I remind you, *you* tried and failed, which is why we sent him back to Allende in the first place."

Kane throws up his hands and shrugs a half-hearted apology.

"Fix this. And do it in a way that doesn't draw any-more undue attention. I don't need to remind you, but I will: your contract's at stake."

"Need I remind *you?* You're not the only govern-ment agency in the world who's shown interest in my work."

"Did I just hear a threat, son? You make that kinda call, you'll be dead before you hang up the phone. We clear?"

Kane stares, defiant. His lips part. He stops the words.

"I'll take that as a yes. We're burning daylight. Let's get on with it. I assume you've made progress, seeing as you're within a razor's margin of your deadline."

Kane tilts his head sideways; a menacing smile creases his lips, his black eyes narrow. He rises slowly out of his chair toward the frosted inner wall. "In fact, I have."

Kane flips the switch only after two cleanings and a visual inspection. The wall's frosted tint evaporates, re-vealing a well-dressed woman seated in a wheelchair in the room adjoining the north wall of the atrium of-fice, two tables, a camera, and a man in a lab coat.

"What am I looking at here?"

"Watch and learn," Kane tells him.

Gullen watches the man in the white lab coat place two blank pieces of paper on the table in front of the woman in the wheelchair, one near her right hand, the other near her left. He next holds up two more blank pages, until receiving a nod from Kane, then disappears from view below the table.

Gullen resists the urge to smack the smug smile from Kane's face as he leans over Gullen and sets down a file.

"Hers, I assume?" Kane nods. Gullen pushes it away. "Don't need to read it. Get this show on the road."

Gullen sees the woman in the wheelchair move her right and left hands across the pages in front of her, clearly penning something with each. He sees what appears to be movement in the lower half of her body, which is obscured from his view by the table. He looks away, having seen what he thinks is enough. "Synesthesia. For your sake, and that of your company, I hope you have more."

Kane raises his index finger once more, the man in the lab coat removes the false front from the table, retrieves two new pieces of paper, and moves to the back of the room where he places the papers in precise order underneath the camera mounted to the desk, panning each, once, then again.

"They're passages from her favorite book. *The Cabinet of Curiosities*, Preston and Childs the authors." Kane holds up a hardbound copy, one he had autographed.

"She's a person with paraplegia who can write with her feet. *That's* what you have?"

"Different chapters, Grey. Chapters one and two with her hands. Three and four, I don't need to tell you. Go ahead, have a look." Kane slides the hardbound book across the table to Gullen.

Gullen selects only the third and fourth chapters to audit, looking carefully back and forth between the book and the monitor displaying video from the observation room. The writing is not only exact, it's also neat.

"Let me remind you of your deliverables," Gullen says, pushing the book aside. "One, technology-based alter development. Two, complete mission programmability. Three, non-traumatic verbal erase codes. Four, alter invisibility, meaning the subject can't become self-aware. Your company was engaged to create assets and soldiers here. Not sideshows. Show me assets and soldiers, son."

"Fair enough. But first, a word about the science."

"You're trying my patience here. Need I remind you that I have people I report to on this?" Gullen says. "Make it quick. Then show me deliverables."

Kane draws a short breath, exhales his indifference as he rotates his chair one-half turn, and stares casually out the window. "As you say. You obviously can't see it, but she's wearing a human body skin-textured suit. We utilized human robotics cooperative learning embedded with machine learning to generate a synergy of suit and human. There's a precise high-resolution coupling of the piezo resistance-embedded movement suit to the human. It is this that enables us to achieve a higher neuromotor performance capacity than even an Olympic-level athlete exhibits."

"Cut the theatrics," Gullen snaps. "What I saw is someone write with her feet. Impressive. Hardly Olympian."

Kane glances over at Gullen, then away in boredom. "We've used internal models allowing us to forward the precise biomechanical movements needed by the feet to execute fine motor dexterity through the smart material she's wearing using predict-and-actuate models."

Gullen thumbs out another Prilosec. "I've heard enough. Show me proof of the work my agency pays you for."

"As you say." Kane points the long, manicured nail of his right index finger at the once frosted window, then gives a nod to the woman in the wheelchair, who grins in response. Without even a falter and so fast the movement barely registers, the woman bursts to her feet and leaps toward the glass, directly at Gullen.

Gullen masks his surprise. "That's a great jump scare, Kane. What's the point?"

Kane gives a two-finger signal to the technician inside the room who responds with two knuckle raps on the door behind him. Delacruz and Wilfredo enter on his cue. The technician places his back against the farthest wall. "Just watch."

Delacruz and Wilfredo charge forward.

Kane conducts a silent symphony with his hands; the guards are tossed like rag dolls into the observation room window.

"Now we're getting somewhere. I report to the Director tomorrow. Is she *programmable*?"

"But of course," Kane responds.

"And the recall?"

"No trauma required," brags Kane.

Gullen checks his watch. "Two things. Help me solve the Conduit issue. And hit the fucking deadline. I have a flight to catch. I'll show myself out."

"Before you go, a small favor," Kane says. "I've caught wind of an uprising within Paradign. Two troublemakers I would like to silence. I wonder if you could be of assistance?"

Kane shows Gullen two photographs, both taken by drone on the night he announced his father's death.

Gullen frowns. "It's already in motion. Now finish your fucking work, son."

***

DR. KATT

I should never have agreed.

Katt dials the number he was instructed to but hangs up before the call connects. He runs hands through his thinning grey hair.

I should have never let him see her.

But he had.

I just wanted to free her. Like Bish almost had.

What if I just don't report it? How would they know?

He scoffs at his own stupidity. It's the *agency*. Of course they'll know. They always know. It's their job to know. And it's not wise to run afoul of them. It's career suicide.

Katt logs off of his computer, a five-note melody plays as the screen goes dark. He slides Miriam Hill's file into the bottom right drawer and locks it, trades his lab coat for a white winter parka. His hand is on the light switch when the desk phone rattles to life, jolting him from his thoughts.

He runs back to answer it, knowing who's calling.

"Dr. Katt speaking."

"Miriam Hill had a visitor today, did she not?"

"She. Um. I intended to call you after I finished with her case file."

"I'm sure you did. Confirm please, Nathan Badger?"

"Yes," Katt replies, now more than ever concerned about coming implications.

"Miriam will have a second visitor tonight; he's on his way as we speak. He'll be arriving this evening by 8:00 p.m. You're to stay until his work is complete. He'll provide you credentials. He is to have unlimited access to Ms. Hill. Alone. Understood?"

"Miriam is given her last round of medications at 7:30, which includes something to help her sleep. Surely you understand how important routines are to my patients."

"See to it she is *not* given those medications tonight."

"With all due respect, I never agreed to something like this."

"We don't require your agreement."

"Then I deserve to know why you've decided to send someone?'

"It's in the interest of national security. That's all you need know."

"I need your assurance then that no harm will come to my patient."

"That is the goal. One last thing, anything of note you observed about Mr. Badger during his visit?"

The line goes dead after Katt answers the question. *What have I done?*

***

CAVE

SORRENTO VALLEY, CALIFORNIA

"Where are you right now?"

At the crossroad, thinks Cave, torn.

She raps a knuckle on his forehead. "Hello. Is anyone in there? McFly?"

"Very funny," Cave says, gently guiding her hand back to her lap.

"No, seriously, Michael. Where were you?"

"No idea what you mean," Cave replies unconvincingly.

"You can't talk about it can you?" She pops up two peace signs, makes a series of quotation marks in the air. "It's the job, honey. The jaaaaaaahhhhhhhb."

"You knew there'd be times."

"Yeah, I did. And you know what times like this call for, don't you?" She pokes him in the ribcage.

"Not tonight, babe."

"For *sure* tonight. Here she comes."

She digs a wriggling finger into his ribcage. Nothing. "I must break you!" Cave looks away. She inches up into his armpit, his most vulnerable spot. Nothing.

Cave takes her finger gently in his hand, guides it up to his lips and kisses it.

She takes his other hand in hers and does the same. "You should talk to me."

A somber silence shrouds the air between them.

She kisses his cheek, takes his chin in her hand and turns his forlorn face to hers. "You can trust me."

"I know," he says before kissing her long on the lips. "Go to bed, babe."

"You don't need to carry whatever this burden is alone. Come upstairs with me. Mr. Barry White's waiting."

Cave cradles his face in his hands.

"Babe? Barry. Come."

He finally breaks. "What if you had to make a choice between what you love, what you believe and what you know?"

"I'd choose what I love. I'd choose you," she says, taking his hand and guiding him up from the couch. "Now let's go."

And with her words, Cave knows what he must do.

***

13

CAVANAUGH

OLD TOWN, SAN DIEGO
JANUARY 7

She pours over Daniel Mazer's toxicology report and all she can find on the Pellen tragedy.

What's the connection? Cavanaugh asks herself after filling her glass with two cubes and two fingers of Gentleman Jack.

"Whaaaa!" Nixon lands claws first into Cavanaugh's lap. "Easy buddy."

He does small circles, nudging her hand with his nose.

"I know, boy," she tells him before getting lost again in her thoughts.

There would be investigations. The police, the press. Maybe both.

She thuds keys, taps her mouse and skims through seemingly endless digital records. A wet ring forms on the coffee table, her drink fades from deep amber to a watery yellow.

Finally, a new file holds promise.

Police suspected, never proved, that Lena Tanninger's accidental drowning might not have been accidental after all, when they ran across an unpublished article she'd been working on while doing the customary search of her home.

"Dear God," Cavanaugh mumbles to Nixy as she skims through the article.

'Til Death Do Us Part. The Tragic Death of Laura Weston, and the Cult She Tried to Leave Behind.
BY LENA TANNINGER

In the early morning hours of July 6, 2014, a young woman entered Tipsy McStaggers, the landmark Irish pub in Austintown, Ohio. Within minutes she'd be dead by her own hand. Was this desperate act the result of a state of despair and deep depression, or was her suicide caused by something else?

"I can't believe she's gone. She had a smile that would light up a room. Everyone loved to be around her. I miss her every minute of every day." Six months after, her mother, Gina Weston, still grieves the loss of her daughter. And holds tight to her claim that while her daughter held the gun, a force greater than her pulled the trigger. "Laura had been afraid for her life after she left them." By them, Gina Weston means Paradign.

Laura dropped out of college during her sophomore year at Youngstown State University in 2012, months after attending her first Paradign event. Her best friend Barbara recalled this time in her friend's life. "She went all the way in. After the first event Laura got hooked, and then she just went fanatic on me. I almost didn't know her."

By all reports from the Paradign members who would speak to me, they saw Laura as a bright and shining new star in the organization she'd quit college to join. According to Gina Weston, her daughter's concerns started to rise soon after being elevated to Doyen, a coveted position within Paradign, one responsible for leading the local chapter, or Causa.

"She called me one night, sounding frightened. She wouldn't speak loudly; she was afraid of being overheard, she said she needed to get out. I told her I'd come and get her, and we made a plan."

Gina Weston drove through the night and into the early hours of the next morning. Later, after a two-hour nap, she arrived at the address where her daughter had planned to meet her. She waited there for several hours before her cell phone rang. "Mom, go home. I'm where I belong." Laura hung up. The words will forever haunt Gina Weston as they were the last she would ever hear from her daughter's lips.

In the months following she received only one email. The subject line read, "I've found a way out."

The email went on to detail something Laura called "Schema Realignment" or SR. She described it as the erasing of memories. Turns out, it's not the first time Paradign has come under scrutiny for its SR practices.

In August of 2013, police in a rural Oklahoma town outside of Oklahoma City were called to the site of a domestic altercation spun out of control. The husband, Paul James Pellen, held his wife and children hostage. He made his demands known to a local newscaster.

"I can't stop my thoughts. The weight of everything I've ever done is crashing down on me. I'm going to do something bad, something that can't be undone." KOCI investigative reporter Linda Carello recalled the chilling phone call.

Hostage negotiators were unsuccessful in talking Pellen down. Before the standoff could be brought to its end, he'd shot and killed his wife and critically wounded one of his two children before turning the gun on himself. The second Pellen child died on the way to the hospital.

My attempts to reach Paradign for comments have been largely unsuccessful, other than the following statement, sent to my email:

"We deeply mourn the loss of Laura Weston. She was a part of our family for many years, and we will miss her. Out of respect for her privacy, and in consideration of her family, we respectfully decline any further comment, but send healing thoughts to her family in their time of need."

We may never know the reason that Laura Weston took her own life on that fateful night, but we can honor her memory by asking one question: Is it time to look more closely at Paradign?

"Maybe it *is*," Cavanaugh tells Nixy, directing her browser to Paradign's website.

She sees the bright, happy couple greet her in a high-quality video on the website's hero banner. Clearly they're actors. They're dressed all in white, the glowing faces of what we're meant to believe are their children beside them.

"We'd talked about divorce. Nothing worked between us, and the children knew it. They'd seen all the fights. Our life experiences had given us a set of tools. Most of them dulled over the years."

The woman speaks for the couple. Her husband smiles, nods in agreement, first to her, then the camera. The wife's voice, sweet as honey, drips on in the background.

"It's so easy to get hooked. Get caught up in what *they* want us watching. What's Kylie wearing? Who is Tana dating now? What's the latest political scandal? It becomes the answer to everything. I'm bored, tune in.

We're fighting, tune in. The kids are acting up, tune in. And while we're all tuned in, our lives are incrementally taken from us. It isn't until we awaken to the world *within* that things in our own lives begin to change."

Here it comes. Cavanaugh lights a cigarette, and finally pays attention to her drink.

"After we completed the Serenities, things for us blossomed. Paradign taught us the answers we need are all within reach. If we can just reconnect with ourselves, with our past. If we can just reach deep enough within to see the choices we've made, and rewrite them, we can change what we do tomorrow for the better."

The husband finally speaks. "That was five years ago. This is now." He plants a long kiss on her cheek. "Thank you, Paradign."

The hero banner fills with cornfields. Then beaches. Then a sunrise. The bright promise of a new day, all delivered by Paradign.

She watches the next video roll. It's grittier. Dark, messy hair falls in front of a face marked with blemishes. Pale skin stretches over a skeleton with hollow eyes. It's the face of an addict; Cavanaugh recognizes heroin's distinct signature. The narrator tells of the day he'd found hope as the camera pans across a gymnasium.

Two men jump, one tips the ball. A pack of five sweaty guys fight for it. One knocks it out of bounds.

The former addict, now holding the ball, pauses and speaks to the camera.

"I'd lost everything. My wife. My kids. It all went here," he points to his right arm, just below the bicep.

"You don't see any new scars there. Not anymore. That was the old me. This is my life now."

He smacks the ball and the players all move. He tosses it in, pushes through two defenders and raises his hand. The ball meets it. He takes a jump shot. The ball ricochets back and forth on the rim before bouncing out.

"You can't win 'em all. But you *can* win more. That's what Paradign taught me."

"Is that what they taught Daniel Mazer?" Cavanaugh says aloud, takes a long draw, then snuffs out the half-finished cigarette in disgust. "How about Laura Weston, or the Pellen family?"

Her mouse pointer hovers over the Submit button on the Contact Us form for a long moment before it slides to the right and clicks cancel and she walks off angrily to bed.

Ω

The black Toyota Camry drives slowly past her a second time.

"Hello, handsome," she says.

The man reaches over, unlocks the passenger door, and flings it open.

"Challenge Me" plays over and over again on the bumpy dirt road leading to his house.

"Make you a plateful of my nachos," the man says, cranking the radio up, singing along. "Wreck my car, that challenged me. Cheat and steal, all night long. Cha-ha-ha-haha, cha-ha-ha-hallenge me."

"Fifth Street!"

Cavanaugh jerks up from the bed, hands and arms protecting her face.

"Fifth Street!" She screams out. Nixy screeches, runs off to a corner. Eyes full of tears, she rips at her shirt sleeve.

When the adrenaline fades, when she's sure she's alone, she accepts the fact that there's no going back to sleep tonight.

Fine. Fuck it.

She stumble-steps through the dark bedroom until hitting her pinkie toe on the edge of the bed-chair she'd carelessly left in the path to the door. "Ow, fuck." Nixon follows her out to the cold living room.

As the small, insufficient living room wall heater hums back to life, she trudges into the kitchen, grinds four tablespoons of Kona beans, and groggily dumps the fine powder into the Mr. Coffee machine on the counter she'd needed to do a vinegar rinse on since last year. She spills a full third of the grounds on the counter.

The machine groans as it spits out transparent brown in fits and spurts. She pulls the carafe out too soon, thin brown liquid rolls over the burner and onto the counter, disappearing into browned grout-canals.

She returns to her desk. Nixon makes a dash across the cold apartment floor and leaps into her lap.

She taps in her password, fires up a browser, and returns to the Paradign site. This time she fills out the contact form.

An email arrives shortly after. A welcome letter from Doyen Michael Cave with an invitation to visit Anlon Hall, the San Diego Causa, and a link to an external intake questionnaire.

"No coincidence," she says.

***

KANE

Jeffrey Delacruz checks his watch. It's 6:55 a.m. He's five minutes early.

He sits down on one of six empty chairs lining a glass wall.

Precisely at 7:00, a tiny, balding lab technician motions him into a room. Jeffery senses the little man as an uptight, unhappy shadow of whatever he may once have been.

"Retraining," Jeffrey says, eyeing an area more resembling a private patient room at his physician's office than what he'd expected. "Is this? Am I in the right place?"

"Have a seat there, please." Jeffrey accepts his clinical dispassion.

"Uh, here? This is like an exam table or something."

"Not something like, it's exactly one. Please sit down." The technician checks his watch and clipboard before crossing his arms and waiting impatiently for Delacruz to comply.

"Now," he says, checking his clipboard again, "recent illness, fever?"

"No sir."

"Seizures? History of epilepsy in your family?"

"Wait, what?" Jeffrey gets up from the table. "What's going on here? And what's *this* for?" he asks, pointing at the electrode-lined cap on the metal rolla-way cart near where he was seated.

"Mr. Delacruz," lab coat guy says with all the warmth and personality of an embalmed frog, "shall I inform Mr. Kane you won't be participating today?"

"Wait a minute. Hold up. No. I need this job. No." Jeffrey grabs lab coat guy's arm, who takes a step back, clearly shaken by Jeffrey's sudden reaction. "It's just… What the fuck is all this?"

"Language, Mr. Delacruz. I'll thank you to use proper language during our sessions." As he finishes speaking, Jeffrey sees the technician's tongue flick around his mouth nervously, like it's chasing an insect.

"Can you just tell me what we're going to be do-ing?"

"Mr. Kane has developed a new technology he's calling the KI Alpha program. He wishes to implement it as our new on-boarding procedure. You'll be one of our first," the technician says, waiting for Delacruz to return to the exam table.

The technician seats the electrode lined cap on Jef-frey's head before turning a computer screen to face his patient.

"This is an interactive experience, Mr. Delacruz. Us-ing the mouse and keyboard, you'll complete all the modules I've marked for today's session. Let me know when you're ready to begin."

Jeffrey nods and soon after is greeted on screen by an avatar who introduces herself as Willa.

Ω

Jeffrey awakens, confused, disoriented. "Musta. What? How… I must've fallen asleep?" Alastair Kane stares back at him through the glass wall in front of the exam table.

"That is all for today. Same time tomorrow, Delacruz," the technician says.

A confused Jeffrey stumbles out of the room as Kane returns to his desk to view the technician's summary.

Patient Jeffrey Delacruz began his interactions with the KI Alpha program at 7:06 a.m. At 7:14, Delacruz completed the ethics review and answered all control questions in the affirmative. Patient asked to produce childhood memory, first stimulation of occipital lobe followed at 7:15. Patient visibly disoriented. The first of six suggestive modules occur here.

Kane skims down to the EEG readings, taking particular interest in the firing patterns in the amygdala region.

He'll do.

***

NATHAN BADGER

WHEATON, ILLINOIS

Ring around the Rosie. A pocket full of posies.

Five children's hands interlock. They form a circle around me.

"Dance with us, Nathan."

The bearded man watches from the dark corner of the dark basement room. *"Yes, Nathan. You must dance."*

I'm surrounded by gurneys. Metal tables holding headsets lined with wires.

"I don't want to," I scream, and bolt toward the door. It's locked, the footsteps behind me grow louder.

My tiny fists slam into metal.

Thuuhck. Thuuhck. THUUHCK.

"Let me out!" I scream.

A muffled voice from the other side of the door greets me. "Good morning."

"Help me," I answer back weakly, afraid to look back over my shoulder. Afraid of what the Doctor will do to me.

Thuuhck. Thuuhck. THUUHCK.

A tiny hand touches mine. Our fingers interlock.

"You have to dance. We all have to dance."

My eyes fan down toward the floor when I see two tiny stick legs covered in milky-white leggings.

"My name is Miriam," the little girl tells me.

Thuuhck.

Thuuhck.

THUUHCK.

"Housekeeping," a voice calls out to the slow sound of a door handle turning.

My eyes fly open, the cold-shower smack of reality hits me like a two-by-four.

Miriam Hill knew me.

Miriam Hill knew the rhyme.

Daniel Mazer knew the rhyme.

Kenneth Bish knew the rhyme.

Abby knew the rhyme.

And I knew the victims who died with Bish. They were my friends. I danced with them.

"Come back later," I yell, just as the door slides open and slams into the security lock.

I sink back in the bed as the door to my hotel room closes.

There are things hiding inside me. Things locked away in a dark closet somewhere deep in the recesses of my mind. I've always suspected them, denied them. I know that now.

It stops today. I will have answers.

Let your training take over, Nate.

What are the common denominators?

Bish's alleged victims were all Theosophists. Bish was a Theosophist. Maybe Miriam Hill was too. The house where the massacres took place is walking distance from here. This could be where we all met.

My flight boards at 10:20, I have precious little time and precious less to go on. I pack, drop my keycard on the lobby desk and sprint to the car.

Siri guides me to the parking lot.

Nervous knots twist in my stomach, causing me to stumble as I jog-walk up a gently curving red brick path to the entrance of the three-story brick L.W. Rogers Building.

My hand touches the door handle.

I've held it before.

I know I've held it before.

Haven't I?

Pulling it open brings a vision of children running past me. My five friends running past me.

Someone loudly clears their throat, spinning me back to the moment. "Excuse me," they say.

I don't know how long I've been standing here holding open the door, letting in the cold morning breeze. I just know that inside a workshop is underway in a corridor between the two staircases leading up to the library, and several of the attendees are glaring up at me.

I slip past their chairs. One woman creases her eyebrows, tilts her head, and after what appears to be a moment of reflection, she smiles.

I smile back, absent, distracted. My feet carry me upstairs as though they know where they're taking me.

They stop in front of the librarian's station. Our eyes meet, I stare back blankly.

"May I help you," she finally asks.

"I um," I stammer. A vision of Miriam walks slowly toward me. Another girl follows. A new child steps forward. They're all here now. All five of my friends form a circle and begin dancing.

Ring around the Rosie. A pocket full of posies.

"Sir?'

Ashes. Ashes. We all fall down.

The librarian rounds her desk, tissue in hand. "Here'" she says, concern tightening her lips.

"I'm sorry. Thank you," I say, wiping the blood from my face. One by one, each of the children fade away into dust.

"Yearbooks?"

The librarian looks back, confused.

"Photos from past events," her eyebrows press down in a question. "Do you have them?" I ask.

Her head tilts to the side, the question gone, replaced by suspicion. "You're the second person this morning to ask me." She looks up her nose through her glasses and points. "Third to last aisle, right-hand side. Toward the back."

The patter of tiny shoes from in front of me. Tiny feet. Children leading the way. Five little children. Leading the way.

Two-thirds of the way down the row, the footsteps stop and I find what I now know I've come for.

I run my finger across the yearbook spines and count back.

1991.

1990.

1989.

1988.

1987 is missing. As is '86 and '85.

I bolt back to the librarian's stand. "Three years' worth of yearbooks are missing from the shelf. 1987, 1986, 1985. You said someone else was here looking for yearbooks."

"I'm afraid you're just a few minutes too late," she exclaims, after a nose-bobbing review. "Someone checked them out just after 8:00 this morning."

"Tell me the name of the person signing them out," I demand.

She glares back defiant. "I most certainly will not."

I stand there an awkward moment staring, eyes pleading, before accepting the fact that I'm too late.

"Thank you anyway," I call out over my shoulder on the way down the stairs.

I reach the car, lungs stung by bitter cold air, close my eyes and bring myself back the woods.

They're here. They're hiding someone in here.

The winds howl a warning. They tell me I must stay on the path. That I'm only safe on the path. They tell me I'm late.

Just as I was taught as a child, I visualize lighting the first candle in honor of Mnemosyne and things remembered. Its flickering flame cuts against the blackness, illuminating the portrait of two children, of my first kiss with Claire, her auburn hair pulled back into pigtails.

I open my eyes to a plan.

Claire Lemley. My first kiss.

She's not hard to find online.

Claire Lemley graduates Cum Laude from Northwestern University. Claire Lemley announces her engagement. Claire Lemley is now Claire Corbin.

Facebook photos of a freckle-faced child and her freckle-faced mother, whose hair is no longer pulled back into ponytails. The photo is recent, taken on the grounds of Olcott Lodge. Another, a school play at Lincolnwood Elementary, Claire's daughter Clarisse is dressed as a woodland fairy.

I type in my credit card number, the BeenVerified website informs me there's only one Claire Corbin in Evanston.

I tell Siri Claire's number on the way to the airport. It rings six times before the voicemail greeting. "Claire, my name is Nathan Badger. We knew each other as children. I need to ask you a question. When you get this message, please call me. I'm just leaving Wheaton, my flight boards at 10:20."

***

CAVANAUGH

OLD TOWN, SAN DIEGO

She checks the stove's digital display. It's one hour before she reports downtown.

She pours herself a cup of burnt-smelling coffee, grabs a stale piece of bread from a sagging bag inside a cabinet, and sits down at her computer to read over the document Paradign sent her.

INTRODUCTION

This report seeks to define two important principles of self-concept: self-image and projection. Self-image illustrates the "you" that you see, your values, judgments, the core principles guiding your behaviors and governing your actions. Projection is you, as seen through the eyes of others, how you perceive your behaviors are judged by others based upon their own unique values and life experiences.

By understanding the variances and commonalities between these two important concepts, we get a glimpse into our own unique internal wiring and the knowledge we require to effect change in this wiring.

Copyright 2009-2028 Paradign Performance Systems (PPS)

Nixy nudges against Cavanaugh's leg until she picks him up. The printer hums to life, startling him, as it always seems to do.

She'd taken many personality tests over the course of her career, and though the category names differed from Myers-Briggs to DISC, from Predictive Index to Rembrandt to this one, the narratives all sounded the same. From *you thrive on challenge, constantly seeking out new and unique scenarios that test and push the boundaries of your skillsets and knowledge,* to *you hold others around you to the same high standards you expect of yourself. Your workstation is neat, orderly, you often wonder why others don't approach their work in the same efficient manner you do.*

"Maybe this one will be different, Nixy," Cavanaugh says as she pulls the report from the printer. "Let's see, shall we?" She reads the report's narrative aloud.

"In the Self-Perception measure, Drew's defining dimensions are Persistence and Process. Both are two full sigmas above the norm-line, which represents the average measure of all PPS participants. These dimensional rankings exceed those of ninety-three percent of the PPS sampling. Ratings for Personability and Patience fall one-and-one-quarter sigma below the norm-line, indicating Drew as a person who places higher value on process and data than people and feelings.

Notable changes are observed in the line graph displaying Projection. Here, there is a significant rise in the Patience dimension. A decrease in the Persistence dimension, within one-standard point of the increase in Patience, indicates Drew may feel less autonomous and more reliant on the actions, approvals and authority of others."

Cavanaugh reads the rest silently, anger building. Clearly Ward's decision had had an effect. The report makes this clear.

Not anymore.

She palms her mouse and scrolls down the digital version of the report until she lands on the hyperlinked accept button at the bottom of the page.

Badger was right. I'm getting this case back.

She clicks the *accept* button, triggering an auto-generated email with instructions, an address and a new questionnaire she must complete before attending her first SR session.

She compares this to the prior email she'd received. This is not the address to Anlon Hall, nor is Doyen Cave copied.

Interesting.

***

NATHAN BADGER

AMERICAN AIRLINES
FLIGHT #296

"My name is Dr. Brown," the bearded man announces. "Miriam, I'd like you to please lay down here. Nathan, you'll be next to her here. Then you."

He points to the next empty gurney. Ellen, Charlie, Manuel and Eddie and the boy are already cinched down and deep asleep, though the room is bright. Far too bright. Not a single shadow to hide in.

"We agreed," a disembodied voice snaps. "He's to be treated like the others."

I lay still on the bed as I'm strapped down, as electrodes are pressed against my temples. Look for heroes on the white ceiling. Find none.

When he's finished preparing each of us, Brown walks a wobbly duck-duck-goose circle around us to the words of a song, touching our heads one by one as he passes. "Ring around the Rosie, a pocket full of posies, ashes, ashes, we all fall down." His hand lands on Miriam last. "It will be you."

"Leave my friend alone," I demand, trying in vain to pry myself out of the straps. Brown cuts a piece of duct tape from a spool on the table nearest me and slaps it over my mouth. The bitter taste of glue stings my tongue.

"Now, Miriam. You're angry with s-someone in the room. You're angry with someone, Miriam. With one of the boys. Which one are you angry with?"

"No, I'm not," she protests.

Her back arches, she lets out an excruciating scream.

"Mmmeeeee! Mmmm mmmmeeeee!" I yell through the tape, try to push it away with my tongue.

"Just t-tell us who you're angry with."

"I, I told you I'm—" A second scream stabs my eardrums.

"Mmmmm!"

"Who are you *angry* with, M-Miriam?"

She surrenders before the next jolt of electricity is administered. "I'm angry with him." I lean up enough to see her point at the nameless boy lying strapped to the gurney on my right.

"You shouldn't pick me," the nameless boy warns in a whispered, nasally threat. A tear crawls down Miriam's pleading face as she stares at me, eyes begging me to take action.

I push harder at the tape with my tongue.

"Take this," Brown says, "and show him your anger."

Miriam's eyes now filled with tears. She's trembling, I watch her fight against all instincts to do the thing asked of her.

"Stop this now," cries the disembodied voice.

"Do n-not interfere," replies Brown as a massive force strikes the boy, causing his back to arch up in the air, and his face to wrench against agonizing pain.

"Enough I said!"

"When you are angry, you hurt others," Brown tells Miriam before turning his attention to the nameless boy, "And you, when you are hurting, you cut."

"When you are hurting, you cut."

You are hurt.

You cut.

Cut.

CUT!

Branches spread across the floor to the gurney I'm strapped to, climbing up. Taking hold of me.

"Sir?"

They stretch toward my neck and clamp down like a vise.

"Sir!"

The flight attendant shakes me awake. "Wha-where?" The front of my shirt is covered in blood.

"Lean your head back." She covers my face with a cold towel. "This will help."

I reach into my pocket and take hold of the ring, repeating *Cuimhne,* the word I learned as a child. The woods are dark. There's an ominous chill to the wind whipping up fury in the trees lining the path.

A flash of lightning strikes in front of me.

Charly and I playing in front of a tent.

An adult's hand reaching down to Charly.

Ellen, alone, crying.

Dr. Brown brings us down to the basement.

A boy in the shadows holding a knife.

When you are hurting, you cut.

"Mr. Badger, we'll have medical staff help you after we land. Just lean back and try to relax. Press the call button if you need anything else."

A porcelain mask shatters to pieces on the floor.

"Ladies and gentlemen, as we start our descent, please make sure your seat backs and tray tables are in their upright position. Make sure your seat belt is securely fastened and all carry-on luggage is stowed underneath the seat in front of you or in the overhead bins."

A boy walks toward the closet, knife in hand. Miriam's shuddering sobs echo inside.

"Let me see," the flight attendant says, removing the towel. "Better, looks better." My thoughts come back to focus on the reassuring smile she gives me before moving down the aisle to reach her seat at the front of the plane and strapping herself in.

The woman next to me stares out the window. I've made her uncomfortable. Across the aisle, a man shuts down his laptop while checking his phone. Rows and rows of others move their seats into position, stow their items.

I sit motionless, numb, unsure how to process what just happened.

Outside my window, the harbor lined with boats grows in size. We thud onto the runway.

"Ladies and gentlemen, welcome to San Diego, where the local time is 4:06 p.m. We ask that you please stay seated once the plane has landed as medical staff will be boarding to help one of our passengers."

The seatbelt light goes off to the sound of a ding. Lookie-loo passengers scan all the rows until they spot me, bloody towel pressed against my face.

The paramedics arrive as the last head rotates back. The first fixes his dull, laboring eyes on me. His left slightly droops, the outer rim of each sclera is lined in red. His nose resembles that of an aged cage fighter, crooked as Lombard Street, pressed flat to his face. The second paramedic, close behind him, pushes a wheel-chair. He stands no taller than five-four. The sleeves of his uniform are rolled up to the elbows, exposing the familiar *Kouf Mem* symbol of Krav Maga.

Crooked Nose removes a penlight from his pocket, clicks it on. "Follow the light, eyes only please."

I push up and out of my seat, the compress drops to the floor. "It's a nosebleed. I'm fine." Kouf Mem pushes a button on his two-way radio. He mumbles something, a response squeaks back and he motions his partner back a few steps.

They exchange words, Crooked Nose returns. "We'll secure your luggage and have it brought to us. Please," he says, motioning to the chair.

"Don't need it."

He places a hand on my shoulder. "Airport regula-tions, sir."

I have my tactical pen as a weapon. Let's see where this leads.

As I'm being wheeled through the airport, I take my cellphone off airplane mode. One missed call and a text message including a photo. Both from Claire. She's sent a page from her scrapbook, it's her and me as children, clothes covered in mud.

Ω

A man in his early twenties dressed in a bright or-ange Tommy Bahamas Hawaiian print shirt, cut off tan shorts and flip-flops with a beer bottle opener molded into the underside watches the last bag being taken off the carrousel by an airport security guard.

He picks up his guitar case, slides the strap over the telescoping handle of his wheeled suitcase and heads outside of Baggage Claim #1 to a grey metal bench before sending a text.

Across the street, a Hispanic woman, mid-twenties, dressed in a hunter-green business suit waits impatiently for the crosswalk light to turn. She checks her cellphone, looks up at the sky and lets out a frustrated sigh.

The light changes. She follows a pack of travelers toward the lower-level entrance of the San Diego Airport. The man in the Hawaiian shirt spots her, smiles and winks. She winks back, then swats her hand through the air as though shooing him away before she answers an incoming call.

She finds the designated smoking area nearest Baggage Claim #1 and has a seat at the bench. A man opposite her puffs on a grape-flavored cigar. She checks her phone again, taps in a text, then takes out a Vape pen from her purse.

His ride now arriving, the man in the Hawaiian shirt grabs his things and rushes toward the waiting car. He throws the guitar and his suitcase in the trunk and hops in the back seat. He nods to the Hispanic woman as they roll by her. She nods back.

"You guys figure out what happened?" he asks.

"Badger had an issue on the plane. EMTs took him off. He's still there," says a man dressed in sweatpants, a Lakers tank top, white knee-high socks and a pair of Kobe's.

"All dressed up for nothin' I guess," Hawaiian-shirt guy says.

"Elena's in position by baggage claim. We have the other exits covered as well. They'll alert us when he leaves."

"And then what?"

"Then we await further orders."

The call from Elena comes minutes later. "He's on his way now. Run a trace to see who he's talking to?"

"It's already done. Out."

Ω

"After all these years," Claire says. "You missed the beautiful celebration of life we held for Ellie. So, um. I'm sorry. It's horrible."

"You were close to her?" I ask.

"We stayed in touch. The Society hosted a beautiful tribute to her. I'm home today with Clarisse. She has a fever. I can scan and send it to you if you give me your email address."

"Please. And Claire, I have no words for what happened," I tell her. But it's a lie. I do have words. Words like anger, like betrayal. Like retribution. Ellie is dead. My friends are dead. And I need to know why.

I get straight to the point. "I've been to see Miriam Hill, and I need your help."

***

14

CAVANAUGH

DOWNTOWN SAN DIEGO

Cavanaugh surveys the comings and goings at the two-story post office across the street, wondering which, if any, will become the next to go missing. Ragged men, weather-worn women, dirty-faced children wait in a line forming at the base of the steps leading up to an open door on the second floor, where a greeter guards stacks of foam plates and utensils.

Nearby her, a ground-floor door opens at a four-story condo complex. A couple emerges, dressed from toe to head in flip flops, shorts, unzipped down jackets, matching sweaters underneath, Christmas scarves strung around their necks. Her chullo is black and brown, adorned by a row of alpaca-shaped figures. His explodes in patterns of pinks, purples and oranges. Their Frenchie snorts and wheezes toward Cavanaugh, testing the boundaries of his leash.

Cavanaugh is reminded of the life she almost had.

"Nietzsche, here boy," the man calls, treat in hand. Nietzsche reaches Cavanaugh's leg; she calculates exactly how much drool she'll later have to launder out of her pressed pants. To her relief, the dog's owner yanks it back before drool reaches wool.

Farther up the road, signage announces the latest restaurant to open in a revolving door location where three concepts came and went in as many years. It used to be a ramen place Cavanaugh frequented at least twice a week when she worked downtown. Her ex-fiancée had taken her there.

They had really good noodles, she tells herself, pushing the memory aside.

She stops before the metal gate she was instructed to enter. It opens into a walkway between the dumpy strip mall's rear graffiti-tagged doors and an adjacent building. The last graffiti-tagged door on her left matches the address she'd been given.

She enters the code from the email she'd received and pushes her way inside, and into a small square chamber. No receptionist. No waiting room furniture. Only two metal doors, one straight ahead, one to her right, which is cold to her touch.

A sound emanates from behind it. The muffled chanting of a strange, single word. Cavanaugh finds herself keeping count.

One, two, three times it repeats.

A curtain of brilliant sky-blue lights cascade down the right wall of the square, revealing a virtual keypad.

Six. Seven. Eight. Nine times it repeats.

She enters her six-digit code.

The chant continues. Twelve. Thirteen times.

The chanting stops.

Her detective's instincts ignite; she presses an ear to the cold metal door.

Then a different sound.

"The basement is off limits, Drew Cavanaugh," a pitch perfect computerized voice calls out to her from the top of the stairs.

What Cavanaugh sees next steals away every other thought. Rotating laser lights beam down from the ceiling, forming the projection of a female in her mid-fifties, mixed descent, Spanish, Middle Eastern possibly. "My name is Willa. I'll be with you today." A welcoming gesture from the projected hands. "Please join me?"

A complex, wheeled apparatus guides the laser projector above the doorway at the top of the steps. Apprehensively, Cavanaugh follows it. There, the thing that is Willa motions first toward the row of closed doors to her right, then to the ones on her left. Cavanaugh counts six on each side.

"These are our orientation rooms, Drew Cavanaugh. Please select one and I'll meet you inside." The laser image begins to fade, particles of dust light up in the air surrounding it until it's gone.

"Excuse me. Uh, Willa." No answer.

"I'm talking to a laser," she mumbles to herself.

"You have questions," Willa's voice emanates from overhead. "Please select a room so I may answer them."

The wheeled apparatus squeakily trails behind Cavanaugh as she walks down the hallway lined with doors, looking alternately across the hall to one, then the next. She stops at the second to last one on the right, pausing a moment to take a deep breath before entering.

Here we go.

"The invariant right," Willa says, materializing in the front of the room.

"Sorry?" Cavanaugh says.

"You're right-handed. Statistics would indicate a room on your right to be your choice."

"What else do you know about me, based on your statistics?"

Willa stands still, silent. Her shape glitches, a crease slides down the projection of her body, cutting Willa's face, breasts, torso nearly neatly in half. "Nothing else statistically important for tonight's conversation," she eventually replies.

"Then what *is* important for tonight's conversation?"

The crease slides down the projection of Willa's once again. "Why you chose me, of course."

"Why I chose? Explain what you mean." Cavanaugh sits down in the room's only chair, lightly taps a finger against her neatly pressed pants.

"I see you're impatient," Willa says.

Cavanaugh stops tapping, gives the dark walls and ceilings a once over for cameras before getting up from her chair.

She sidesteps to the right; Willa mirrors her movement. She steps left, Willa mirrors again. Cavanaugh gives the room another once over, still finding no cameras.

"Drew Cavanaugh, what would you like to master today?" Willa asks.

"Not master. Learn. I read an interesting article covering a closed case involving SR treatments like yours. Do you have access to this information?"

"We're here to talk about you. With permission, I'd like to discuss the PPS report you received. You've experienced significant shifts between Self-Perception and Projection. I'd like to learn why."

"My questions first, Willa. Starting with this. What *is* SR?"

"Schema Realignment begins with uncovering self-limiting perceptions."

Cavanaugh moves back to the chair, sits. "Explain...Please."

"I've studied you, Drew Cavanaugh. You have a degree in criminology from UC Irvine. My records indicate it is a most reputable program."

Caught momentarily off-guard by the memories flooding back, she sinks down in the chair, then as an afterthought finally acknowledges. "Graduated with honors."

"After, you joined the San Diego Police Department. You advanced through the ranks to detective quite rapidly. I can project the press release of your promotion to detective if you'd like."

"I know what it says," Cavanaugh snaps back.

"And *I* know how it ends," Willa's curt and emphatic reply. "There's a two-year gap in your employment history, during which you traveled. Rome, Venice, Florence. You took time off to recover, did you not?"

Defenseless, Cavanaugh reflexively tugs at her shirtsleeve. Feels the scars on her wrists start to burn. Watches the life she nearly had fall to ashes before her.

"Show me, Drew Cavanaugh," Willa demands.

"Show you what?" Cavanaugh jets up from her chair. "This?" Pulling up her sleeve, exposing her scars. "How would *you* know, Willa? My injuries were never made public."

"Oh, but they were. By you. There are many old photos on your social media profiles. You spent weekends with friends. You played volleyball on the beach. You once had a love. Then one day, no more photos of friends. None of you with your love. Everything changes. Even the way you dress. Long sleeve shirts replace short sleeve blouses. Bright colors fade to grey, brown, and black. You went to Italy alone. These are the last photos you posted. Tell me, why you haven't deleted your profile?"

Cavanaugh is slow to say the words aloud, but she does. "So I never forget what I lost."

"There's more to life than burying yourself in your job. Coming home to an empty apartment where you work into the late hours every night. Drew Cavanaugh, it's not working. You have so much to give, so much insight, life experience. You need to be back on the beach playing volleyball. Traveling. Loving someone."

"Not open for discussion, Willa." Cavanaugh feels her throat tighten and bolts toward the door. Wheels roll above her.

Memories strike her like gut-punches. Memories of how it all changed after Havens.

How her fiancée stopped touching her after she was released from the hospital. How their plans to start a family were suddenly gone. How she watched him pack the last of his things. How awkwardly each call went when she told friends and family their wedding was off.

"You don't have to hide anymore," Willa says before Cavanaugh shoots out the exit door nearly breathless. A man in a grey hooded sweatshirt stands in the shadows, looks her up and down. She glares back, adrenaline coursing through her veins, fists clenched. The man's eyes fall to the ground.

She finally calms when she arrives home to Nixy.

But still hears Willa's words.

You don't have to hide anymore.

Maybe you're right.

Cavanaugh pours a half glass full of Gentlemen Jack and clicks open the bookmarked Paradign page. She reads the announcement above the video of the former addict, now basketball player.

Join Us for the Third in a Series of Lectures on The Serenities, led by Doyen Michael Cave. The lecture begins at 7:30 p.m.

Tonight.

* * *

NATHAN BADGER

HIGHWAY 67, RAMONA

Claire confirmed it.

Miriam Hill lived most of her life in an institution. Muted. Silenced, until she met Kenneth Bish and the dominoes toppled. Edward Shea is dead. Ellen O'Bannon is dead. Charles Breen is dead. Manuel Ortiz is dead. Four people whose lives are connected to mine are dead. Murdered. Four childhood friends I didn't remember having.

But I remember now.

Landmarks on my drive home fly by. Mount Woodson. The Rashelica Winery. The rodeo field. My car turns right onto Dye Road. I'm long down San Vicente before I first take notice of my speed. And ignore it.

There's a delivery truck behind me, I click my right turn signal before rounding the corner, passing a few parked cars on the side of my road and pulling up and into the now open garage.

The truck beeps its way up the long driveway behind me and stops within a foot of the garage door.

"Package," the driver announces, after getting out of his truck. "I need a signature."

"You have the wrong house," I tell him.

"You're Nathanial Badger, correct?"

I slip a throwing knife from my wall safe into my pocket. "I am. Wait there."

He unclips a digital pad from his belt as I approach.

I take it from him and glance at the delivery ticket. Looks legit, though I don't recognize the return address. Once I've signed, he leans in and whispers, "I'm Agent Michael Cave with the FBI. Act normal."

We square up on each other.

I slip my hand in the pocket holding the knife, offer the driver a smile, then whisper back. "Prove it. And no sudden moves."

"Can't." He points at the house, then the garage, as though he's asking me where he should make the delivery. "Please go to the back of your garage. Close the garage door when the packages are inside."

"Not before you show me some identification."

He nods, as though to confirm. "We're being watched. One of the cars parked on the road. Now please go inside."

The rear door of the truck slides up. Cave steps inside, comes out holding a very large, but apparently light box.

He carries it inside; a man and a woman slip out the back of the truck behind him and slide under the garage door as it closes.

That's when I see her.

Kah-thuhm.

I was lied to.

Kah-thuhm. Kah-thuhm.

It's coming again.

Kah-thuhm. Kah-thuhm. Kah-thuhm. My pulse trips along like the foot of a coked-up drummer.

"What are you doing here, Maibel? If that's even your real name.," I say, pointing a shaking finger in accusation.

She looks back, solemn. "Hello, Mr. Nathan. Let's go inside."

I don't budge. "You didn't answer my question."

She reaches for a card, my eyes flash back in warning. Her hand freezes midair. "My name *is* Maibel Ross. I'm a Senior Agent with the Violent Crimes Against Children Task Force at the FBI. We need to talk."

My eyes burn into hers. "You lied to me at the hospital. *What* do you want?"

She glances over at the man, who nods back at her. "You went to see a woman in Wheaton. I've spent the better part of my career following the man in her drawings." Her eyes harden. "The same man you were sent to in Bogotá."

"You *knew* about Bogotá, and you didn't come forward?" I charge up to her, she casts a glance at the man and holds up her palm. I size him up, athletic, alert, calm. Trained. No matter. He's mine if he makes a move. "All record of that flight was erased. I was never on it. Your doing?"

"No. Not our doing," she assures me.

"Bullshit. This has all the earmarks of an FBI operation." Adrenaline courses through my bloodstream like a dozen wild horses at the whip. The man with her notices, takes a step back, appearing to ready an attack.

I point a warning finger at him, he backs off. "Someone tortured Abby. You let me the police think I did it."

"Mr. Nathan, we *know* who's responsible."

"Then give me a name and address and go. You have no currency with me."

"It's not that simple. Let's go inside and talk, please." She motions again toward the door.

"I'll ask you again. Who took Abby?"

"You need to hear what we've come to tell you," the man with her says.

His tight fitting, color-mismatched outfit reveals the tone body of a runner. He's in his early sixties, if a day. He has the face of an academician, completing the look with wire-rim glasses and a grey-specked red mustache. There's a genuineness to his demeanor that in other circumstances I might find disarming. Not today.

"Let me guess, Eastcott is it?" I ask, casting a sideways glance.

"Dr. Richard F. Eastcott," he says, offering his hand. I don't take it.

He makes a show of studying my shirt. "Nosebleeds, I assume?"

"What of it?"

"You've had new memories, haven't you?" a mild look of curiosity forms on his face.

"Yeah, I have. Again, what of it?" I glare at one, then the other.

"It fits," his cryptic response.

I've had enough. I direct what I say next to the FBI agent. "Listen to me. I respect law enforcement. I respect the FBI. But you lied to me at the hospital. Why?"

"Not here," she replies, pointing toward my front door. "Please trust us."

"Tru—" Anger freezes the word on my lips. We stand there in an awkward standoff until I can again speak. "*Trust* you, you said?"

"Yes," Eastcott replies. "You need to trust us. And you need to hear what we've come here to say."

I lock eyes on him and hold an uncomfortable stare. Resolve hardens his.

"Fine." I slam open the side door, disable the alarm with my phone and make a show of gesturing them inside.

This is when they first see my shrine. They exchange glances again. "As expected," Agent Ross says as she takes a seat at the dining room table, digs into her bag and hands me an old black-and-white photograph.

The children in it stand before a shrine just like mine.

"What I'm going to show you next comes from searches conducted in the homes of several convicted felons made after their arrests."

She lays out each piece of evidence one at a time. "Police found this in Samuel Moore's basement. This one in Daniel Mazer's bedroom. This one is from Paul James Pellen's dining room."

All shrines, just like mine.

For a brief moment I'm back in the woods. Back where it's not safe. Back where my memories are guarded.

"Who are they?" I ask, nerves dulled.

It's Eastcott's turn. "You have a very specific collection of books too, don't you Mr. Badger?"

"Enough with the questions." I pound the table once, shoot them each a warning glare. "Answers, remember?"

"Maibel, show him."

She lays down three new police evidence photos.

They're of bookshelves filled with copies of The Wizard of Oz.

"May I see yours?" Eastcott asks.

I take him into the living room. He pulls several out, one at a time.

"Collector's editions, I see. Each purchased one year apart to the day, December 15th. But where is this year's copy?" he asks.

"I'm late," my reply.

***

CAVANAUGH

The Serenities

Through the hardship, character. Through the pain, clarity.

Through the unplugging, awareness. Through the awareness, rebirth.

Through the rebirth, deliverance.

Serenity Four - Awareness

I am the author of me.
I am the composer. I am the conductor.
I am not part of your world.
I am of the one I create.

Cavanaugh folds the flyer she just read once, then again, and shoves it into the back pocket of her jeans.

Suppose we'll all be chanting this together.

She takes in the room, expecting to see seats filled with New Age hippie men dressed in hemp-woven shirts sporting man-buns, women with matted hair and hairy legs named Dharma or Sage, wild-eyed former junkies-turned-zealots who'd traded up for a new addiction.

Instead, she sees everyday people. Men whose ties match their socks. A row full of college-aged kids. A husband and wife waving to their young child, who looks out at them from the nursery room window, surrounded by rainbows and a few other children.

She even sees a sharply dressed woman in her mid-forties she recognizes from a front-page article she'd read as Cheryl Ganbergh, COO of Jentaine Technologies, one of the largest military contractors in California.

She watches a handsome man, mid-thirties, emerge from an adjacent door and bound onto the stage. Doyen Michael Cave, she guesses, the name CC'd on the first email she received.

"Good evening all. And a special welcome to our first-time members," Doyen Cave says, glancing down at the notecard he's holding. "Sparrow, where are you?" A girl seated to her far right raises her arm, a hint of underarm hair peeks out from her sleeveless blouse.

I fucking knew it, Cavanaugh thinks.

"Welcome, Sparrow." Cave glances down at his notecard a second time, "Drew Cavanaugh. Raise your hand please, Drew." She'd been dreading this, still she reluctantly raises her arm. All eyes fall on her.

"Welcome to both of you," Cave says. "We have an incredible session tonight. So glad you could join in." He clicks a button on the remote, and a screen behind him fills with the four-line affirmation. "Tonight, we continue our series on The Serenities, with an exercise you'll each participate in, one I think you'll all find quite revealing. Before we get to it, we'll begin as we always do. Please prepare."

All around Cavanaugh, the unbuttoning of buttons, the loosening of shirtsleeves to expose the matching taupe-colored Mala beads each audience member is wearing. Cavanaugh puts her head down and thinks of her scars.

"Drew," Doyen Cave makes his way from the stage to her. "This is for you. We'll each repeat today's discernment 108 times silently." He hands her a set of Mala beads. "You can begin whenever you're ready," he says, before slipping off toward Sparrow.

Cavanaugh studies the room full of Paradignists mouthing the affirmation, turning a single bead in full rotation after each recitation.

"I am the author," she begins, now surprised by a sudden wave of anger toward Ward.

Fucking case closed, she repeats while spinning her beads.

When enough heads are raised, Cave breaks the silence. "I am the author of me… but are we really? Awareness. How much of it do we actually have? We think of ourselves as mindful beings. We choose to believe that the decisions we make come from a place of inner control, with supporting rationale. But do they?" Cave paces back and forth on stage. Intensity builds. His steps quicken. "We spoke of stimulus and response in our last session. How many of you completed the assigned lifework?" Every hand but two in the room go up. "Very good. Now let's get started. First, please join me in welcoming my facilitators for tonight's exercise."

From behind a curtain at the back of the stage, six people emerge. Two of them white men dressed in identical, impeccably tailored navy-blue suits, matching oxford brown lace-ups, styled black hair parted on the right. Both clean shaven, both holding briefcases in their left hands.

The other four, two loving couples. Two men in their early thirties hold hands and wave at the audience. Opposite them, a radiant black woman fidgets with her wedding ring as she looks adoringly into the eyes of her husband, who looks to be of Scandinavian descent.

Cave taps on the microphone lightly, once, then again. "Ladies and gentlemen, what matters most to you? What will you stand fast for, what are you willing to sacrifice for the greater good, the higher purpose? We're about to find out. Please count off by twos."

A chorus of *ones* and *twos* fills the air until the person seated in the very last chair in the back of the room, Cavanaugh, calls out, "Two."

"Thank you all. Those of you in Group One, please assemble in there," he says, motioning to the empty room next to the nursery. "You'll be joined momentarily by these two couples." He points to a second empty room. "Those of you in Group Two will be joined in there by these young businessmen. Go now," he says to the growing rumble of chairs, "you'll receive further instructions inside."

Cavanaugh notices a man noticing her as she stands. He smiles. She blushes and turns away to join her group, who've already settled into a room that looks like the bullpen of a telemarketing company. Motivational posters line the wall, and familiar grey-carpeted cubicles semi-separate one group from the next.

Glengarry Glenn Ross plays on the television set mounted to the wall. The scene with Alec Baldwin at the chalkboard.

Cavanaugh take a seat in the last open cubicle and straightens the seams of her dress pants.

"Mind if I join you?"

Cavanaugh glances up at the man. They lock eyes before she looks away. "Sure." She feels heat flush her face once again, unsure why.

He offers his hand. "My name's Jerry."

She looks up. Steel-blue eyes meet hers again.

"Um. Drew."

"Nice to meet you, Drew. Are you enjoying your first session?"

"Jury's still out."

"As it should be," he replies. His good-natured way, his manner disarms her. "Let me know if you reach a verdict."

"You'll be the second to know," she says with a smile, then blushes again, surprised at how nervous she feels.

Businessman One passes out papers. Cavanaugh gets a red one, Jerry's is yellow.

Businessman Two speaks in a commanding baritone voice: "If I can have your attention. Your attention please." He removes a Montblanc from his breast pocket, using it as a pointer. "Those of you holding red papers. Those with red only, please read the instructions carefully. When you've finished, report outside the front door for a briefing. Those with yellow sheets will wait here. Let's go people."

Cavanaugh scans her red paper and her pulse starts drumming in her ears.

What the hell? she thinks, when she reaches the end. *This can't be right.* She sneaks a furtive glance at the people around her to see if they're having similar reactions, but everyone is too busy reading.

An uneasiness crawls up from her gut as she settles in to read the paper again.

***

BADGER HOME
RAMONA, CA

How could they know about my books?

Ross, Eastcott and I reconvene in my dining room. I get there first and slip into the chair at the head of the table, leaving them to take the seats to my left and right. They may have ambushed me in the garage, I'm not going to let them keep calling the shots.

It's time for those answers I'm promised.

"Tell me about your memories," Eastcott says.

"You wanna know? They started at the hospital. The campfire I told my *nurse* here about. A bearded man pulling a girl from a campfire. Pulling Miriam from a campfire. I had more on the plane. Of me, my friends. The same bearded man. He was conducting experiments on us. That what you're after?"

"Yes. Mr. Badger," Eastcott answers, pointing at my shirt. "Precisely what I'm after. The nosebleeds come after these memories?"

"I think we both know the answer," I tell him.

"Would you like to know why you're having these nosebleeds?"

I can count on one hand the number of times in my adult life I've not felt in control. The first, Bogotá. The second, in the driveway with Abby. The third, yesterday, seeing Miriam. Today, right now marks the fourth. And I don't like how it feels.

My foster parents once told me I suffered a traumatic brain injury. A neurologist once told me I lost memory.

"I would *like* to know *everything*," I finally respond.

"And you will." Eastcott stares out the window, appearing to organize his thoughts. His next words animate him. He begins pacing the room like an attorney giving his opening statement. And I'm the jury of one.

"Understand this," he says. "What we know and what we can prove are two very different things. Let's focus on what we know. Agent Ross will tell you the origin story. It explains *how* we know."

Eastcott stops pacing. Agent Ross touches my hand.

"This may not be easy," she says.

"The truth. Now," my reply.

"What started all this?" she begins. "A document purge was ordered in 1973, the goal of it to erase all record of joint experiments the Central and Defense Intelligence Agencies conducted. Unfortunately for both, nearly twenty-thousand records survived and were released by way of a Freedom of Information Act filing, though heavily redacted. A handful, including the black-and-white photos I showed you, documented the goings-on at the Naval Air Weapons Station, China Lake. Specifically, the experiments conducted on children by a man named Dr. Sebastian Allende."

I close my eyes and picture the drawings. The dance. Him. "Lemme guess," I say. "This doctor has a beard."

"Indeed he does." Eastcott's glasses slide down to the tip of his nose. "His work at China Lake continued until sometime in 1984 when the program was officially shut down. What we know of his methods inform us that the children who were experimented on underwent severe traumas as part of what was labelled The Conduit Program. All memory of the things done to them, we suspect, were hidden behind these severe traumas, creating a dissociative amnesia effect. The mind, you see, protects us from reliving traumatic events as a natural defense mechanism."

He points again at my bloody shirt.

"I spent many sessions with two of the three people with shrines in their homes we referenced earlier. At the end, one drew a picture of a bearded man. The others recalled a man named Dr. Brown. That's as far as I could get."

"You pointed at my shirt. Come out and say it. Give a name to what stopped you," I tell him.

"Each had adverse physical reactions, some quite severe."

"I said, give it a name."

The Agent's lips purse. Her eyes soften. "I think you know."

"What are you. What?" I leap up from the table.

Kah-thuhm.

The little moments I've grown to question.

Kah-thuhm. Kah-thuhm.

Little moments I lose, snatched away like a seashell in high tide.

Kah-thuhm. Kah-thuhm. Kah-thuhm.

My foster parents lied.

The neurologist lied.

I tear the off bloody shirt. Throw it at the Buddha statue.

"I told you this may not be easy," Ross says.

My breath becomes staggered, short. I gasp for air. My throat closes.

A word echoes through the room around me.

There's a television set bracketed to the dining room wall. It's the same size as the one in the room in Bogotá I was kept in. It begins a slow turn, then fractures into a trio.

Cuimhne.

Three screens melt into one.

Cuimhne.

My breathing slows.

Cuimhne.

Concerned faces stare back at me.

"Cuimhne," Eastcott repeats.

Agent Ross leaves, returns to the dining room with a clean shirt from my closet.

"Please put it on, Mr. Nathan" she says, with a reassuring shake of her head.

"I'm fine," I tell her.

Eastcott looks to Ross. She nods.

"Was there anyone else in your dreams other than the bearded man, Ms. Hill and your friends?"

"There was a boy," my reply.

They exchange knowing glances again.

"Mr. Nathan, do you know of the events involving the Celestial Temple?" she asks.

"Bolsiver? Yes," I reply.

"We believe this is where Allende went after China Lake. We have evidence indicating he was there at the end. When the bodies burned. When the blades were unsheathed. When the bullets were loaded."

"And he didn't stop it," Eastcott adds.

"He made it out alive. How *lucky* for him," I say.

"Yes, he escaped. Not alone. Our evidence suggests Allende helped a man and two young children escape. A boy and a girl."

"You are suggesting it's *the* boy?"

"The one in your dreams? It's highly likely," Eastcott answers.

"So they escaped to Wheaton. Why?"

"We have theories, but they're not what's important. Here's what is: The man Allende rescued from Bolsiver, we now know, went on to found a New Age belief system you're no doubt familiar with. Paradign."

"Call it what it is. It's a cult. You're saying Allende rescued Cathal Kane?"

Ross touches my hand. "Yes, Mr. Nathan, he rescued Cathal. Richard, please show him what you brought back with you."

Eastcott produces three yearbooks from his satchel.

I study the covers. "From the Theosophical Society. You were there."

"We needed confirmation." Eastcott opens the first of three books, this one dated Summer Recess, 1985. "You see?" he asks, pointing to a photo of me and my now dead friends. "And here," opening the next book, this one from 1986.

"I already know I was there."

"That's the point. *He* knows you know," Ross says. "And when you went public about researching your new book, when you asked people with stories about our government's involvement in cults to come forward, we think it raised alarm bells."

"You're telling me I caused this? All this happened because of my book? Abby? My friends?"

"I'm sorry," Ross tells me. "I warned you."

"I'm fine. We done here? I have a doctor to find."

She closes her eyes and goes silent. Eastcott stares at the floor.

"What?" I demand.

"I'm sorry," she says. "Truly sorry."

"Sorry for what?"

"For what we're about to tell you next," she replies. "But you need context first. Alexi Kostov. Do you recognize the name?"

"The Russian magnate," I reply. "Yeah, I do. Why?"

"Kostov had strong Kremlin ties. They turned him by surfacing evidence of his extramarital affairs. Threesomes, BDSM. Nastier things. Kostov's father-in-law sat on the board of Sberbank. Kostov had a lot to lose if all this got out."

"Yeah, like his life," I say, remembering the news coverage. "He fled the country. They found him dead in a hotel room in Brazil. What *about* Kostov?"

Ross pulls another file from her bag. "This is the only other recovered photo from China Lake. You see what's in the background?"

A shrine. Bookshelves. Books. Five young girls.

She points to a girl in the photo. "This one, the girl on the far left, and the one next to her. Both were sent to Kostov. Both are institutionalized now. They have no memory of what happened. Of Kostov, or of anything before him. We only know of their involvement from surveillance photographs taken at a hotel he used for his dalliances. The women experienced complete amnesia, the wiping of their hard drives if you will. The China Lake papers called it Gamma programming. Erase codes. *Human* erase codes."

"Like Miriam Hill," I stammer out, the weight of it stealing my breath.

"Just like Miriam Hill," Eastcott answers.

"What about the other girls?" I ask.

"They're all dead. Suicides. Omegas. It's important you know how they did it."

"They used knives, didn't they?"

"You're starting to understand."

"Am I?"

"Have you ever been to Brazil, Mr. Nathan?"

"I don't talk about those days."

Eastcott points to my shrine. "Were you?"

"I believe you heard me. I don't *talk* about those days.

Because those days never happened. I wasn't there when the in-country asset who grew up in the Rocinha favelas watched her oldest brother and uncle get zipped into bags.

I wasn't there when the last bullet was fired, when the unflinching brutality of *the Chagas* reign ended.

I wasn't there.

"Next subject. You know all this about Allende, why the fuck haven't you done something?"

Ross' eyes begin to water. "I presented my findings," she tells me. "Everything I've just told you, so much more I can't tell you. They called it my Suspect Zero theory. Before I could take it public, they took my husband Carl and presented me with a choice. See Carl go to prison or back off the case."

"They who? CIA? DIA?"

"DIA."

"I see the inference here. Give it a name. You're saying the DIA is responsible for taking and torturing Abby?"

"No, Mr. Nathan. We think they *sent* her to you."

"Sent her?" It hits like a punch in the gut. The day we first met. How she knew my coffee order.

"Do you remember the exact date you met Abby?"

"What difference would that make?"

"Humor us," Ross says, taking out a new file labeled *Betas*.

"Sometime last July," I reply. Hearing myself say it, it becomes clear. Crystal clear. "Right after I announced my research for the new book on my website."

"We have a working theory. They sent her to find out just how much you knew, how much you'd remembered. And to influence you to stop your research."

"So, if you're right." I say, working it out in my head. "If you're right, that still doesn't explain why she was taken. Unless."

They both wait for me to connect the dots.

"Unless when she couldn't stop me, they took her. And punished her. Punished her right after I did the *GMA* interview."

"And you were sent to the master programmer. Allende. In Bogotá."

Ross opens the Beta file. Removes a photo of Abby and, behind it, what appears to be her psychological profile.

I rest my head in my hands. It takes time for me to come to even accept the betrayal. Once I do, Ross hands me the photo.

"What happens now?"

"We help you remember more. It could give us the proof we need, and it may prove to be a safeguard for you. Richard will stay back and work with you. We see where it leads us, what else you remember."

"You want me to let him inside my head, there's a price," I tell her, crumpling Abby's photo into a ball and winging it as hard as I can at the wall. "I get Allende."

Ross and Eastcott exchange glances again. "This is about the greater good, Mr. Nathan. If Richard's successful, we may be able to bring our case against him out of the shadows and fully into the light of day. Maybe one day he'll be made to atone for what we suspect he's done. What he did to my Carl, to so many others…"

"And I'll be there looking him in the eyes when he atones. Maybe with my hands on his throat. Maybe something else there instead. Maybe the edge of my blade."

Her response: "That's not how this works, Mr. Nathan."

Mine: "It is now."

"One step at a time," Ross says before sending a text. Her phone lights up just after. "Michael's pulling up now. Walk me out, Mr. Nathan."

She stops just outside of the front of the door and turns back to me. "You were right about the drugs, by the way."

"What drugs?" I ask. The answer hits me as the last word leaves my mouth. "The drugs they found when they tested mine and Abby's blood. How do *you* know about my theory?"

She taps away at her phone screen. "I just do. I emailed you the hospital tox reports. I also sent you Miriam Hill's 1987 admission report. Call it all a show of good faith."

I open the email on my phone and confirm. The chemicals in our systems match. Two of them at least.

"Notice there's a third chemical on your report only. Compare it to Miriam's admission report."

I find it and look up the drug Anectine on my phone. "It's a muscle relaxer."

"One apparently administered to both you, *and* on a day long ago, Miriam Hill. As I said, a show of good faith. Good luck with Richard, Mr. Nathan."

She slips out the front door and into the garage. I follow behind her, just in time to see Cave slide open the rear door of the truck. A new cardboard box sits just in front of the garage. She hands me more files from her briefcase before slipping inside the back of the truck. The Beta file. Others.

And I stand there alone in my garage, trying to reconcile what I've just learned.

I *was* in Brazil. Kostov was too. And he's dead. Someone killed him.

Was it me?

I return to the dining room to find Eastcott has taken three items out of his briefcase: a syringe, a metronome and a strobe light.

"What's all this?" I demand.

"What may lead us to the answers we're both af-ter."

* * *

"Explain to me what Anectine does to a body. And be specific." I grab the first of two remaining bottles from my backpack. One I'll soon make him drink. The other for me, filled only with water. "I'll remind you to remember how this works."

The question catches him off guard. He does a poor job disguising it. "Muscle relaxer," he finally says.

I wind up. Deliver the pitch. Water bottle number one, mine, flies out the window. "I said *be specific*!"

"No!" he yells.

"What part of *remember how this works* confuses you?" I let it sit for a moment. "There's one more left. Now, shall we try this again?"

"It causes a feeling of drowning."

"I saw Miriam Hill's admission records. Severe panic attacks. The feeling of suffocating. Of being underwater. You used Anectine on her. Confirm it."

He doesn't hesitate. "Y-yes."

"Why, Doctor? Why this particular drug? And let me warn you before you answer, I've done my homework."

"I n-needed her silenced."

"Because of what had been done to her. Because of what the *boy* did to her. Yes?"

"Because of what had been done to all of you."

"The *boy*, Doctor. Yes?"

"Yes."

"So, to be clear. Miriam Hill did *not* have a mental breakdown."

"I've already told you."

"No, you haven't. So let me tell you. You gave her something to kill the pain in her legs, then you hypnotized her. Maybe having her focus on the syncopated clicking of a metronome. Maybe the flashing lights of a strobe. How am I doing so far?"

He nods.

"Say it." I demand.

"Y-yes."

"When she's under, you ask her about what the boy did to her. And when she answers you truthfully, what do you do?"

"She's t-told holding onto this memory will bring about her death."

"By whom is she told?"

"Me," he says.

"You tell her remembering what actually happened, the truth, will kill her. And you prove it by injecting her with Anectine. She thinks she's suffocating under water, dying. And you let her believe this, you maybe even reinforce it with additional doses. How many times did you re-inject her?"

"H-how do you know this?"

"*How* many times did you inject her?"

"It only took once." He gags. Chokes. Spits out a mouthful of mucous. Rapid-fire coughs explode from his mouth, sending new spittle through the air.

"A child's brain is so susceptible. So easy to scramble. This is what you referred to as Gamma programming, isn't it?" He nods. "Here, have a fucking drink." I let him down half the bottle. "Tell me about Betas. And I won't remind you again."

Once the coughing subsides, he sits up as straight as his bindings allow him. "How long does it take to start working?"

"The antidote?" He nods. I glance at my watch; make like I'm doing some serious calculating. "It takes about *answer my fucking question* long, that's how long it takes."

His face twists in anger at my response. I point to my watch. He gets it.

"We labeled children who'd experienced sexual trauma. Rape, incest, s-sodomy, all. Any. We labelled them Betas."

I reach over and pull out the files Ross gave me from my backpack, open one and slap down the first sheet inside. "Michael Graden, guilty of imprisoning his five-year-old daughter and wife in makeshift cages police discovered in his basement. One of yours?"

"I-I don't know."

"I'll answer for you. Yes." I slap down the second piece of paper. "Lauren Kind, convicted of having sex with two of her eighth-grade students. One of yours?"

"You wouldn't be showing me if she weren't."

"You're catching on. And just so we're clear. Both of these came from a file on Betas. Confirm this for me, Doctor. Betas are the sex slaves your experiments created. Kittens. Butterflies. Honeypots. You used the one's you successfully programmed how?"

"Politicians."

"Specifics, Doctor."

"We used them to compromise politicians."

"Not just politicians. Assets too. Assets like Alexi Kostov."

"How do you *know* all this?"

"We've covered that already, remember? There's one other Beta I want to talk to you about. We'll save her for last." I set Abby's file face down on the floor. "For right now, tell me, how did Kostov die?"

"I don't know."

"You don't? Let me refresh your memory," I say, opening a new file. "You called these Deltas. Scott Harden, he received a second life sentence while already incarcerated after beating his cellmate to death." I smack down the sheet of paper from the file. "Samuel Moore, we talked earlier about him. Paul Pellen." I slam his down harder. "Him too. What are Deltas, Doctor?"

"Sometimes the solutions had to be physical."

"I'd describe it a little differently. You bred violence into Deltas. You made them into assassins."

"They were used for necessary... exterminations."

"Necessary exterminations. What a *kind* way of putting it. How many of these *necessary* exterminations were your products responsible for?"

"However many it took," he finally admits, pulse in his neck pounding like a jackhammer. A new fit of coughing erupts. He clutches his stomach.

"Judging by the sound of things, you could use a little break. Here," I say, handing him back the half-empty bottle. "Drink it while I tell you a story."

He downs most of it. *Good.*

"This didn't come to me on my own, mind you. I had help. Ready for it?"

His fat chin jiggles.

"A young boy arrives at China Lake. He's frightened. He has no family, no friends. The boy goes through a process called *softening*. He's placed in an electrified cage. You called them *Woodpecker Grids*, I believe."

He looks up from the bottle. No sign of regret. "I didn't choose the children. They were b-brought to me."

"*Shut up*! Just. *Just* shut up and drink." He does. "You electrified the cages because electrocution interferes with the brain's ability to file away memories. Instead of whole events, it fractures them into pieces. Confirm it."

He sets down the now empty bottle. "It was a long time ago."

I smack his face hard. "So, that's a yes?"

"Yes."

"Pay close attention, because this is where the story takes a twist. The cage is so small the boy can only squat, never stand or lay down. He spends the next three days watching random light sequences on the paneled flooring flash. Waiting for the *bad* sequence to come and his cage to light up. Waiting for the electrocution he knows will follow. When he's too weak to take any more you let him sleep. But not a long sleep. Not a recuperative sleep. We're talking two hours, maybe three. How am I doing so far?"

He closes his eyes and slowly nods his head. "Yes."

"Tell me what came after. Tell me what you did to *me* after."

"I didn't choose you." Defiance. Denial.

I grab hold of my blade and carve a thin line down his quivering cheek. "*Tell* me."

"Your Delta training came after."

"Why? Why me?" I demand.

"Greater good," he cries, as his face knots up in pain. As the thin red line widens. As the first drop of fresh blood hits the floor.

"Greater good. And who exactly killed Kostov in the pursuit of the greater good?"

A small chuckle builds into laughter.

"You've remembered the beginning; you know nothing of what came after. And guess what? You may never know how we used you. You gave me the antidote. You've lost your leverage, Nathan."

"Hold that thought," I tell him as I flip over the photo I'd set aside.

His smile fades.

"I told you I *know*. I know all about your habits. How do you think I caught you? Tell me, how long after you took Abby away from Bolsiver did the molestations begin?"

A tear weaves its way through the now widened red line down his cheek. A pink drop of water hits the floor.

"A day? A week? A month?"

Another tear forms and makes its way down.

"Where is she? *Where is Abby and her brother?*" I demand.

"I-I don't know."

"But you do know this: Abby is your creation. And you had a hand in sending her to me. Say it."

No response.

I give him a matching red thin red line on the opposite cheek, then pick up one of the empty water bottles. "Got another secret to let you in on. The shot I gave you earlier tonight wasn't poison. It was Amytal. Truth serum. I'll admit, you resisted it better than I'd expected."

His face whitens. "You're lying."

I shake the empty bottle again. "After I escaped you in Bogotá, I drove home, all the while trying to understand what had happened to me. I was so thirsty from the drugs you administered. I had months before I came back for you to think. Plan. You know what I thought about? I thought about that empty water bottle rolling around on my passenger floor on my way home. It's what gave me the idea. Call it my inspiration. The bottle holds the real poison, dear Doctor. Things aren't always what they seem. *You* of all people should know this."

"So the syringe, it's the real antidote?" A look of desperation mixes with the blood-pink sweat on his face.

"Your last chance, that's what it is. Let's try a new topic. See how you do."

***

15

CAVANAUGH

Having overheard the others as their verbal paper cuts transcended to spoken sword slashes, having endured a brutal negotiation of her own, Cavanaugh's fuse is lit as she leaves the meeting room.

Sure, she won. Sure, the other side lost. She's left feeling oddly satisfied and disturbed all at once.

"Heard you in there," Jerry says, slipping in beside her.

"Yeah. Heard you too."

"Hope you won't hold it against me," he says.

The other group spills out from their meeting room. A few high fives, a few pats on the back. If the other group were sugar, Cavanaugh's group is the day-old coffee it's added to.

The two groups intertwine and find their chairs, now with papers and pens on each.

Michael Cave clicks a button on the remote he's holding, cueing up an old Coca-Cola Christmas ad. He calls the audience to order when it ends.

"Anyone from group number one, please tell me your assignment."

A random hand shoots up, tossing a voice over the room: "To negotiate a labor dispute."

"Group number two, how about you?"

A few voices chorus the same.

"Correct, each group had the same assignment. One side of the table held the group of factory CEOs who had to take what they negotiated to the factory's owners whose plants had been immobilized by a union strike. On the other side, the union's shop steward, armed with a list of demands including more overtime, increased benefits, including five more sick days per year for each member. Now, how many of you reached an accord?"

Every hand raises, some more reluctantly than others.

"On the pieces of paper you found on your chair, please write down which group you were in, which role you played, and the outcome of your negotiation," Cave instructs, eyeing his watch. "You have up to five minutes. Go."

Some in the audience write whole paragraphs; some nudge neighbors to show off their answers. Cavanaugh takes mere seconds to list out her answers.

Group Two.

CEO.

Fired them all and brought in the scabs.

She sends Nathan Badger a text while she waits for the others to finish.

You were right about Mazer. What else you got?

She checks emails, reads the news on her phone as the remaining minutes tick by.

"And time!" Cave shouts. The group collectively looks left then right for someone to pass their papers to. "No," he says, "you hold onto them. And without looking at a single one, I'm going to tell you what the majority of them say. Ready?"

Cavanaugh sits up in her chair.

"Group Two, we'll start with you first. Your negotiations were zero-sum. Owners, you didn't acquiesce to the demands of the union. Too costly, too much impact on the bottom line. Show of hands, how many of you CEOs came to terms with the union rep at your table?"

One hand rises.

"As I suspected. And the rest of you told the union to pound sand, didn't you? You knew you had replacement crews at the ready, ones you'd pay half-wage to during the heated negotiations to follow, all the while squeezing every nickel it takes from the pockets of the union members until they concede to a much more reasonable set of demands. And all because of the three words of instruction the owner of the factory, in your cases the well-dressed businessmen, all because of what they told you."

Surprise winds its way through the other half of the room.

"And those of you in Group One. CEOs, how many of you fired the union workers?" This time not a single hand is raised. "You reached some sort of compromise, all of you? Really? Tell me, what were the instructions you received from the factory owners in your group?"

A woman in the back of the room yells out, "Protect the company."

Cavanaugh shakes her head in surprise. *Same instructions.*

A steady stream of murmurs builds in the crowd, as Group Two, for the first time since the exercise began, starts interacting with one another as anything more than adversaries.

"In Group Two, businessmen led you into a room. We played the movie *Glengarry Glenn Ross* on the television set. We hung motivational posters. We even put-up cubicle walls. Not so for Group One, right?" Cave says, pointing to a man in the front row. "What movie played in your room?"

"Norma Rae," the man answers.

"That's right, *Norma Rae*. A movie about the sanctity of worker's rights and the need to form unions to protect those rights. A movie depicting the real human struggle faced by workers in the textile industry, some who just barely scrape together the money for meals. Can't heat their houses for days at a time. But hey, that's not what businessmen care about. They care about bottom lines. They care about winning. They care about the Cadillac, not the steak knives. Watch this commercial again." Cave once again clicks his remote to cue up the Coke commercial he'd just played.

He lets silence hang for a moment after it finishes. "Santa Claus. Presents under the tree. Families coming together to share the holidays. What else does this commercial make you think of?"

"Time off of work," one man yells out, which prompts a round of applause.

"Yeah? Well, guess what? You've been *primed*," Cave says. "You've all been *primed*. Group Two, the businessmen, where are you? Raise your hands." Cave nods to each one of them, passing a quick smile to Cavanaugh. "I want you to think about why all but one of you fired your workers. And consider how Group One kept the plant open, even though it required some costly concessions. And while you're considering, I want to bring up someone you all know from the audience. Cheryl, will you join me on stage please. Folks, the exercise you just participated isn't some made-up scenario. It happened to Cheryl. Cheryl, the stage is yours. Tell them about what *you* awarded *your* workers."

A surprised Cavanaugh catches herself on the edge of her chair as the newly appointed COO tells her story.

Cave returns to the stage to wrap up the evening. "Some of you may be wondering, why this exercise? Show of hands." A few tentative hands raise. "Do we have any guesses?"

A voice from the back, "It's like those subliminal ads they used to run in the movies."

"Good. Anyone else?" Cave stares straight at Cavanaugh, who lets the hard, metal chair swallow her.

"Programming, folks. Awareness, folks. All these subtle cues are made to influence our thinking, often without our knowledge or permission. And this is what makes our Schema Realignment system so powerful. So necessary. Because SR is about you taking back control. About giving you the power to decide what goes in, and more importantly," pointing to his forehead, "what comes out.

Cavanaugh's the first to the door once he's finished. Cave's right behind her.

"Coming back next week?" he asks.

"Well played. And maybe."

"I'll send you the research I did for tonight's presentation if you like."

Cavanaugh digs out a card, scribbles an email address on the back. "Use the personal address. They frown on me getting stuff like this at work."

Cave takes a long look at the card, "I will, Detective. Here, let me text you my number so you have it. I give it to all the new members."

Cavanaugh notices Jerry walking toward her and the exit. He stretches out his hand.

She takes it. And this time doesn't blush.

"I'm glad we met, Drew," he tells her. "Hope to see you again."

Yeah, Jerry. Me too.

She watches him go, then turns back to Cave to thank him and say goodnight. She sees the look on his face and can tell something's wrong. He looks like he's just seen a ghost.

"Everything okay?" she asks.

"Yeah, oh," he replies, clearly shook, staring at his phone. "Really late, my wife."

He pushes past her and out the front door of the Causa. "Let's go everyone. I need to lock up."

Before Cavanaugh can take a step, Sparrow places a hand on her shoulder. "Hi Drew, I'm—"

"Yeah, Sparrow. I heard."

"Can I walk you out?" Sparrow asks, blinking her giant brown owl eyes twice.

"Actually," lying, "I'm just on my way to meet some friends." Cavanaugh shoots a glance at her watch.

"I just want to ask you about something. Won't take a minute." Sparrow leans in and whispers, "Have you gone to SR?"

Cavanaugh nods.

"Upstairs or down?" Sparrow asks.

"My code was for the upstairs. Now, if you'll excuse me."

"Just curious is all. My code worked for upstairs *and* down," Sparrow tells her.

Now you've got my attention.

"Mind if I walk you to your car?" Cavanaugh asks.

"I didn't drive here."

All the better, Cavanaugh thinks.

***

MICHAEL CAVE

All color drains from Cave's face as he again reads the text he'd received again. *Come home. Alone* from an anonymous number. With it, a photo of a red beam of light cutting through the night sky and into his bedroom window.

His motorcycle roars to life and screams down Broadway, sounding like the amplified, mechanized bleats of a sheep. Siri dials Missy's number again, no answer.

"Fuck." Another yellow light turns red, trapping him. He looks left, then right, then left again before twisting the throttle and flying across. A chorus of horns fill the air. Cave cuts through the traffic like a Hollywood stunt man.

When he reaches his street, he pulls to the side of the road several houses away, parks. The sound of Missy's ringtone startles him.

"Babe, you okay?"

"Why wouldn't I be, McFly? Maybe I should ask you the same."

A burst of red light momentarily blinds him. He slams his eyes closed, recovers, and opens them to find the beam gone. "Sorry, nothing. Just a little wound up, I guess. Big night at the Causa." The light returns, crawling the sidewalk to his feet, moving up his legs. It comes to rest on his chest, dead center. The man he'd once spoken to in a limo moves toward him, face covered by a hoodie, index finger held to his lips. "I, um,

I'm almost home, Babe. Need me, uh, can I, should I pick up anything?"

"Do you remember the bottle of red I like. I'm trying to think, hang on." Bottles clank in the background as Lucas Sturgeon mouths the word *Josh*.

"Honey, you can't have wine."

"Not for me, bonehead." Bottles continue to clank. "Wait, found it. Josh, the Cabernet."

Sturgeon nods his head, pointing a finger at the ear bud in his ear, letting Cave know he's listening.

"Of course, babe. Anything else?" Eyes locked on the man in the hoodie.

"Just you. Hurry, I bought a chick-flick on iTunes."

Sturgeon motions Cave to end the call. "Gotta go. See you soon."

They stand staring at one another. Cave breaks the silence. "What do you want?"

Sturgeon reaches into his pocket, withdraws a piece of paper. "You'll be asked to ID a police sketch. When you are, give the person asking you this."

Cave glances down. "An address?"

"It's that simple, Michael."

"And if I don't?"

"Excellent question. Let me show you a video."

Cave leans in, the light from the phone reflects the hooded man's head and face for a moment, just long enough for Cave to study it further. The man catches him, grabs Cave's chin. "Here," he says, yanking off the hoodie. "Memorize it this time. And if you see this face again, it'll be followed by a muzzle flash. Now watch the fucking video."

The camera pans the square chamber. A curtain of brilliant sky-blue lights cascades toward the door to the right. Down the stairs.

"You know where this is?"

Cave shakes his head. "No idea."

"You will."

The camera's view plods down the last steps, turning right, going through a series of doors before zooming in.

"Is the man okay?" Cave sees blood draining down the man's arm, down his hand to his fingertip, to the pool below the steel table he lies motionless on. "What have you done to him?"

The camera view widens, then zooms in to the opposite corner of the room, where another man sits strapped to a chair. His left eye is swollen shut, his right stares forward.

"Someone's going to discover this scene tonight, Michael. Whose fingerprints and DNA would you like forensics to find? Yours? Or this guy's?" Sturgeon points to the paper with the address.

Thinking of Missy, Cave gives the only answer he can.

"Good talk, Michael. Now go get that bottle." The red beam trails back down the sidewalk. The hooded man turns to go, then turns back and adds, "We have an insurance policy. Don't make us use it."

Cave stands frozen, still processing what he'd just seen on the video as the man disappears, as the light disappears, as a car in the distance speeds away.

Ω

Alastair Kane's private line rings twice before he answers it.

"The FBI's at his house as we speak. He visited Miriam Hill. He's piecing it together. It may be only a matter of time before he remembers everything. Can you *fix* this or not?"

"Not even a hello, or a *how are you doing*?" Kane says dryly. "My, I thought we were closer."

As Gullen roars out his reply, Kane imagines how red Gullen's face must now be. "Perhaps I wasn't clear. Conduits *cannot* remember."

"Just take him out and be done with it." Kane smiles at a thought. "Or, if you prefer, I'll do it myself. Say yes."

"Like you handled those friends of his in Wheaton? That was a bloodbath."

"Bloody, but effective I might add."

"Might you? You left fingerprints in the safe room, Kane. You're getting sloppy. And it's a no-go on Badger. My orders are specific. He stays alive. We take him out and another participant starts remembering, we're right back where we are now. This needs to be resolved, once and for all."

"I *do* have one idea."

"Spell it out."

"Alters have their own unique EEG patterns. And the traumas they're buried beneath have their own signatures too."

"Which means what?"

"I recreate the traumas. I trigger the memories myself."

"And?"

"*And*, you say? The alters, Grey. One's awakening. I can find it."

"And then what?"

"Then I encourage it to close its eyes again."

"We *only* get the chance to test your little theory if we get him back in your hands. As I said, the FBI is with him right now. I have men watching the house. They'll take him if the opportunity presents."

"Why go through all that trouble? We both know how persuasive *she* can be."

"You and she had your shot. We both know how that turned out."

"Yes, unfortunately she failed me and had to be punished. This time will be different."

"Make it count. Am I clear?" Gullen replies.

"Crystal. And Grey. The favor I asked you for regarding the little rebellion of mine?"

"It's in play," Gullen replies, and fills Kane in on only the necessary details.

"You've inspired me. I have a new idea for Badger's funhouse. An Ascension."

"I'll inform my men. And Kane. Make sure Cathal knows nothing of this."

"Trust me, he won't," Kane says before hanging up. He then pushes an update to the KI Alpha program before taking two vials from a top desk drawer. A mask, a knit cap and a transmitter from the bottom drawer. He puts all the items in his hand-stitched leather satchel.

Downstairs, Kane's assistant places the last of eleven shipping labels on packages addressed to Scion

Bank, Epsilon Investments, the Grœbeck Fund, Tet-
raTech, Sequence Analytics, the Cohagen Group,
Atrium Foodservice, Jentaine Technologies, Turning
Leaf Media, Zephyr Metrics and Howard Regence, Inc.

***

CAVANAUGH

ANLON HALL
JANUARY 8, 9:10 P.M.

"You need a ride home? We can talk on the way," Cavanaugh motions Sparrow to the passenger side of her car, moves around to the driver's side and fires up the ignition as Sparrow climbs in. Sparrow gives her an address.

"Your code opened both, that's what you're saying?" Cavanaugh asks.

"I, um, I thought they were testing me. You know, choose up or down."

"How far down did you go?"

"I just went down a few steps before the laser person showed up and told me to come upstairs instead."

"So you didn't see anything?" Cavanaugh asks, typing the address Sparrow had given her into Apple Maps, then shifting the car into drive.

"No, but I heard something. It sounded like moaning, or, I don't know, maybe chanting."

Cavanaugh thinks of Mazer as she pulls out. A plan forms. "You know, I didn't have the best SR experience my first time. Got personal. Told that bitch to fuck off at the end."

"Willa?" Sparrow asks.

"You had her too?"

"I did. You wanna talk about what happened?"

"No. But I *do* want to go back." She pauses. "I'm sure my access code's already shut down. Maybe we can go together sometime?"

"Why not?" Sparrow replies.

Cavanaugh glances over at her car mate, who smiles an imperfect smile back at her. "Can I ask you a question?"

Sparrow chuckles. "I mean, should I be worried. You being a detective and all. I heard Doyen Michael call you that, you know. Your secret's out."

"Guilty as charged." Cavanaugh chuckles too. "I want to know why you came tonight?"

"Because I fell in love."

"Your, um, love interest is a member I take it." Cavanaugh states.

"See, there you go being a detective. Yeah, he is. In Italy."

"Long distance relationship."

"Not for long. I leave in the morning to go spend two months with him."

Morning. Italy. *Fuck. Think Drew.*

Got it.

"Can I ask you something else? And don't be afraid to say no."

Sparrow turns toward her. Nods.

"I mean, don't you want to know what's down-stairs?"

"As do you I take it."

"As do I. So here's my question. You've probably got packing to do tonight, right?"

"Of course. You want my code, don't you?"

"I'll make you a deal. You give it to me, along with your number. I'll call you and tell you what I see after."

"It's a plan," Cavanaugh's car mate replies.

"So Sparrow, you have a last name?"

"Not anymore."

The inadvertent chuckle bursts out before Cavanaugh can stop it. "Just Sparrow, then."

They arrive at Sparrow's condo complex. Cavanaugh navigates the tight, winding descent to the downstairs parking garage and into a guest parking spot

One car door opens.

"What's your cell number, Detective?"

Cavanaugh gives it. She gets a text in return.

EXPERIMENTAL SR FACILITY
SAN DIEGO, CA

A lone man in the shadows raises a crack pipe to his lips as Cavanaugh enters the code and waits for the locks to release. A grey hoodie covers his face and head, his hands shake. *Another addict gets his fix,* thinks Cavanaugh.

She drums at her hip where her holster and weapon should be. She's naked here, nothing but fists to protect her. The man appears content with his crack pipe. Still, she watches him until the locks disengage.

She steps into the square chamber. A curtain of brilliant sky-blue lights cascade down the right wall of the square, revealing the floor-to-ceiling virtual keypad to her right.

675-309

The blue lights fade as a panel slides up into the ceiling and lights illuminate two flights of stairs. One leading up, the other, which she takes, leading down.

She screams only once as she enters the room at the base of the steps.

16

PALOMAR MEDICAL CENTER
JANUARY 9, 6:45 P.M.

Christoph Hansen lived a difficult life. Growing up, the oldest of two children pressed his face to the carpet and watched through the gap below his bedroom door as the lights to each bedroom went dark on many a night, and on many a night heard the heavy padding of feet down the hallway from his father's bedroom to his younger sister's. Christoph tried to protect her once. Only once.

The beatings he suffered after weren't done by just his father's hand. There were instruments involved.

He dropped out of school after ninth grade and managed to keep it from his parents for the first three full weeks of what would have been his sophomore year at Brawley High School. Each day he hid among the haystacks until they left together for work, then snuck back in the house to eat cereal, watch cartoons, and plot his escape.

His father, a grifter disguised as a Christian, sang hymns on Sundays, cheated and stole from his business partner and relatives Monday through Saturday, and beat his children when the need arose, as it did when he learned of Christoph's school absences. As always, mother stood silently by her husband and watched. She cleaned when he told her to, cooked what he told her to, and each night buried her pitiful life in a bottle of cheap, blended red wine.

Christoph ran away at age 17, at 18 he volunteered. Days after completing basic training, the *Gulf of Tonkin* incident occurred. He boarded a plane bound for Vietnam a week after graduating advanced soldier training.

On November 14, 1965, the First Cavalry Division touched down at the base of Chu Pong Massif, within strolling distance of three regiments of the PAVN. Three days later, a Medivac helicopter carried Christoph away. Part of his leg stayed behind.

A prosthetic, a small monthly disability check and his nation's gratitude awaited him when he returned home.

Father, however, made no attempts to see his son, the war veteran.

Years later, the sister he once tried to protect couldn't find him to tell him when their father had passed. He already lived on the streets by then.

On the day of his 71st birthday, Christoph was taken. And shown a photo of his sister, a red laser dot on her forehead. His programming followed.

Seated today behind the police sketch artist is the woman who found and saved him.

"You're sure?" Cavanaugh asks one last time.

Christoph pushes the answer through his near toothless mouth. "Him."

She calls in a favor before she leaves. Christoph will have a warm meal and a roof over his head for as long as he needs to fully recover from the torture he suffered.

She arrives at the Causa in time for tonight's session, the final Serenity. But that's not what she's here for.

She's here for Cave.

As he takes the stage, she flashes her badge. "Ladies and gentlemen, the Causa is closed for the evening," Cavanaugh orders.

Cave reaches into his pocket. Holds the slip of paper he was given.

He thinks of Missy at home. Of his new baby Miles. Of his life as he knows it.

And waits breathless to know which set of fingerprints have been found.

"Recognize this man?" Cavanaugh says, holding up a copy of the sketch artist's drawing.

In that moment, Cave knows whose prints were found.

Ω

"What do you mean, a crew is on its way? I broke this case. *Me*." Cavanaugh opens the door of her car. Slides in and slams it closed.

Ward pauses a beat and exhales a long breath before answering. "You did good, kid. You saved a life; you maybe solved the case. We'll handle it from here, the team's only three minutes out. Go home, spend some quality time with that cat of yours, or whatever it is you do to relax."

"With all due respect, sir--"

"Have a good night Detective, and great work here."

"Hey, how'd you get the team there so fast?" Her answer, a dial tone.

She opens an app in her phone. Types in numbers and letters.

Her car speeds away, heading to the address she'd been given.

Eyes fixed on the house, Cavanaugh slams the car into park and reaches into her glovebox, fingering through it until landing on a half-finished pack of stale Dunhills. A hand shaking with anger pulls a cigarette out from pack, the other shaking hand lights it. Her window slides down before the first waft of smoke reaches it.

She takes a long second pull and watches the movement in front of Elder Dean's home.

They haven't even yellow-taped the scene.

Cavanaugh slams a new lung full of smoke, pitches her cigarette out the window, then pulls out her iPhone, tapping the camera icon. She pinches the screen to zoom in on the house.

Two people emerge from the doorway. Both plainclothes. They walk down the front stoop toward a black sedan parked in the driveway.

They appear to be rustling through papers on the front passenger seat. One of them raises a wrist to his mouth and talks. His head pivots toward the front door. Cavanaugh traces the path of his eyes until her camera meets the female peering out from inside.

You got to be kidding me.

Now outside, the woman she knows as Sparrow holds a wrist to her mouth. Sparrow nods: her eyes dart in the direction of Cavanaugh, who ducks down in her seat, glancing up to check if the coast is clear every few seconds.

She doesn't hear or see the woman approaching, crouched below the windows of the car. She doesn't see the hand reaching through the open window.

Fifty-thousand volts race through Cavanaugh's body before she slumps unconscious in the front seat. Sparrow pushes her body over to the passenger side, slides in and slips the car into reverse.

* * *

WISSUM

"That went well," Dorien Wissum says to himself as the last employee leaves.

The staff meeting was worse than he expected. He watched surprise turn to shock, and shock turn to anger. ARMR's Carlsbad office was opened specifically to service the Kain Industries contract. Once the papers are filed by his lawyers, the Kane contract ends.

And the Carlsbad office ends with it.

Wissum rubs stubby fingers through his beard, thinking of Melina, his favorite at Casa de Matías. He can taste the red ball in his mouth, feel the leather straps cinched tight around the back of his head. Feel the sting of her whip, the pinch of her stiletto heel on his back.

See you soon, Melina.

Wissum makes the first of three calls before jetting down south.

"Cary, Bradley and Dickers, how may I direct your call?

"Diana, it's Dorien. Put me through."

"Just a--"

He pulls the desk phone from his ear, thuds it twice against his palm. "Hello? I said put me through." Nothing but static. "Hello? What the fuck?" Wissum thuds the switch-hook, nothing. Dead. The phone line is out.

He fumbles out the iPhone XR from his pocket. No service.

"What the fuck do I pay you people for?" He says, firing up his laptop for a VoIP call with the guys from IT.

The building's internet is down too.

Wissum raises the shutters and looks across the parking lot to the neighboring building. Still lights on there, and cars in front. A good sign. He can use one of their phones and make the three calls he needs to make. One back to the Cary, Bradley and Dickers office to tell his attorney to move forward with his action against Kane Industries. One to Renato in Cartagena so he can prepare for Wissum's visit. The last to his pilot to start his preflight inspection.

Wissum packs his laptop and briefcase, types in the alarm's arming code into the side exit keypad.

He doesn't register the pin prick on the back of his neck, or the fact that he's caught as he falls.

Two men, both dressed in black, load him next to Cavanaugh in the panel van waiting just a few steps away.

* * *

CAVE

FBI FIELD OPERATION OFFICE, SAN DIEGO
JANUARY 10

A two-word email arrives in his inbox just after he finishes his run. *4:00 pm* is all it says.

Cave pushes papers, his mind elsewhere. The address was instructed to give led investigators to the home of Elder Dean, who was a revered leader within the Paradign body, an outspoken advocate for the homeless, and the best friend and loyal companion of Paradign's founder, Father Cathal.

As of today, he's also the subject of a citywide manhunt.

Dean's fingerprints were found at the scene of the homeless man's torture, not Cave's. And Cave himself led police to Dean's home.

He takes out his wallet, flips it open to the photo of Missy, then thumbs out the one behind it. The sonogram photo.

For the next hour and forty-five minutes, he does not check for typos, nor does he verify procedural integrity. At the appointed time, before he rises to leave for his meeting, he scribbles a message on a Post-It, which he affixes atop of the stack of untouched papers.

$$\Omega$$

"You remember what I told you about the Badger case. About what happened to his girlfriend."

"She was kidnapped and tortured."

"And he was arrested for it. On the day before he was taken into custody, a psychiatrist visited Abigail Ashford in her hospital room. He told staff he was there under the authority of one William Ward, who, coincidentally, was in charge of the detective investigating Badger's case. The detective had been to see Miss Ashford the day prior, she'd spent several hours alone in the room with her. I have a copy of Cavanaugh's affidavit in support of an arrest warrant. Care to read it?"

"Or you can give me the Cliff Notes version," replies Cave.

"According to the detective, Miss Ashford described Badger as a blackout drunk and indicated there was a history of unreported abuse. She also indicated Badger had planted cameras throughout the house. She claimed he liked to record her so he could relive the events. Claimed he'd watch them on his computer. One day later, she retracted all of it to the psychiatrist Ward sent."

Cave lowers back down into his chair; he's starting to follow. "You think she'd been coerced."

"Ward. Let's talk about him. Last December, he plopped down one-hundred-fifteen thousand cash on a used forty-two-foot Cruiser 380 Express. Just to be clear, that's a full year's wages for him. We checked his bank accounts, credit cards, investments, what little he had of them. You see where I'm going with this, don't you?"

"Can't say I do."

"They can be quite persuasive. Sometimes they use a carrot. Sometimes, like with you, they use a stick."

"Am I missing something here?" Cave asks.

"You are. Your phone."

Cave goes white, knowing she knows.

"I saw the text, Michael. You showed me some very damning circumstantial evidence regarding Dorien Wissum. Now he's gone missing. You need to start talking."

"I had no choice."

"There's always a choice. I had one when Carl was taken. You have one now. We *will* protect you. We *will* protect Missy. You've been compromised, stay that way. Play all sides. Do it for me."

"This is three-dimensional chess we're talking about here. Paradign, you, them. I have a baby on the way."

"And you swore an oath to do a job. So do it. You're in play. Stay that way."

Cave rises, strips the badge and ID from his wallet, and tosses them on the table. "Here you go. We're done here."

"I don't want your badge, Agent Cave."

"Funny thing is," Cave scoffs, shakes his head, "right now, neither do I."

***

17

KANE

NUESTRO HOGAR
JANUARY 10

Kane's fingers wrap tight around the steering wheel of his DB5, imagining for a satisfying moment holds Gullen's neck in his hands as he listens to Gullen updates him on the initiative and confirms the readiness of the special room.

His fingers relax and peel away, relief washes over him. Gullen has solved his little rebellion problem, leaving only Father, then Badger to deal with.

You first, old man. I have something special for you.

Kane's DB5 rolls along the winding driveway, passing the black oak, pecan, and rosewood trees lining it. He parks, arranges two things on a table just inside the front door, and makes a quick stop in the kitchen, pouring grape juice into a plastic cup with a straw. He empties the contents of a vial inside it. Jeffrey Delacruz arrives and takes his place at the door before Kane thumbs open a security app on his phone to unlock Father's door on his way upstairs.

"I brought you something to drink," Kane says as he enters the room.

Grey-veined hands clutch bed sheets. A sunken chest rises and falls in strained movements. Air escapes through Cathal's lips, forming weak words. "The truth. Bolsiver. I-I've told."

"I know." Kane's hand flies toward his father's face, stopping just before striking him. "And you thought what? You thought you would change things? Save your strength and drink," Kane demands, holding the plastic cup to Father's face and pointing the straw at his dry, cracked lips.

Cathal musters the strength to push it away. "Protect Paradign," he manages to say before a furious, rapid-fire bout of coughing erupts.

"I already have." Kane waits until the coughing subsides, then jams his father's head back and empties the contents of the cup into Cathal's mouth. A satisfied smile worms its way across Kane's face as his father gags. As he tries not to swallow. As he fails. As the realization of what he was just been given becomes clear on his father's face.

Kane reaches into a pocket, retrieving his phone and noting the time.

Even now, the eyes of his father offer Kane forgiveness. "Will it come quickly?" Cathal asks.

Kane makes no effort to shape his face into the look of regret he once practiced. His face only shows contempt and impatience. "Two hours," he replies. "I imagine your tongue may feel a little heavy already. Has it numbed yet?" Cathal sucks in a breath, but before he can speak Kane taps a finger on Cathal's forehead. "Just move your head. Can you still feel your tongue?"

Cathal wills his mouth to open, his tongue to move. He tries to form words. None come.

"Can't speak? Good. Because now you will listen."

Kane opens a Chrome browser window on his phone. He slides past articles until finding the one he's after. The one with a photo.

"Open your eyes, Father. Open them and see."

The article's headline reads "Citywide Manhunt Underway for Suspect in Homeless Murders." Cathal reads it in wide-eyed disbelief.

"I'm assured they found very incriminating evidence in your beloved Dean's home. I'm also told a victim described him quite accurately to a police sketch artist."

Cathal fights again to speak.

"You fled Bolsiver as my parents burned and did *nothing* to help them. Now *you* know how it feels to lose someone you love. We're hosting our own little Ascension. After, I'll be the one to guide Paradign. Just as you prophesied when you gave me my new name. Alastair, defender of mankind. Fitting, wouldn't you agree?"

Kane watches tears form in his father's eyes.

"You cry only for yourself, old man. I'll leave you in the knowledge I've given you now, but before I go, my dear sister would like to say goodbye."

Through the door comes Abigail Ashford. She slowly approaches the bed.

Amelie, Cathal's mouth fights to say.

She leans down to kiss her father's forehead, then places an envelope on the nightstand next to his bed, one she'd marked with a kiss.

Kane places something in the closet next to their dying father's bed before the door seals shut and he steps into the next room to prepare it.

He reaches his office on Torreyana Road before giving Abigail Ashford permission to send out a text.

***

Miss Me?

Her text message includes an address, a gate code, and instructions: come alone.

Eastcott's prepping for the next round with his metronome and strobe light. He won't get the chance to use them again.

"Time for your part of the bargain. Where do I find Allende?"

"Even if I knew, I couldn't tell you," Eastcott responds.

"Then I hope you got what you came for, because we're done here."

Eastcott holds up his hands in protest. "I need more time."

"Time's run out." I show him the text.

"This, I assume, is from Miss Abigail?"

"You don't want to give me Allende, maybe she can."

"Surely you know this is likely a trap?"

"Not the first one I've walked into," I yell over my shoulder as I head into my office and grab my kit from the closet. Everything's there: the old iPhone 8 I use for recording, a GPS tracking device, a tactical pen, a laser pointer, several of my favorite blades and a roll of black electric tape.

I turn to leave; he's blocking the door.

"Stop and think for a minute, Mr. Badger."

"Think about what? You got something to say, say it.

"It may not be *her* you're going to see.

"I'm counting on it," I tell him, pushing past. "Show yourself out."

Ω

NUESTRO HOGAR

I park a half mile away from the address, prep my iPhone 8. Six home button taps and one for good measure on the camera icon, the screen goes blank. I'm ready to record. I'll have audio of what happens inside. It could come in handy.

I break into a jog, arrive slightly winded at the gate and tap in the key code. It works. I advance along the winding driveway until I reach the front entrance of the mansion, but out of view from the front entrance where a uniformed guard is stationed.

I grab my tactical pen, my weapon, then the GPS tracker from my kit. If Allende's not here, there's a chance I can track him through her. I stash the rest in the bushes

When I get near the front door the guard turns toward me. He's armed.

"Hands up," he instructs.

"Delacruz, is it? I say, reading his name tag. He nods. "Get on with it, Delacruz."

He does and finds the pen, inspects it, then makes the mistake of giving it back. He doesn't find the tracker I stuffed in between my shirt and the small of my back.

Now I'm allowed to go in.

A small table sits in the foyer next to a coat closet door; there's a strange looking knit cap and a clip-on transmitter on top.

From the ceiling above, a camera whirs in a semicircle until it points directly at me.

"We've been expecting you, Nathaniel. Put them both on if you want to see her," a voice from the camera above me instructs. Whoever's behind it, Allende I suspect, is using a voice-altering device.

"Is that you, Doctor?" I ask.

"All in good t-time. Put them on please."

It's then that I notice what's lining the inside of the cap. I pick it up and hold it to the camera.

"There's no fucking way."

"The electrodes are n-not meant to harm you, Nathaniel."

My response? I wind up and underhand pitch it back on the table.

"Mistake number one," the voice says. "Delacruz?"

The guard is fast, I'll give him that. He's locked, loaded, and drawn, weapon is aimed center mass. I could deal with him if he were a step or two closer.

But he's not.

It's check. It's not checkmate.

I raise my hands in the air, take a small step forward, gauge the angles. How I'll move. Which hand traps the weapon. Which fingers I'll shove in his eye sockets.

"I'm chambered and ready," Delacruz warns, backing away.

"Duly noted," I tell him.

There'll be time. There'll be opportunity. Just need to be patient and ready.

"Nice place you have here, Doc," I say, lowering my hands to waist-level. "Which room can I find *you* in?"

"Nathaniel. You're sp-spoiling our fun. Just put them on," the voice instructs.

"Fun? You mean fun like when you strapped me to a gurney? When you electrocuted Miriam Hill? That the kind of fun you're talking about?" I cast a sideways glance at Delacruz, who taps his index finger on the trigger three times and smiles back at me. "He experiments on children, Delacruz. This the kinda guy you really want to pull the trigger for?"

He pauses, thinks it over. Good, I'm already in his head.

"Put them on, Nathaniel."

"Tell Delacruz here to stand down first."

"Once you do as you're told. And Nathaniel, someone waits for you upstairs. If you hurry you may just get there in time."

"In time for what?" I demand.

"Why, to save them, of course."

"Is it her?"

"Time is n-not on your side, Nathaniel."

Delacruz nods, points his weapon toward the stairs, then back at me.

No time. No choice. Make a decision.

I take my chances, slide the cap on my head. Slip on the transmitter. Wait for a burst of electricity. None comes. In its place, a slight buzzing sound.

"Before you g-go upstairs" the voice says, "let's reach an understanding, shall we? Say yes."

Ω

The van door slides open, Lucas Sturgeon and Sparrow exchange nods as the two others with them pile out. They drag Elder Dean's and Wissum's limp bodies out of the van and through the delivery doors.

Inside the vehicle, Cavanaugh stares back at Sturgeon in wide-eyed panic. Duct tape seals her mouth shut; it muffles her screams. Her wrists bleed in thin lines from the plastic straps she can't fight her way out of.

Just as they'd done earlier, Sturgeon and Sparrow place gas masks over their faces. He removes the spray bottle from his jacket pocket, douses her with chloroform, and waits for her to slump like the others had.

Cavanaugh's body falls to the floor of the van. Sturgeon hoists her over his shoulder and carries her back down the hallway to the room on the right, where her body joins the two others who are already there.

Sparrow and the two operatives guard the entrance and grounds. Sturgeon takes his place outside the delivery doors, weapon in hand, awaiting his orders.

"Rules, Nathaniel, are important to me. When they're broken, trust is b-broken. You understand? Say yes."

"I said make him stand down."

"Very well," the voice responds. "Jeffrey?"

Delacruz holsters his weapon and turns toward the first-floor hallway.

I mouth the words, "Good boy."

He smiles, taps a finger on his holster.

Good boy. I want you edgy. You'll make mistakes that way.

"Rules, Nathaniel. Say yes."

"What rules?"

"I want to see how that brain of yours works. You will not interfere. Say yes."

"You overestimate me."

"Do I? I'll be monitoring your brain's electrical activity. The hippocampus, neocortex, and amygdala are all stimulated by the act of remembering. There are other regions if stimulated, however, which, when they fire, w-would indicate you to be lying. Be intelligent in what you choose to do, because I'll know."

"I'm hearing an implied threat. Give it a name."

"Try to deceive me and you'll never get what you've come here for."

"What exactly is that?"

"Answers. The truth about you. You understand what I mean, don't you? Say yes."

Miriam Hill. My childhood friends. China Lake.

My real past.

"Yes," I reply.

"Then we have an accord, no interference?"

I give the camera a thumbs-up.

"Good. Then best you hurry."

I bolt up the steps and turn down the hallway. A second camera moves above me, tracking my progress as I reach the open door and enter the room. The door slams shut and locks behind me.

I freeze. My mind denies what my eyes clearly see. A man lies in bed doubled over in pain, there's a puddle of blood-soaked vomit on a pillow near his head. The man's jaws squeeze tightly together. His muscles appear to spasm. Beads of sweat form and fall from his forehead.

"What have you done?" I snatch the phone from my pocket, jam fingers into keys.

Nine-one-one.

Send.

Nothing.

"You're wasting valuable time," the voice tells me. "Your cell service is blocked. Permanently blocked. What you hold in your hand now is an expensive paperweight."

"He needs help. Call an *ambulance*," I demand.

"He'll be dead before one could arrive. Now listen to me carefully. He's ingested a lethal dose of aconite. I've hidden the antidote in the next bedroom over. If you really wish to save him, you'll need to give me something."

Frantic eyes search the room. I bolt toward the door.

"Tuh-tuh, Nathaniel. I'm sure you heard it lock. Besides, we spoke about rules. You must give me a something. A memory."

The man in bed closes his thick-lidded, red-tinged eyes. A shudder moves through his body. "Unlock the door," I demand.

"Give me a memory first."

"What memory?" I yell, staring at the man. Helpless to help him.

"Oh, how beautifully your brain lights up at the stress you must be feeling. I wish you could see the patterns I'm reading, Your brain's a Christmas tree."

"I said *what* fucking memory?"

"Why, a memory of him, of course. I trust you have something in your pocket to help you in producing this? A ring perhaps? Say yes."

The man in the bed gags on his own vomit. Time's running out.

"Yes."

"I suggest you use it. Ticktock, Nathaniel"

I shove the phone into my pocket and take hold of the ring.

I focus my breathing.

One eight count in.

One blood-filled exhale through my nostrils.

I say the word.

Cuimhne. Remember. *Cuimhne.*

Cuimhne.

A foul wind rustles the leaves, branches slice through the night air.

Cuimhne

Wheaton. The house.

"M-Miriam, I'd like you to p-please lay down here. Nathan, you'll be next to her here. Then you."

"We agreed. He's is to be treated just like the others."

I lay still on the bed as I'm strapped down, as an electrode is pressed against my temple. Look for heroes on the white ceiling. Find none.

Allende walks a wobbly duck-duck-goose circle around us to the words of a song, touching our heads one-by-one as he passes. "Ring around the rosy, a p-pocket full of posies, ashes, ashes, we all fall down." His hand lands on Miriam last. "It will be you."

"Leave my friend alone," I demand.

"Now, Miriam. You're angry with someone in the room. You're angry with someone, Miriam. With one of the boys. Which one are you angry with?"

"No, I'm not." She arches her back and lets out an excruciating scream.

"Mmmeeeee! Mmmm mmmmeeeee!" I yell through the tape.

"Just tell us who you're angry with."

"I, I told you I'm—" A second scream stabs my eardrums.

"Mmmmm!"

"Who are you angry with, Miriam?"

She surrenders before the next jolt of electricity is administered. "I'm angry with him."

"Stop this now," cries a disembodied voice.

"Do not interfere." A massive force strikes the boy, causing his back to arch up in the air and his face to wrench against agonizing pain.

"Enough I said!"

"And I said, do not interfere Cath-"

My eyes fly open. "Cathal was there when we were experimented on. Me and my friends. We were strapped to gurneys. Electrocuted. Miriam cried out for help. Cathal tried to stop you. Now where *is the anti-dote*?"

"More. Give me more. Describe the room, Nathaniel. Describe *me*."

I squeeze my eyes shut, search the memory again. Call out what I see.

A fat, bearded man.

Gurneys forming a circle. A circle ringed with my friends.

Wood-grain paneled walls.

Darkness.

Sterilized instruments lined up perfectly next to a jar filled with a solution.

Only one window. No one out there to save us.

Enough.

"You got what you asked for. Open the door," I demand.

I hear the sharp snap of the lock disengaging. "Very good. Your reward waits for you."

I bolt out the door, grab the syringe left for me on the nightstand in the next room.

I arrive back in time to see a last shudder escape from Cathal's mouth. And to watch his life end.

I wipe the blood from my face and stare down at the floor.

"You've passed the first test, Nathaniel. You didn't lie. You see, when you lie, the anterior cingulated-"

I cut the voice off. "You killed him."

"*Did* I? Or did *you*? Try to be faster next time."

"There won't be a next time," I snap back.

"Oh, but there will."

For the first time I notice the envelope next to Cathal's bed. There's a kiss mark on the seal, just like the one Abby left on the sliding glass window of what once was our bedroom.

I rip it open. A keycard falls to the floor.

"Would you like to know which door it opens?"

"Let me guess. It will cost me a memory."

"Open the closet door, Nathaniel. There's something for you inside."

One hand on the pocket with my tactical pen, I swing open the closet door. And see the porcelain mask inside.

I've seen it before.

"What a beautiful array of reds. Your amygdala is glowing bright like the embers of a campfire. Please have a seat on the bed next to Cathal and put it on."

The mask feels like hot steel in my hands

"You were the lucky one that day."

My eyes squeeze shut. My temples pound.

"They made the other child's mask out of wax. Do you remember holding the lighter to it?"

Another image flashes.

A child screams.

Under his chin, the mask starts to melt.

And now I know.

"Tell me what you remember," the voice demands.

I open my eyes. "I remember Allende speaks with a slight stutter. What happened to yours?"

Locks disengage. "The door you're looking for is on the first floor. Hold the keycard up to the mirror at the end of the hall."

I place the keycard in the center of the mirror as instructed and wait, ticking off the seconds it takes for the locks to disengage with the clenching and unclenching of my jaw. A chill draft rolls over me as I run down the steps and reach the basement floor.

"Here I am, Nathaniel."

Frosted glass fades partially to reveal a room to my left with several rows of chairs and what appears to be three seated figures, all dressed in black.

"Here I. Am."

The frost fades further, revealing faces nearly covered by hooded black robes. The one seated in front near the podium has a microphone pinned just under his beard.

"All for you, Nathaniel. A front row seat to our glorious *Ascension*."

Inside the room, a head shakes vigorously back and forth, up and down, side to side until the hood falls away. Emerald green eyes, panicked, stare wide-eyed at me. A mouth covered by duct tape fights to scream.

It's Cavanaugh.

A flame ignites inside the insignia carved into the floor. It moves like a snake below their feet. Below her feet.

"Why's she in there? What is this?"

It takes me a second to process. I jam the handle. The door's locked. I step back and thrust a front kick into the door. Another. Nothing.

"Open it," I demand.

No answer.

"I said open it."

The flames rise.

"What the fuck *is* this?" I say.

"What will you do, Nathaniel, with the choice I present you? I wonder." A thin veil of frost forms back on the glass.

"Let Cavanaugh go. She's got nothing to *do* with this!"

"It's not me you need to convince. It's her."

Down the hall, the faint click of heels grows louder. I reach back and slip the tracker into my palm.

Abby, dressed head to toe in black leather, appears at the end of the hallway wearing nine-inch come-fuck-me heels. She saunters toward me like some B-movie villainess. Glossed red lips form a seductive smile. Cashmere-painted fingers play across her breasts, down her body.

The sight of her hits me like a chill arctic wind, numbing all feeling. But only for a moment.

She reaches me and places both hands on my shoulders. Tries to press her lips into mine.

Not a chance, Abby.

I stop her just before our lips meet. Take hold of her shoulders, slide my hand under leather and slip the tracker inside.

Then I push her away.

She moves her mouth to my ear, kissing it. "Avenge me," she whispers, her hand gently stroking me. "Inside are the men who took me, Nathan. Avenge me." Her lips move to my neck, I push her away again.

"Listen to me, Abby. Inside that room is the detective who tried to help you. Whatever the fuck this is, she's not part of it."

"But she is, my beloved," the woman I once thought I loved says.

Abby removes a keycard of her own from her pocket, placing it on a pad mounted next to the door of the room. A plate slides up, revealing a dial, she turns it a quarter turn clockwise. Flames rise up still higher from the floor.

"The fuck *is* this?" I yell.

"Avenge me, Nathan. Do it, and we'll make love. Right here, right here next to the flames you can have me." Lips try again to press into mine. I pull away. "Don't deny us what we both want. Turn the dial."

"Fuck you, Abby. Fuck both of you. Open the door."

She turns the dial further. The flames rise higher.

My *God*. Now I understand.

"No," I yell, pushing her away.

She stumbles back. Recovers her balance. Smiles.

"Make your choice. Me or them." She moves closer.

"Them," I say spinning back the dial. The flames fall to the floor.

"I *let* you inside me." Her lips quiver in anger, betrayal. A storm brews in her eyes. "Pathetic," she says.

The voice overhead orders Delacruz downstairs.

He takes up a stance bang opposite me.

"Truly pathetic." She slips out a new pendant from beneath leather, slides it open, and blows white powder at Delacruz's face.

Ω

Sturgeon watches from a crack in the service doors, awaiting the order to take his friend out. His hands shake as he taps an update into his phone.

Drug administered to guard.

Sturgeon thumbs out and dry swallows two pills once he presses send.

G2X Deputy Gullen stares at his laptop, still awaiting the email confirmation from Kane. Smoke billows from the exhaust of his idling limo.

Impatient, he dials Kane's number again. As before, and the time before that, no answer. *You're playing a dangerous game, son.*

Seconds drag on like minutes until a new text message lights up Gullen's phone. A smiley face emoji. Acid builds in his throat. He shakes three Prilosec pills out of the bottle.

Another message from Sturgeon: *Intercede?*

Gullen thuds a response to Kane's text: *Do you have it?*

Sturgeon again: *Urgent. Intercede?*

You'll know when you know. Kane's cryptic response.

"I'm not the one you play fuck-fuck with," Gullen mutters as he taps out a new text.

His orders to Sturgeon: *Negative. Regroup. Proceed to the following address and await further instructions.*

Gullen swallows three pills. He initiates his contingency plan on the way to Torreyana Road.

His first call is to Commander William Ward. His second is to an operative waiting in a cul-de-sac near the Goff halfway house in North Park.

"You heard the lady," the voice says. "Do it. Take the dial. Embrace us with flames."

"I asked you a question earlier. What happened to your stutter?"

Dead-eyed Delacruz stares forward at me. Abby's lips twist again into a smile. "Last chance," she tells me, slowly turning the dial.

They will be burned alive.

Have to stop this.

Buy time, Nate. Buy time.

"Next question. Why did you show me the mask?"

"To remind you. This will help. Dear sister?"

On cue, she turns the dial again.

"Abby, *no*."

She places a hand on my shoulder, leans toward me and whispers in my ear. "Be a man. Do it for me."

"Nobody's dying here today. You hear me. You *hear* me?" I yell toward the camera. "Now tell me about the porcelain mask."

"Feeling what you believe is your own face on fire can bring a certain clarity. You delivered this clarity."

"Clarity to who?"

"*Cuimhne*, Nathaniel. Remember. And give me the memory. Do it in time and perhaps I'll allow you to intercede on your friend the detective's behalf."

"Is this really necessary?" Abby asks, looking up at the camera.

"Quite," the response.

"Get it over with, then," Abby tells me.

"Step away from the dial first," I tell her.

She holds her hands in the air and takes one step back.

I need to hurry.

I cup my hands over the dial to shield it, then summon the memory.

Cuimhne

Cavanaugh's eyes plead to me.

Cuimhne.

I look down at my hands. At the blowtorch I'm holding.

Flames. A blowtorch. The blowtorch in my hand.

A child is seated in front of me. He's visibly shaking. "You let them die," he cries out.

A bearded man. Allende taps a syringe, then sticks the needle into the boy's arm.

The blowtorch ignites.

Allende presses a wax mask into the boy's hands. "This mask holds your secrets," he tells the boy, whose chin falls to his chest. "Now place it on your face."

The boy struggles to lift it. His hands are shaking. He stares forward in fear. Fear of me. Of what I'm holding. I register a pinch on my arm and nearly drop the blowtorch I'm holding.

"This memory is a lie," the man in the lab coat tells the boy. "You were never there"

The boy's head falls; he slumps over.

"We will teach you what happens when you remember a lie."

Allende snatches my arm. Pulls me forward.

"Do it," he demands.

I resist. He overpowers me.

The boy's mask begins to bubble. Melt.

"Nathaniel, open your eyes please."

I try to pull away. They've restrained me.

"Abby, help him open his eyes."

I fight back. Allende's lab coat catches fire.

I come to when Abby slaps my face sharply a second time, and the cold muzzle of a weapon presses against my temple.

"We were just kids. I tried to stop it," I tell the voice.

"Then as now, you have failed. The flames will be like an old friend who's come to visit you, Nathaniel. Watch."

I judge the angle of my attack.

Abby takes hold of my chin, pulls me toward her. Spits in my face. "He said, *watch!*"

I jerk my head clear and trap Delacruz's arm under my armpit, forcing the weapon to point behind my back.

The voice above screams *Althraigh!*

Delacruz's eyes widen at the command. The dead eyes affix.

With purpose.

On me.

From the corner of my eye, I see Abby take the dial in her hand and spin it violently clockwise.

Robes ignite.

"Abby, *no!*"

Black smoke rises. Cavanaugh fights to break free. The others do not.

I push away from Delacruz in an effort to stop her. Inside, flesh begins to burn. Cavanaugh's face freezes, she's in shock.

A somber piano piece plays over the speakers above, the macabre soundtrack of flame ravaging bodies.

I slam my fist into the window. Once. Twice.

Delacruz takes advantage and lands his first blow. This one to the base of my skull.

My knees buckle.

He shoves the weapon toward me again. I direct it away, get up. Pry it loose from his hold. I hit him with a left cross. His nose shatters.

"Back away," I tell him. He zombies forward.

I slam the weapon into his temple. He falls.

Inside the last shred of Cavanaugh's clothing melts away, exposing her bubbling skin.

Delacruz gets back up. Zombies forward again.

I step back, fire a shot at the glass. It shatters, black smoke seeps through the cracked glass as Delacruz reaches me. I hear Cavanaugh's screams, hear the sizzling flesh.

I squeeze the trigger again. A perfect red circle appears between Delacruz's eyes. Grey matter explodes from the back of his head. His eyes deaden again, and he falls.

I turn the gun on the woman I once thought I loved.

"Abby, step away."

Our eyes meet. Lock. Just for a moment before she obeys my demand.

I snap the dial back, the flames fall. Abby snatches the cap and receiver off me before I leap through the window. The window takes a bite of my leg.

I'm met by a molten blast of sickly-sweet air.

What once was Cavanaugh is now blackened flesh, charred bones and muscle, a small swatch of matted, smoldering hair.

When I turn back, Abby's gone.

I sprint down the hallway and through the back service doors. Vanished.

I turn back toward the house but freeze when I hear the pounding of footfalls down the stairs. I duck into the bushes near the kit I stashed earlier and take cover as police cars arrive.

***

18

KANE

"This is one-one-five," the van driver says, "we need a path cleared to the destination. Running one mike off schedule."

"Roger that, one-one-five. Out."

The driver punches the gas. The van speeds to forty, forty-five, fifty. His foot bears down harder on the gas pedal. Sixty-five. Seventy. Sturgeon and Sparrow shift in their seats.

As Ward had been instructed to ensure, red lights change to green, there are no police vehicles in sight as the van rounds the corner and turns onto Torreyana Road, pulling up next to Gullen's stretch black limo.

"Thanks for the assist, boys," the driver says, holding the radio receiver. "We've made the staging site, over." The driver slams the van into park.

"Roger that. Be advised, power will be cut in T-minus-five mikes. Out."

Sturgeon calls the group to order. "Hand signals only from here," he says, then waits for each to acknowledge.

Three men and one woman exit the rear door of the van, and form on their leader. Sturgeon sorts them into two teams, then points out the ingress.

Grey Gullen looks on from the limo, assessing the scene.

Ω

KANE INDUSTRIES
TORREYANA ROAD, LA JOLLA

Upstairs in his office, Kane admires his computer screen, noting the beautiful symmetry of the life energy that unites and unifies us all.

It worked. Genius.

Kane types out an email

State-dependent memory, Grey. Such an easy answer to the Conduit puzzle. Allende should've known this.

Badger's Delta programming. Then amygdala over-stimulation, as was Allende's protocol. And therein lies the flaw. The Conduit flaw.

A flaw only Kane knows how to exploit.

He touches a long nail to the keyboard. He then deletes the email letter by delicious letter.

The file transfer of Badger's EEG goes from computer to USB memory stick, the computer screen dims.

Time for more important things.

Kane activates a new update to the KI Alpha program. The encryption code timer counts down toward eleven tonight.

A faint sound registers with him: feet shuffling down the hallway leading to his atrium office registers.

Red lights pan across the empty workstations and his assistant's desk, beaming through the sliding glass door and fish tank, all eventually coming to rest on him.

Kane lifts his palms to the sky and rises slowly up from his chair. Through the doorway four figures emerge. They're all dressed head-to-toe in black, each of their faces is covered. Sheaths of throwing knives drape from shoulder to torso. Glocks at the hip.

Such a dramatic entrance, Kane muses, ticking off the seconds with an impatient swing of his finger.

"It took you long enough, my arms were starting to get tired. Won't you have a seat."

Gullen storms into the room and up to Kane, unleashing a backhand that spins Kane's head a full ninety degrees. "A fucking smiley face? The director is *not* pleased."

"Oh, Grey. Where's your sense of humor?"

"It's right here." Gullen backhands him again. Kane shows bloody teeth back.

"Let me ask you a different way." Gullen draws his Glock and presses it into Kane's forehead. "Were you successful in sequencing Badger? Yes or no."

"Put down your weapon and let's talk about it."

Gullen clicks off the safety. "Yes or no?"

"All right. Yes. I finished up just before you arrived. Now can you put that thing away so we can have a reasonable conversation?"

Gullen lowers it slowly, calls over his shoulder. "It's a go."

Ω

They'll find my fingerprints at the scene. I have an insurance policy, the recording.

The recording of the sound of flames devouring Cavanaugh's skin. The recording of her as she screamed through charred, black lips.

The recording of a death she did not deserve. Nor did the others, whoever they were.

One thing's for sure. Allende was not one of them.

Time to go find him.

I need a few things from home before I vanish.

The drive there happens of its own volition. Out of instinct I park on my street several houses away. I check parked cars along my road. All belong to neighbors. All empty, unlike the day with the FedEx truck.

It's only when I enter the courtyard and see Eastcott's face through the dining room window that I know something's wrong. His glasses are mangled, they hang from his face by one temple. Dried blood crusts under his nose. One eye's near swollen shut.

His one good eye stares forward across the table.

There's someone inside with him.

I slip into the garage, kit in hand. Grab a few more throwing knives from their hiding spot behind the door. They'll do nicely.

Time to assess.

Trained operatives would've searched the place. They would've found my stash of knives. Trained operatives would have posted observers on my route. They would've reported in. Whoever's inside would know I'm coming. Do they?

I step back behind the door. Pull it close to my body. Watch through the cracks for any shadows. Listen for the sound of movement.

There is none.

I slide out from behind the door, watch for signs of movement inside.

There is none.

I lower myself down on my stomach, and low crawl to the east end of the courtyard and lay prone in the mulch. Still no movement inside.

I inch my way to the master bedroom window and pry out the screen. The window's locked, as it should be.

Can't slip inside. I'll need to draw them out instead.

I take a prone position again and start work on my plan.

Inside, two hands slam down on the table. The man they belong to leans forward, yelling at Eastcott. Short in stature. Muscled up. Tatted up. Wearing an eyepatch.

It's Carlos Najera, the drug thug extraordinaire, free as a bird.

A second man appears from the direction of my office, his weapon slipped into a shoulder holster, a silencer pokes out from its leather. He walks behind Eastcott, grabs a handful of his hair and slams his face into the table. The man lifts Eastcott's head again, pointing his bloodied face at Carlos, who waves a silenced weapon at him.

A third man emerges from the direction of the living room. His weapon is also holstered, it too has a silencer. I wait long enough to be sure there aren't more of them.

I prop my laser pointer on top of a rock, and stare down the shaft, adjusting the angle. I pull out the roll of tape and rip off a small piece.

The man takes hold of Eastcott's hair again.

In one fluid motion I snap the tape over the pointer's *on* button. I stay just long enough to see the red beam hit Carlos' forehead. He drops to all fours before I slip out of the courtyard and to the right. I leave the wooden side entry wide open on purpose, quickly unlock one of the two locks on the tool shed doors, tuck in behind the back of the shed and wait.

I hear the side door to the garage bang hard against the wall. I hear footfalls, and the crunching of mulch. By now they've found the pointer. Next, they'll search the grounds.

Perfect.

One takes the left side of the house. The other, the right.

They will never meet in the middle.

I hear the one who'll die first approaching, see his long shadow fill the sidewalk. Listen as he checks the shed. Hear his footsteps as moves toward the back patio.

I let him get a few steps past me before I take aim and throw. My knife finds its purchase, deep in his neck.

I'm on him before panic turns to realization in his eyes, covering his mouth before he can scream. I trap his hand before he can raise his weapon, he fires anyway. A flash of smoke, the silencer spits out a bullet. I strip it from him before he can fire again and jam it into his forehead.

A desperate hand reaches up to his neck, pulls out the knife. Blood and blade come at me. The silencer spits out another bullet. I catch him as he falls and shove his lifeless body into the toolshed before closing and locking the door.

Ω

"I took the liberty of having a press release drafted. It's relevant to what we're about to discuss next. Sturgeon?" Lucas steps forward and holds up his phone.

For Immediate Release

Kelly Williams
Kane Industries
1-858-555-7566

Kane Industries Mourns the Loss of Its Founder/ CEO Alastair Kane

San Diego, Ca: *Kane Industries is reeling from the tragic death of its Founder/ CEO, Alastair Kane, after what police suspect to be a murder-suicide. Police discovered the body of his adoptive sister, Abigail Ashford, by his side. No other details are known at this time.*

The company will temporarily cease operations until a replacement is named.

"Short and sweet, wouldn't you agree?" Gullen says.

"I don't do well with threats."

"Really? Well, I don't do well with people who fail me."

"I already told you, Grey. I was successful."

"I hope for your sake you were, because you won't get another shot."

"Another threat?"

"No. It's a fact. Badger's already dead, or soon will be."

"I see. You gave your goon here the go-ahead," pointing a long fingernail at Sturgeon, who balls up a fist in response. "Another team took him out then?"

"Local color. An old score to settle. My hands and those of my associates are clean."

"You made some adjustment, dear Grey."

Gullen nods.

"Interesting," Kane replies. "So have I."

Ω

I edge up to the side of the house, check reflections in windows, listen for movement.

No sign of guy number two. Not yet. Give him time.

I dart past the end of the sidewalk and take a prone position behind a thicket of roses.

Guy number two steps onto the other end of the patio, near my office.

I move the silenced weapon into place and wait.

I shallow my breath.

He raps on the dining room window. Carlos opens the sliding glass door and sticks his head out. They exchange rapid-fire words in Spanish. I don't have to speak the language to know what is said.

Carlos' head disappears. He closes but doesn't lock the sliding glass door behind him.

Looking like he's imitating a cop show he saw, guy number two slides behind a patio column, pokes his head out, then rolls behind the U-shaped outdoor sofa.

The snout of the silencer trails him. When his head pops up again, I take my shot. His lifeless body hits the wooden deck with a thud.

I still. Wait. One-thousand-one. One-thousand-two.

The sliding glass door opens again. Eastcott appears, a gun pressed to his temple, Carlos behind him.

Ω

"You're as arrogant as you are stupid."

"Oh, Grey. The questions you could soon be asked."

"What's your end game here, son?"

"Tell you what, *son*. You get rid of your little goonies here," Kane makes a shooing motion. "Then we can have a meaningful conversation. Just the two of us."

"Fuck that. Talk."

"Whatever you say, Grey. So let me see if I'm tracking you here. Your plan is to fly me, fly *us* to some undisclosed location where you've set up a lab. You'll have an ample supply of subjects brought in, any age I choose. How am I doing so far?"

"I said, what's your end game here?"

"Patience, Grey. Let's just talk this through. If I provide you proof that my sequencing theory works, you let us go home. We're cleared as suspects. We go about our lives as if none of this ever happened."

"And if not, yours and your sister's bodies are discovered in some seedy hotel. That is the plan."

"And now there's a new one."

"I'm going to give you one chance here. Pull the Ki Alpha update from your network. Now."

"You're just being unreasonable. Let me tell you how this works. If I don't log into my computer every day before 11:00 p.m. and enter a code, the update goes live. And every participating KI Alpha member across eleven companies learns all about the things you've been doing. You think a Conduit regaining memories is an issue? That's child's play, *son*. Let me tell you what happens from here."

Ω

"Nathan. How you been?"

"Let him go, Carlos."

He fires a shot in my direction. And misses. Not by much.

I rapid-fire three quick shots at the stucco wall behind him. He falls to the floor, pulling Eastcott on top of him. I slide down the hill and tuck under the patio.

"Where have you gone, my long-lost compadre?" Carlos calls out in a singsong.

I don't respond.

Floorboards creak above. "Your friend here is getting in the way of our reunion. I think it's better if it's just you and me."

I study the seams in the decking, watching for movement directly above me.

"I've waited a long time for this, Nathan. Show yourself or I shoot him."

I edge my way under the sound and draw my weapon.

"No? Okay. Have it your way."

There's a scuffle above. Shots ring out. One. Two. Three. A body thuds above.

I dart out from under the deck and climb up the railings, weapon pointed.

Carlos lies on the ground, writhing in pain, holding a bloody, limp arm.

The gun shakes in Eastcott's hand. I pry it away from him. He pulls out his cellphone.

Carlos pushes himself across the floorboards toward the weapon he dropped. I reach it before him and kick it away, then grind my heel into one of two bloody wounds. "That's for Johnnie. Now, I got a question for you."

"Fuck you!" Spittle flies from his mouth.

"Is someone else coming?"

He stares up at me, smiling in painful defiance. "You won't be so lucky the next time."

"Lucky? You brought amateurs. What'd you expect? I'd just waltz in the front door and into your trap? Now answer me," I say, driving down my heel with all my force.

"You're a dead man," he grunts out. "One day, when you least expect it."

"So not today, then? Good. Gives us time to talk." I lift up my foot up from his arm, and stomp down again. Harder this time. "By the way, you're in no position to level threats, or haven't you noticed?" His screams nearly drown out my words.

"I apprised Agent Ross of what's happened," Eastcott says, stuffing his phone back in a pocket.

"She's sending a cleanup crew." He heads into the house.

"Hear that, Carlos? The FBI's on its way."

"Fuck them. And fuck you."

Eastcott returns with a torn bedsheet and hydrogen peroxide. "I need to clean it and stop the bleeding."

"See how this goes? The man *you* held a gun to is helping you. Who do you think your God is smiling on now, you or him?"

"I'm straight with my maker."

"Maybe you were. Not after today. I'd say you've strayed pretty fucking far from your path."

Eastcott kneels down at Carlos' side. "Nathan, one of your knives please." He douses it with peroxide after cutting away the injured man's shirt. "This will sting."

The blade draws a circle in flesh around the bullet wound before digging in

The drug dealer's cries nearly drown out the sound of a van backing into my driveway.

"You got this?" I ask Eastcott.

"I don't know, Carlos. Do I?" Eastcott asks. "Or would you prefer I let you bleed out?"

Carlos closes his eyes. Nods his head.

I sprint down the walkway lining the side of my house. There's blood seeping out from the toolshed.

The van is labeled *Ken's Karpet and Flooring*. There's an 1-866 number on each side, a logo below it.

The last of four men dressed in logo-ed jumpsuits climb out of the van. Ross pulls in behind them.

Ω

"First, I do it here. At Kane Industries. And I'll have as much time as I need to integrate Badger's mapping."

Gullen doesn't respond.

"We're burning daylight here. And you don't have that much of it left."

"Fine. Now call it off."

"Oh, you didn't think I'd finished now did you? I own the IP."

"We fund the entire project. Now you want the technology. Horse shit."

"It's a licensing deal, Grey. Kane Industries holds the license, we grant you the use. That way," Kane gestures toward the door, "that way you won't be tempted to send your associates. Wait, I left out the most important part. Kane Industries receives full written indemnification for the use of our work product. You put all this in writing, I'll enter the code."

Gullen takes out his phone. Reads a text.

"I have a better idea." Gullen taps a few keys and shows Kane video of his sister at gunpoint.

"What makes you think I care what happens to her?" Kane asks, trying his best to look unfazed.

"Here's how this goes. You'll leave tomorrow for a sabbatical. Before you go, you announce that you need to mourn your father's death. You appoint an interim CEO, one of my choosing. Are you following me, Kane? You seem distracted."

Kane bluffs. "Maybe I don't love her as much as you think I do?"

"She likes it when you scrape those hideous nails of yours down her back, remember?"

"She does. So will others."

"Fair enough. Excuse me for just a second while I give the order."

"One question first," calling Gullen's bluff. "Do you think you'll prefer the top or the bottom bunk in your prison cell?"

"Good one, Kane." Gullen raises the phone to his mouth, waits until the number he'd dialed connects. "Do it."

Kane's face goes white, he springs out of chair and has Gullen by the neck before he can reach his weapon.

A slow smile spreads across Gullen's face.

Kane draws back a fist as Sturgeon bursts into the room alone. Gullen holds up a hand.

"Go ahead. *Do* it. It won't bring your sister back. Or maybe she's not dead. Maybe that was a warning. Kill the update, Kane."

Ω

Michael Cave places his ear against Missy's stomach. "I don't hear anything."

"So, Mr. Supreme FBI Agent. This is the best excuse you can muster?" Missy tucks her middle finger behind her thumb, lines up the shot, and releases.

"Ow. Hey!" Cave rubs his forehead. She waits, plans the next shot.

Again, she thwacks him.

"You really want a piece of me?" Cave asks.

She lands a third shot for good measure. A small red welt forms on his forehead.

"It's a war you want then?" Cave shows her his weapons. Two middle fingers drawn. Ready to fire. "I need only give the command, Milady."

"Michael, seriously. Talk to him. He's your son."

His hands fall to his side. "You're gonna have a great life, Miles," Cave says, in the direction of her protruding belly.

"That all you got?" Missy asks, crooking an index finger, inching it toward him. "Because if it is, maybe you should *say hello to my little friend*?"

He catches her finger mid-air. His eyes start to water. "You'll always be....Um. I'm sorry," he says before breaking down.

"Michael?"

Cave's head falls to her lap. "I'll protect you."

Missy strokes the hair from his tear-filled eyes. "Protect me from *what*, Michael?"

He lifts up his head, their eyes meet. He says nothing.

"Michael. Protect me from *what*?"

His lower lip quivers.

"Michael?"

He takes her face in his hands. "Do you trust me?"

"I don't know. You're scaring me," she replies. She blinks once, again. A single tear falls, she makes no effort to wipe it away. "What's going on?"

Play all sides. Do it for me.

"Michael, *what's* going *on*?" Though she fights it, fear overcomes her. "Michael, *what*?"

In this moment his decision is made.

"Three-dimensional chess," is his cryptic reply.

Ω

"What happens after?" I ask Agent Ross, who's sitting across from me on my patio couch, watching her men hauling away a green tarp. The body from the toolshed.

"After *what*, Mr. Nathan?"

"After this?" pointing at my blood-stained deck. "After him?" Nodding toward Carlos, who's inside in the dining room, out of earshot, now guarded by one of her men.

"This never happened. My men will see to it."

"I thought you were covert," I say.

"I have my ways."

"Guess I owe you one then."

"No, we're even. I could've done more for you."

I pull out my phone, show her the text I'd received from Abby. "I saw her today. I wanna know who owns this house." If the news has already broken, she'll already know the answer. And the police may already be on their way.

Time to find out.

She takes out her phone and pads in a number. "I need a property check run." She reads the address from the text aloud. "Tell me the name of the current owner, and any information you can find on other people who may be living there too."

She sets down her phone. "What did she say to you?"

"It's not what she said. It's what she did."

Ross's cellphone chimes. She picks it up and thumbs through an email attachment. "Man's name is Alastair Kane. CEO of Kane Industries. Why?"

"Anything else come up when you had the address run?" I ask.

"*Should* something have?"

"I'll answer your question in a minute. You told me you wanted Eastcott to work on me. He did. You want more?"

"Anything that can help us, yes."

"And what if I could give you those memories right now? What would you give in exchange?" I ask, pulling the iPhone 8 from my pocket.

"Are we negotiating here?"

"Always," I respond. "I'll track down this Alastair Kane myself. Eventually. My guess is Abby will be with him. Here's what I need from you. I need a location for Allende. I want him first."

"I don't know where Allende is now. We assume somewhere in Colombia still. Maybe Bogotá. He has certain habits to feed. Wherever he is, he'll *need* to feed them."

"You tell me everything you know about his last known location and these habits. Do it and I'll have a story to tell. Do it not and we're done here. We *are* even, remember?"

"Even if I were to tell you, I can't sanction you going after him. And I damn sure can't protect you if you go on your own."

"Who said I need protecting?"

"I told you before, you don't know who you're dealing with here."

"Yeah, I do."

"It's not the time to be cocky, Mr. Nathan. I could have you taken into custody right here. I'd be doing you a favor."

"You can try."

"Say you take out my four guys. What then? Resisting a federal officer? You won't make it out of the airport once I send the alert."

"Then help me and I'll tell you everything I've remembered."

Ross pads an order into her cellphone. Three men post around me.

I look over at Ross, tilt my head. "You sure you wanna do this?"

Three men await their next order.

Ross stares long at my iPhone.

PRESENT DAY

"Call Me the Breeze" blasts through speakers une-quipped to handle the volume Gullen demands of them. Today is a first. The Director has summoned *him* to the hill to testify.

Get your shit squared away, Gullen. No loose ends.

He thumbs through the Conduit e-file.

Past the article detailing an explosion at sea. Past the one-paragraph obituary of Commander William Ward and his family. Past the investigating officer's findings of a faulty fuel line being the cause.

Check.

He thumbs past the status update on Kane, and the photos of his sister Abigail Ashford, alive, held captive.

Check.

With Michael Cave under his thumb, and his peers inside the FBI applying new pressures on Ross, there's just one more order of business.

Finding Nathan Badger.

Two-hundred-forty-one days ago, Badger crossed the U.S.-Mexico border and entered Tijuana on foot. He took a taxi to Adelitas, where, in the company of a lady for hire, he paid for a room at an adjacent hotel.

When his allotted time was up, and security entered the room, they found the woman fully clothed, gagged, and tied to a bedpost.

There has been no sign of Badger since.

No matter. He's a suspect in the murder of Jeffrey Delacruz and wanted for questioning in the horrific deaths of Detective Drew Cavanaugh, Dorien Wissum and Dean Wallace. And he's fled the country. Not the move an innocent man makes.

Gullen's limo arrives at 8:15 am sharp. Nerves unexpectedly on edge, he tosses his briefcase across the back seat before twisting his lineman's body inside.

He lowers the privacy screen. The driver hands him a bag. He opens it, savors the smell before devouring the contents. The nerves start to settle.

He licks each finger after finishing the last of three crullers.

Delicious.

The limo arrives in plenty of time.

He culls his thoughts down from many to one before stepping out. Kane's missteps are erased. Ward's gone. Agent Ross is on check.

There's nothing left to trip him up. He'll be the hero, not the fall guy.

Gullen makes his way up the steps of the Capitol building. Clears security.

He takes a seat on a bench across the hall from where his testimony will take place and waits.

The doors open late. Very late.

A woman in a wheelchair rolls out, dressed in a suit, briefcase in her lap.

"Mr. Kane sends his regards," is all she says.

Ω

HOTEL DEL SALTO
TEQUENDAMA FALLS, COLOMBIA

The morning sun paints the sky in reds and purples. A bluebird trills its song, others join in.

The world is coming to life again after a long sleep, and the clock's running out.

I need more. It's time for bold moves.

"Are you a gambling man, Allende?" I reach into my pocket, pull out the SIM card I'd taken from his phone.

He's doubled over, clutching his stomach. He labors to draw in a stuttered breath.

"Because I am." I open my backpack and remove just two items. The plastic bag holding his cellphone and the syringe filled with antidote. "I'll ask you again. Are you a gambling man? Ticktock, Doctor."

Bloodshot eyes stare back as he nods.

"Good. Since you don't seem to know where Abby and Kane are, a few new questions."

He stares forward.

"Will your people be looking for you?"

No answer.

"I'll take that as a yes. Will they be tracking your phone?"

Nothing.

"Of course they will. If they pick up your signal, will they come for you?"

A pained smirk.

"I see. And I already know your facility is a twenty-six-minute drive. Know what's thirty-three minutes away?"

No response.

"The authorities I placed a call to. Just after I took you, I called in an anonymous tip to the police. They're tracking your phone number too."

"W-what did you say?"

"I told them all about you and your habits." I check my watch, only for show. "Right about now they should be on their way. Here's my proposal: you talk, I mean, really talk. No bullshit, no stalling. You give substantive answers to my questions. I only have a few left. You do that, I put back the SIM card and we see if your guys arrive first. They do, you get your precious antidote. They don't? Well hey, you probably already know what happens to a pedophile in prison."

"Ask y-your questions," he stammers before screaming out in pain.

"Muster your strength. Say it loud. Proclaim it to the heavens. You were at Bolsiver when the Celestial Temple members laid down in suicide circles and took their own lives, yes?"

"Yes."

"You rescued a man and two children there?"

"Yes." He twists in pain.

"The man's name was Cathal. You gave the children new identities. Abigail Ashford and Alastair Kane, yes?"

A few dry heaves. "Yes."

"Cathal's family had money and influence. You needed both. This is why you helped him escape. Yes?

"Yes."

"But he and the children had a past you had to bury first. Miriam Hill knew; you silenced her. Yes."

"I n-never wanted to harm her." A shaky hand reaches out to me and falls weak to the floor.

"Of course you didn't. And after what happened to Miriam, you left the country. Cathal went on to found Paradign. You helped him remotely, yes?"

Allende body goes rigid. His eyes widen. He starts to convulse. A payload erupts from his mouth, coating the wall opposite him.

"You're running out of time."

"Yes," he manages to say before the next volley of vomit.

I place the syringe near his feet, just out of his reach. "Why?"

Panting, he wipes his face with a shirtsleeve. "A new way."

"Tell me all about this *new way*, Doctor."

His shoulders hunch forward. He convulses. I look away as he wretches again.

"Ticktock," I tell him when he's finished. "*What* new way?"

"A new way to carry on my work."

"And so Paradign and Schema Realignment are born. Paradign's one-million-plus members. Your new guinea pigs?"

"Yes."

"I wanna hear you say it. Paradign is a government experiment."

He's slow to answer, but he does. "Yes."

"Not going to put words in your mouth. You need to say it. Why?"

His eyes slowly close.

"Doctor?"

Slow, his head moves side to side.

"Fucking *say* it."

"I create government assets. Like you."

"Government assets like me. Like Abby. Like Samuel Moore. Proud of your work, Doc?"

No answer.

"I'm sure you are. Let me let you in on just one more secret." I reach into my pocket and pull out my iPhone 8. "I've recorded every last word. Right here."

"The words of a d-dying man trying to save his own l-life. They'll do you no good."

"That depends. Watch this," I say next, placing the SIM card into its tray, sliding it closed before powering on his phone. A glimmer of hope flashes in his eyes.

"Who gets here first?"

From my backpack I remove the last item inside; a long rope attached to a grappling hook. I secure the hook on the window ledge and toss the rope over the side.

"W-what now?" he asks.

I sit down bang opposite him.

"Now we wait."

Not another word is spoken between us until the sound of sirens break through the still air. A slow parade of vehicles with flashing red and blue lights wind up the road leading to the abandoned hotel.

As they approach, I get up, step over to the window ledge, place a hand on the rope.

"Time to place your bets, Doctor."

* * *

Made in the USA
Las Vegas, NV
09 January 2021

15591290R10223